Hidden in Shadow

Georgia Florey-Evans

Published by Georgia A Evans
Beecher City, Illinois
ISBN-13: 978-0692586655
ISBN-10: 0692586652

This book is dedicated to the most amazing person I know. My husband has stood by me as we became very young parents, when we moved away from all our family and friends, when one precious little boy was taken before he was barely here—through my struggles and illnesses—with no complaints or concern for himself, he has loved me.

I don't have to imagine the heroes in books or on the screen because I have the real hero sharing my life.

Jeff, we've made it through thirty-six years—raising three semi-normal children, spoiling six remarkable grandchildren, and even surviving the most ridiculous dog in the world. RIP Buddy Ray.

I pray we have at least another thirty-six years together. I love you.

Also by Georgia Florey-Evans

Writing as Georgia A Evans
Extended Family **Series**

Book 1 – *Making Memories*

Book 2 – *Counting On It*

Book 3 – *Because of Bob*

Writing as Georgia A Evans
Hearts for Ransom **Series**

Book 1 – *Counting On It*

Book 2 – *Just Practicing*

Book 3 – *Believe Me*

In Shadow **Trilogy**

Book 1 – *Hidden in Shadow*

Coming soon:
Book 2 – *Living in Shadow*
Book 3 – *Staying in Shadow*

After watching a movie about stalking, I was curious—horrified, but curious. So, being a retired teacher and perpetual student (still taking online classes), I researched.

Reports vary, but according to the Stalking Resource Center, over seven million* people are victims each year. Add to that the three million cyber-stalker victims reported by the National White Collar Crime Center, and we're talking about a lot of people.

Because the crime is so prevalent and laws confusing, legal agencies often have difficulty deciding whose jurisdiction a case is in.

I wondered what would happen to a stalking victim if the local police department was the only law enforcement involved. So, Holly Morris was born and placed in the relatively small community of Shadow, Illinois. I gave her a healthy, loving family, a couple of really good friends, sense of humor, and extremely strong faith.

Then, one of those good friends refused to sit on the sidelines. Luke Walker, a gentle man with deep beliefs and principles, had a story to tell.

Join both of them as they discover the power of love over evil, and the power of God over everything.

*This does not take into account victims too intimidated to come forward, or those who feel embarrassed or even guilty. Estimates range from 1.5-3 million unreported stalking cases per year.

ACKNOWLEDGMENTS

My heartfelt gratitude goes to Nicole Gordon for the amazing cover design. Without her help, *Hidden* would strongly resemble a coloring book.

Also…

Thank you to
Detective John Niccum for
answering all my questions
about how to break the law, and
promising to back me up if my
million internet searches for
such things as how to
poison somebody
were flagged.

You never know where you'll find a blessing.

God is our refuge and strength, a very present help in trouble. Psalm 46:1

The Legend of Shadow

During the early nineteenth century, Virgil Clayton Richmond, always seeking greener grass, decided to travel west. Even though she wanted nothing more than a permanent home and family, Betsy traveled dutifully beside him.

After months of trudging through many unpleasant conditions, Betsy was finished with their adventure. The petite, soft-spoken, devoted wife stood toe-to-toe with her six-and-a-half foot giant of a husband.

"I'm through. This is our home."

Virgil, too stunned by his meek spouse's attitude to argue, instead stammered around until he managed a coherent sentence. "Tomorrow, Betsy, when we get to a place I can't see my shadow, we'll be home. I promise."

Though self-taught, the pioneer woman was highly intelligent. She saw through his ruse, knowing even moonlight produced shadows. If Virgil thought he outsmarted her, he was in for a surprise.

Early the next morning, Betsy asked, "May we go for a short walk before we leave? Just to stretch our legs."

Feeling expansive, Virgil agreed.

As they walked by a large oak tree, lush with green leaves, Betsy doubled over, as though in pain.

"What is it?' Virgil leaned over his wife.

She quickly straightened, and with every ounce of her strength, shoved her husband back about five feet.

He was understandably confused. "Betsy?"

Her smile outdid the sunshine. "You can't see your shadow under that tree, Virgil. We're home."

Thus, the farm which later became a settlement, and then a town, still bears the name Virgil gave it: Shadow.

x

Chapter 1

"Helllllp Meeee!"

A blood-curdling scream followed the equally distressing plea. Holly Morris promptly dropped her laundry basket and wildly looked around. It wasn't until the sound repeated that she realized its source.

"So, you set up speed dial for me, did you?" Her feet slipped and slid as she hurriedly raced across the freshly mopped dining room floor. She should have known better than to let a fourteen-year-old boy "fix up" her new smartphone.

The screaming had just stopped when she finally managed to extract it from her satchel. She no more than had a good grip on the contraption when the stupid thing took off shaking like a hula dancer and screamed bloody murder again. Her helpful student would be summoned to her office first thing Monday morning.

"Hello?"

"Good morning, Holly. Is this a bad time?" Her mom's voice was a pleasant contrast to ear-splitting shrieks.

"No." She took a deep breath and willed her pounding heart to slow down. "I'm just doing laundry. It's nothing that can't wait."

"Well, I talked to Anita Walker a few minutes ago. Has Luke told you about his new...?" As her mom began a Luke Walker promotion worthy of the most aggressive salesman, Holly gazed out the window and idly contemplated the various shapes of cumulus clouds. One in the east resembled a rooster, and that could be a turtle in front of it.

When she figured her mom should be winding down, Holly shifted her focus away from a bunny-shaped cloud appearing to hop across the horizon and tuned back in to her mother's words.

"... Dad and I want you and Luke to join us for lunch tomorrow."

"I'm sorry, Mom, but we can't. Luke just took over the youth group, and I promised to help him tomorrow. I appreciate the invitation, though."

"Well, then we'll plan on having you both out for grilled steaks next Sunday." Nobody could ever fault Susan Morris for a lack of tenacity.

"Okay. I'll talk to Luke about it tomorrow."

After a few more minutes of idle chitchat, the women said their goodbyes.

Holly ruminated over her mother's mule-headedness as she gathered the towels that had flopped out of the basket when it fell. While her mom knew perfectly well Holly and Luke weren't actually a couple, she persisted in using every opportunity to promote a romance between them. Susan was wasting her time. As much as their relationship meant to Holly, that kind of love was not involved.

Her gaze went to a framed photograph on her desk, and she picked it up. Luke's dad took it in the high school lobby right after their graduation. Richard Walker was a certified goofball, and he said something that had both graduates laughing. With Luke's arm casually draped across her shoulders and her gown hiding extra pounds, it was one of her favorite pictures.

She carefully replaced it before retrieving the basket and making her way back across the open space between the dining and living rooms. As she sat and folded laundry, her eyes wandered back to the picture.

Holly and Luke started kindergarten together, and as part of a small class of only thirty-four students, it seemed natural for the two "farm kids" to bond. Then, as they grew, Luke was just *there*. He was well-liked, and his friendship helped her through some teenage-induced rough patches. Being a plain, slightly overweight, young woman wasn't easy.

It would have been natural to assume they would grow apart while they were in college. After all, she went all the way to Massachusetts, and Luke stayed put, content to attend a school within driving distance. Even so, when she came home for breaks and holidays, there he'd be. And after graduation, when he bought his retiring grandparents' farm, and she was hired as the guidance counselor for Shadow High School, there he was again.

The sun's rays made it through the picture window and shone on a strawberry-print dish towel in the basket. The sight reminded her of a day not long after she moved back to Shadow. It was the evening Luke took her on their first post-college "date," for want of a better word, and would have made a good sitcom episode.

After a long day of school, she could barely wait to shed her dress and heels in favor of her favorite jeans, faded T-shirt, and bare feet. She had just taken her hair out of its customary twist and was about to give it a much-needed brushing when the doorbell rang. It was all she could do not to shut the door in Luke's face when she found him standing there, amazingly handsome in a pair of khakis and polo shirt.

"I was going to take you out for dinner, but maybe I'm underdressed." His dark green eyes sparkled with mischief.

"Ha, ha." She opened the door farther. "Come in. It will just take me a minute to change clothes."

His expression sobered. "If you're too tired, we can have a pizza delivered."

She was tempted for a moment before good manners kicked in. After working in his fields all day, Luke took the time to get cleaned up. The least she could do was slip into a decent top and pair of slacks. "I'll get ready. Come on in."

Luke laughed all through dinner and continued even after they were on their way home.

"Guess you didn't need to change clothes," he said, taking his eyes off the road long enough to wink.

"Be quiet." Holly stopped scrubbing her pants leg and hesitantly lifted the cloth. Somehow, she wasn't surprised to see an abstract painting of salad dressing and strawberry juice still proudly on display.

"You still have some red stuff between your eyes." The car swerved as Luke reached over and ran his finger across her forehead. "You know, if you wanted a bite of my pie, all you had to do was ask. There was no need to launch a strawberry."

"I did not launch that strawberry on purpose, and you know it, Lucas Ryan Walker." She leaned toward him. "I didn't do any of this intentionally, so stop teasing me."

"Okay." He nodded. "The salad dressing was practically overflowing before you even picked the bottle up. And, the spaghetti was greasy, so it slid right off the fork onto your lap—three times. And, then I tempted you with—"

"Enough!" Holly fought to keep her smile at bay. "You're not exactly Mr. Clean."

"Hey." His smile disappeared. "Fine, Cruella. Not another word."

"Thank you."

"But, next time, just ask for a doggy bag instead of wearing the leftovers home."

After that, they fell into a routine which had now lasted nearly six years. They spent every Friday evening together, and on Wednesdays, he gave her a lift to Bible study. They developed a habit of sitting together at Sunday morning worship, as well, and usually did something for lunch afterward.

Their relationship was unconventional by most people's standards, however; because in no way were they actually dating. They were simply good friends who enjoyed spending time together. Why, Luke had never tried to kiss her, and she didn't know how she'd respond if he did. In fact, other than behavior mandated by gentlemanly manners, he didn't even touch her.

Of course, their shared social life wouldn't last forever. Luke was a charming man with exemplary values. Tall and extremely well-built, with thick, brown hair and a perpetual five o'clock shadow his mother disliked, he was very attractive. The man would have no difficulty finding a girlfriend. She figured if a woman he wanted to date ever came along, he'd let Holly know. The same went for her meeting somebody. Until then, they'd just keep things the way they were. It worked.

She about jumped out of her skin when her phone screamed again. That thing was going to be the death of her yet. She reached across the sofa and picked up the annoying piece of technology.

"Hello."

Her voice was met with silence.

"Hello." Great. Yet another dropped call. Why had she shelled out big bucks for a new smartphone, when she'd apparently be better off with tin cans and kite string?

Then she heard a whisper, so quiet she had to be imagining it—"My Holly." Soft, male laughter filled her ear before the line went dead.

The phone landed on the sofa and bounced between cushions. This couldn't be happening. *Please, God, not again.*

She took a deep breath. Tears welled in her eyes for a moment before she resolutely blinked them away. Okay. That wasn't a dropped call. The laughter was real. The words—she could explain the words. Her imagination formed them from meaningless sounds.

The stack of hand towels joined the washcloths on the floor as she abruptly stood. It was a prank call. That's all.

Holly paced her living room floor and grasped hold of the idea. That's exactly what it was—a prank. Summer break began in eight weeks, and the students were amped. Since she was responsible for quite a bit of discipline, it made sense they would choose her to torment.

She knelt and resolutely gathered the dropped laundry. Now, she was thinking clearly. This was not her apartment in Tullen, Massachusetts. She was safe and sound in her hometown of Shadow, Illinois.

The pieces of terry cloth landed right back on the floor when her phone emitted yet another agonizing howl. All right. This was ridiculous. It was time to show her students another side of Miss Morris.

"Listen, young man, you are breaking the law. I have caller ID, and after I speak to your father, I may very well contact the sheriff." It was too bad she hadn't gotten around to following the one hundred-step directions to activate the application; she would really know who this was.

"You must not have checked it this time, because it's me." A rightfully puzzled Tessa Lincoln was on the phone.

The wind went right out of Holly's sails. Here, she used her "mean" voice and everything. "Oh. I thought you were a student playing a prank."

"Which one? I'll fix him." Tessa had been Holly's defender since their teenage years.

"I don't know." She could compile a list of possibilities, but it would probably end up being a copy of the school roster. No halo-wearing teenagers attended Shadow High School.

"But you said you had him on caller ID."

"I know, but I don't have it set up on this new phone." She picked up a handful of linen and slammed it on the sofa. "I thought maybe he'd mess up and give himself away."

"Wait a minute." Tessa's voice was filled with suspicion. "You had a supposed prank call? It's not—"

"No." She kicked the half-empty basket with uncalled for vehemence, turning it on its side. "There's no way. I'm sure it was just some kids."

"But Holly, if it is, you need to—"

"It's not." Her voice came out harsher than she intended. As she finally picked up the basket and dumped its remaining contents on the floor, she managed to calm down. "It just can't be." If only she felt the conviction as strongly as it sounded in her voice.

"Holly—"

"It was just one call." Holly's determination grew.

"The whole mess started with just one call." As Holly's college roommate, Tessa shared every moment of the nightmarish experience. "I went along with you when you asked me not to tell anybody, but I won't help you pretend it didn't happen at all."

Holly swept folded towels and washcloths off the sofa and dropped to her knees, the lone survivor of a towel-filled tornado. "I'm not pretending anything, Tess. I just refuse to let myself be afraid of something as ridiculous as a prank call."

It was probably just as well that Holly couldn't understand what the other woman mumbled before Tessa spoke again. "Okay. Will you promise me one thing, though?"

"If I can." She knew her friend too well to blindly agree.

"Promise me if you get even one more 'prank call,' you'll talk to Mitch. Tell him everything."

Talk to the Shadow County sheriff. Holly stifled a snort. Law enforcement was so helpful before. *I'm sorry, Miss Morris, but we simply don't have enough information to take any further action. However, should physical contact be made or a confrontation occur, you give us a call, and we'll be there.* Right. And Holly would sit up in her coffin and thank them profusely.

Tessa must have read her mind. "It won't be like Tullen, Holly. We're talking about Mitch, and you know he'll help. You can trust him."

There was probably nothing to worry about, anyway. "Okay."

"Good." Tessa's voice was filled with relief.

"So, what did you call about, Tess?" Her friend wasn't one to make unnecessary calls. She'd be right beside Holly in the "Bring the Telegraph Back" march.

"Oh." Tessa must have needed to shift gears in her thinking. "Have you seen your mail yet?"

"It's too early." She glanced at a clock and was surprised to see it was nearly eleven. "Will doesn't deliver here until around eleven-thirty on Saturdays. Why?"

"I'm sure you'll get the same thing I did." Tessa started speaking faster, a sure indication she was excited. "Jennifer Ewing and Rob Sanders are hosting a ten-year class reunion right here in town, at the high school." The sound of papers shuffling brought a smile to Holly's face. Her friend was the math teacher at Shadow High and had to be the most disorganized person on the planet. "It got me thinking about our classmates. You know, I always thought Sarah Hart would move back and take over her parents' furniture store. And I can't believe Clay Richmond isn't here. He'd have his choice of running an insurance agency or working in real estate."

At the mention of Clay Richmond, Holly developed goose bumps. He was, by far, the most popular boy in their class. With his swoon-worthy blond hair and blue eyes, nearly every girl in the entire high school pined for him. It shamed her to think she was one of them. Of course, he would never give more than a passing glance to somebody like plain Jane, Holly Morris. A man who chose a woman for her looks wasn't the kind of guy she wanted to be with anyway.

"So, I take it you're going to this reunion."

The paper noises stopped. "So are you. We'll go together, or Luke will bring you. Just think how some of those women like Lucy Phillips will feel when they see how you look now."

"Appearances aren't what matter, Tess."

"I know, I know." Tessa's exasperated sigh was a little dramatic. "But you have to admit you've come a long way from the high school

Holly Morris. You were always pretty, but after you lost weight and learned how to fix your hair and wear makeup, you blossomed."

She had to admit most of her classmates would be surprised. Not that their opinions really mattered, but it might feel good to see their reactions. "When is it?"

"Oh, it's not for a month." Unsurprisingly, the excitement had disappeared from Tessa's voice. Patience was not one of her virtues. "I guess they want to give the people who'll travel plenty of notice."

"I'll mark my calendar." Of course, to do that, she'd have to get up off the floor. "I'd better go, Tess. I have another load of laundry coming out of the dryer in fifteen minutes, and I still haven't folded this one." In fact, she'd flopped the towels around so much they probably needed a second washing.

"I need to get busy, too. I have three classes worth of homework assignments to grade, and if writing skills were the only necessary qualification, there would be a ton of doctors in my classes. Scribbles, I tell you."

"Okay. I'll see you at church in the morning."

"Yeah." There was a brief pause. "Don't forget your promise about the phone call, Holly."

Amid the normalcy of their conversation, she had put the unpleasant phone call and horrible memories it instilled completely out of her mind. Nevertheless, she promised. "I'll remember."

"Okay. Bye."

Holly looked around her at the haphazard spiral of towels and washcloths and decided the floor was as good of a place as any to sit and fold the poor, mistreated things.

A class reunion. It was difficult to imagine seeing all the people she attended school and graduated with. Tyler Brady and Sally Young were voted class sweethearts during senior year. Did they even see each other anymore? And what happened to tiny Kim Feldhake? She was so petite her mom had to alter a graduation gown before Kim could wear it. And, Tom Dwer and Kevin Tripp—those two were always in trouble, with Tom being the brains—although not very effecient ones since they were constantly getting caught—and Kevin the brawn. She couldn't remember hearing Kevin speak more than two or three words at a time.

She pictured other classmates as she once more folded laundry. Each of them was bound to have changed during the past ten years.

And as for the identity of her caller, she'd just listen at school. Whoever phoned wouldn't be happy unless he could brag about it.

There was nothing in Shadow to worry about.

Was there?

Chapter 2

"Hey, Clarence, whatta you say? Ready to go in and get some food in our stomachs?" Luke Walker patted the scruffy neck on his five-year-old, Heinz Fifty-seven dog. The large, multi-hued mutt's floppy ears went back as he nuzzled his owner's hand.

Clarence didn't know he wasn't a full-blooded show dog, and he frequently turned up his nose at lesser animals. Luke was accustomed to receiving dirty looks from other pet owners in the vet's waiting room.

Luke's mom, Anita, still had fits about Clarence living in the house, even though Luke had kept him inside since the day he rescued the rambunctious puppy from the pound. She said he was too big and hairy for a house dog. Luke figured she knew he wasn't going to kick his dog out at this stage of the game, so maybe she just felt it was her maternal obligation to object. Besides, as Luke kept reminding his mom, every farmer needed a good watchdog. Of course, should anybody ever break in, that's most likely what Clarence would do—watch. He was a chummy animal unless he was around Holly.

If Holly came out to spend an afternoon, Clarence was never more than a few feet from her. And when Luke's dad started to give her a friendly hug one day, Clarence immediately inserted himself between them, growling ferociously at Richard. Naturally, Luke's mom made the most of the opportunity and suggested perhaps Holly would benefit from Clarence's presence in her home. Well aware of Anita's ongoing campaign to remove the dog from her son's house, Holly politely declined. She doubted her small abode would suit a dog Clarence's size. Besides, he was a farm dog.

Holly. Her radiant smile—the brilliance of a sunrise. And he could see his dreams come true in those perfectly shaped eyes the color of chestnuts. Holly was always pretty, but when she let her long, silken locks of dark chocolate fall tantalizingly over her shoulders and down her back, her beauty took his breath away.

What was he going to do about her? He had been in love with Holly Morris since they were in high school, and she never considered him as anything more than a friend. From her perspective, she was doing him a favor when she chose his furniture and decorated his house, but he intended for it to feel like home to her. Scratch that. He wanted it to *be* home to her.

"I'm a big chicken, huh, Clarence?" His dog looked at him and appeared to nod his head. Or maybe he was excited because he saw his dog food. Luke chuckled as he poured some in Clarence's dish. He picked up the bright orange bowl to fill it with fresh water. "It's not like I haven't thought about kissing her. Many times. It just seems like every time I work up the gumption, she says something about us being friends. At least if we're friends, I get to see her." He set the water bowl beside Clarence's food and then went to the refrigerator and pulled out the fixings for a sandwich.

"See, Clarence, if I tell her how I really feel, it's liable to scare her off." Luke slathered two slices of bread with mayonnaise. "And then she wouldn't go anywhere with me."

Clarence looked up from devouring his food and snorted.

"Well, she wouldn't." Luke finished making his sandwiches. "She'd stop going to church with me and letting me take her out every Friday. I bet she'd even stop going to Bible study with me." He pulled a bag of chips from the cabinet. "Let alone come out here to spend a

Sunday afternoon. Then, you'd never get to see her either. How do you feel about that?"

He sat at the table and began to eat his lunch. In Holly's eyes, they weren't even dating, so there was no way he could ask for any kind of commitment. He was ready now, though. It had taken over four years to get the farm on its feet, but it was earning a steady profit. He could provide a comfortable, stable home for a wife. If he could just get the woman he loved to marry him.

"You home, Son?" Richard Walker's voice came from the back door.

"In here, Dad!" Why wasn't his father spending Saturday afternoon out in the fields?

"Got any more of that stuff?" Richard eagerly eyed Luke's lunch as he walked into the kitchen.

"Yes I do, but Mom will kill both of us if she finds out you're eating bologna and chips. You know what the doctor said."

Richard walked to the cabinet and took out a glass. "Guess I'll settle for some tea then." He pulled the pitcher Luke kept brewed sweet tea in from the refrigerator.

Tea wouldn't fill an empty stomach. "I can probably find something healthier." Luke started to stand.

"No." His dad waved him back down. "I already ate lunch." He scrunched his nose in disgust. "If you can call a bowl of rabbit food with little pieces of chicken tossed in lunch."

Luke hid a smile by taking a bite of his sandwich. His dad's insurance company made him go in for a complete physical. The poor guy's cholesterol was through the roof, so he was placed on a restricted diet. Doc Tindell didn't have to worry about Richard following his instructions; Anita strictly enforced them. They didn't even keep "unhealthy" food in their house anymore.

"Been in the fields?" Luke asked between bites.

Richard ran a hand over his graying buzz cut. "Just came in to eat. Then your mom sent me over here."

That was odd. "What's going on a phone call wouldn't have worked?"

"I have something to give you." An enigmatic smile appeared as he dug into his jean's pocket.

Luke's curiosity was piqued. His birthday had been less than two months ago, and there was no other special occasion he knew of. He finished off his second sandwich and waited.

"Your grandparents mailed this up to me a while back. They told me to give it to you when I thought it was time." The corners of his mouth quirked upward. "Your mom informed me I think it's time."

Both his father and grandpa were jokesters, so it was hard telling what his dad was holding. Luke was probably being set up for a knee-slapper.

"What is it?" This wouldn't be the first time he was the butt of one of their jokes. It took nearly a solid week with no sleep for ten-year-old Luke to discover the masks on raccoons did not turn white at night. And yet another to determine owls didn't yell "who?" and "you" back and forth between them.

"We-ell." It was obvious the older man intended to draw out the suspense as long as he could. "Remember how your Grandpa and Grandma Walker eloped?"

"Great-Grandpa Simmons thought Grandpa was worthless." Heaven knew Luke had heard that particular refrain many, many times. "He climbed a ladder to Grandma's room, and they ran off to get married." And Grandpa didn't know his britches were split until the preacher told him after the vows. "What does that have to do with what you're giving me?"

"After Mom and Pop were married, her father had a change of heart. Suddenly, my dad could do no wrong."

"Grandpa told me that before." Okay. His grandparents had told their son to bore Luke to death. "I still don't understand, Dad."

Richard's eyes twinkled as he continued at his own pace. "What you don't know is my grandpa Simmons gave my mom and dad a present. Something very special that had been in the Simmons family for at least four generations."

And now for the punchline. It was probably a family handkerchief—used, of course.

"He gave them this." Luke's dad held out his hand and opened it. There, lay the most delicate ring Luke had ever seen.

"Take it." His father's voice was soft now.

It was so dainty, Luke was almost afraid to pick it up. Then, it looked even more fragile grasped between his thumb and finger. Upon close examination, he could see the band was comprised of tiny, interweaving threads of silver, giving it a lace-like appearance. The stone was unusual. It was cut with facets like a diamond, but instead of being clear, every color of the rainbow seemed to sparkle in it.

"What is this?" He held it toward his dad. "It's not a diamond, but it looks valuable."

Richard shrugged. "Nobody knows. I suppose you could take it to a jeweler and find out, but I guess none of our ancestors ever cared enough to do that. What it represents is more important."

Luke understood. "Family and love."

"Exactly." His father stood.

"Wait, Dad." Luke rose to his feet. "Why are Grandpa and Grandma giving this to me instead of Ellie or Lucy?" Either of his cousins would love the ring. "And what did you mean about it being time?"

A knowing smile appeared on the older man's face. "Your grandparents love Holly. They'll expect to see that ring on her finger the next time they visit."

"But, Dad—"

"You've been dating for several years, and in love with her a lot longer than that. Don't you think you've waited long enough?"

Maybe he could talk to somebody besides Clarence about his predicament.

"I would ask Holly to marry me in a heartbeat, but she doesn't see me as more than a friend. If I let on how I really feel about her, she's going to end everything." Even saying the words made him sad. "And I'd rather have her in my life as a friend than not at all."

"Have you prayed?" Richard asked solemnly.

"Fervently." He figured the good Lord was probably tired of hearing his sob story, but he kept praying anyway.

His dad's hand felt warm when he placed it on Luke's shoulder. "Well, then, if God means for the two of you to be together, it'll work out. And I don't think he'd put it in your heart so strongly if it wasn't meant to be."

"I hope you're right, Dad." He looked at the ring, already picturing it on Holly's slender finger. "I really hope you're right."

Chapter 3

"Whether we're looking at that homeless person standing on the corner asking for food or money; or a man in a three-piece suit stepping out of a luxury car, who do we see? Who do we *really* see? If we see them as we are supposed to, we'll see God's children, no better or worse than you or me. I pray as we leave church this morning, we'll remember that. Amen."

Pastor Rollins sat behind the lectern as the pianist began to play. Holly looked at the hymnal Luke was holding for them to share, but her mind was still on the sermon. Her job was sometimes challenging . It was difficult when kids like Billy Andrews strutted into her office, all bluster and attitude. She needed to look past the exterior to the uncertain young man behind it, a fourteen-year-old with no idea whether his mom would be sober when he got home from school.

The boy didn't even have his dad to depend on. Cliff Andrews was overseas in the military, on some kind of extended mission with no leave. Instead of finding strength and being there for her children, Gina Andrews chose to lose her worries in alcohol. There were a few times when, had Billy's paternal grandmother not stepped in to take care of him and his younger sister, the children would have been placed in a foster home. Holly had nothing against the system, but familial custody was much better.

"You okay?" Luke whispered loudly as he looked at her with concern on his face.

She tried to smile as she silently nodded. It was too bad Billy wasn't in their church youth group. Luke would be an excellent role model for the teenager.

Luke's eyes searched hers for a moment before he resumed singing. She focused on the words and joined in.

After forcing herself to pay attention to the service, the rest passed quickly. She soon found herself in front of Luke on their way out of the building.

"Good morning, Holly." A bright smile accompanied the pastor's hearty handshake. "I hear you and Luke have a big day planned."

"You know me. I'll use any excuse to spend a day at the preserve."

The minister looked over Holly's head at Luke. "And, I'm sure you're every bit as anxious."

Luke answered him. "I just hope I haven't taken on more than I can handle, Pastor. These teenagers need somebody to lead them on the right path and keep it interesting enough they want to stay there."

Pastor Rollins' smile didn't dim as he responded. "And that's exactly why you're the fellow for the job. You see that need."

Holly glanced at Luke as she finally reclaimed her hand and gave him his turn with the minister. She couldn't keep the smile from her face as she saw the tell-tale redness creeping up toward the brown hair resting on Luke's neck. If he weren't so darkly tanned from spending most of his time outdoors, he'd undoubtedly be as red as a Christmas ornament about now. And with his green eyes, he could really get into the season. A giggle escaped before she could stop it.

"What's so funny?" Luke took her arm and led her out into the sunshine.

"Nothing." She smiled brightly as she fought laughter. He would not be flattered by a comparison to holiday decor.

"Well, I hope you can keep that attitude after we're with the kids for a couple of hours. You know the Chambers boy can be a handful, and in case you didn't notice, Amy Brock isn't exactly dressed appropriately for a fourteen-year-old." Luke's hand felt warm against her back as they walked farther out on the sidewalk.

She thought about the young lady's home situation. "I'm not sure Amy has any other kind of clothes to wear. Her mother provides a wardrobe designed for more...mature females." And much too sophisticated for Holly's taste.

They both stopped talking as the young lady in question walked by. Amy's dress was cut very low and way too short, and if her heels weren't at least four inches, Holly would yodel the Doxology next Sunday. Appreciative glances from too many males, both young and old, followed her.

Luke dropped his hand from Holly's back and stepped around to face her. "I understand what you're saying." With a skeptical lift of his brow, he crossed his arms. "But don't tell me the boys won't get in a dither over that."

"Did Holly tell you about the steak dinner next Sunday?" Susan Morris, with Holly's dad, Tony, beside her, grasped Luke's arm.

"No." Luke uncrossed his arms, and his frown was replaced by a broad smile. "But if Tony's grilling steak, I'm there."

Holly probably ground some enamel off her teeth over her mother's ecstasy. It was too bad Susan couldn't date Luke.

"Plan on coming right after church." Susan let go of Luke's arm and smiled at her daughter. "Why don't you let Luke drive you? There's no sense in using two vehicles, is there? Gas being so high."

"Mom, Luke always drives me when we go someplace." She actually had to point that out? What was her mother up to now?

"You know, it's senseless for Luke to bring you all the way back to town." Susan was trying to look innocent but wasn't quite pulling it off. "Why don't you plan on staying at the farm, and your dad will drive you home first thing Monday morning? Your room is still ready."

Oh. If Susan Morris couldn't marry her daughter off, she'd keep her at home. Holly's dad had finally put his foot down and told his wife their daughter was an adult. He even co-signed the loan for her house.

"I don't mind bringing Holly back to town." Luke seemed to sense her discontent. "If I ask nicely enough, I may even get her to go for ice cream with me after we're back."

Of course, that more than appeased Susan. In her eyes, they would be extending their "date."

"Susie-Q, we need to go if we're going to speak to the Lincolns. You said you needed to ask Teresa about a recipe, and I wanted to run some ideas about pasturing the dairy cows past Max." Tony caught his daughter's eye and winked. Why couldn't her mom be more supportive, like her dad?

"We'll see you next week then." Susan turned and walked beside her husband to where Tessa's parents stood.

"I brought work duds for this afternoon." Luke indicated the dress shirt and slacks he was wearing. "It'll only take me a few minutes to change. Maybe you can catch Tessa while I'm gone."

She had just turned to find her friend when Mitch Landon's twin sister, Melissa, appeared in front of her.

"Did you get your invitation?" Missy practically bubbled over with enthusiasm.

It seemed Tessa had a kindred spirit. "If you mean for our class reunion, then, yes, it came yesterday."

"Isn't it exciting?" Melissa pushed her long, auburn hair back off her shoulders. "I haven't seen most of our classmates since graduation. Aren't you curious how they turned out?" A mischievous grin appeared. "I think it would be funny if Miss Perfect Lucy Phillips has to wear spandex to zip her jeans."

"Melissa." Holly had to fight the smile she felt rising as she pictured the most attractive female student in their class wearing a support garment. "We're supposed to see others through God's Eyes. Weren't you listening to Pastor Rollins?"

"Sure." Missy's smile didn't diminish. "Who says I can't still see her in a girdle?"

"You're hopeless. You know that, don't you?" She liked Missy. Although not close in school, since college they had developed a strong friendship. Maybe it was because they both chose to stay in Shadow. Guidance counselors and accountants were employable just about anywhere, but Shadow was home.

"Thank heavens, Joe doesn't think so." Melissa had been dating Joe Willis for nearly two years. "I think he's about ready to pop the question. Mitch saw him at the jewelry store in Pattinton last week. I can't imagine any other reason for Joe to be at a jewelry store, can you?"

Actually, she could imagine many other reasons for Joe to be at a jewelry store. His watch may need repairs; he could be picking something up for his parents. It was hard telling. She found herself unsure what to say, though. Holly didn't want to hurt her friend, but she had no desire to help set her up for a tremendous disappointment. "What makes you think he'd be getting ready to propose now? It's not Valentine's Day or anything."

"Next Saturday is our anniversary. We'll have been dating for exactly two years. I think it's the perfect time for a proposal, don't you?"

"It would be romantic." Joe had better have something planned for next Saturday, or he was going to have a very upset girlfriend on his hands. "Are you helping at the nature preserve this afternoon?"

Missy wrinkled her nose. "No way. I'm not going to hang around and bait hooks or walk on trails. Worms are disgusting, and I get poison ivy if I so much as look at it."

If that were the case, marrying a man who would soon be the sole owner of a nature preserve might result in some interesting situations. "I'm helping Luke. I guess it'll just be the three of us." She had hoped Melissa would be there. Holly was comfortable enough with Luke and Joe, but the presence of another female would be nice.

"So, when is Luke going to pop the question?" Missy's eyes sparkled. "You two have been an item for what? Six years?"

What was going on? "Luke and I are just good friends. You know that."

"Sorry, but I don't buy it."

Something occurred to Holly. "Have you been talking to my mom?"

"Nope." Missy focused her gaze on something behind Holly. "I just don't think you two would be together so much if you weren't in love. That's all."

"Well, you're wrong." She would just put a stop to this before it got started. "Luke and I are only friends. Friends. You can ask him. He'll tell you."

"He'll tell her what?" Luke's voice came from behind Holly, startling her.

Now, with Luke right there, even the mention of them being more than friends was embarrassing. "Nothing. Are you ready? I still need to stop at home and change clothes."

For just a moment, it looked like he was going to press on, but he didn't. "Okay. Let's get this show on the road."

"Yes. Let's do." Holly ignored Missy's smug smile and set off beside Luke as they headed for his vehicle. Her *friend's* vehicle.

Chapter 4

Luke yawned as he pulled his Jeep into the garage. The day had gone better than he expected. Of course, just as he predicted, the boys had their eyes glued on Amy Brock when they should have been watching their fishing lines. Even the modest clothes Holly brought for the girl to change into failed to make a difference. He honestly thought they were going to run out of bait way too soon since the boys kept letting their hooks get cleaned off.

And, if he didn't know Joe Willis was seriously involved with Missy Landon, he might have been jealous. When Ronnie Chambers pulled his pole back to cast, the hook caught Joe's cap and flung it into the pond. Instead of being upset or scolding Ronnie for being careless, Joe stomped to the edge of the dock and yelled at the worm. "Your head is not big enough for my hat! Give it back, you little wiggler!" Everybody was in stitches, but Luke only had eyes for Holly. Laughter and a smile increased her beauty.

He stood back as he opened the door so Clarence could come out for his nightly romp. As Luke turned to watch his dog, a movement off to his right and down by the machine shed caught his eye. He let the door close and headed that direction.

"Somebody out here?" He wasn't certain, but his impression was of something too tall for an animal. "Who's there?"

Luke stopped in front of the machine shed. Something didn't seem right. He moved closer. That was it. The door, which he kept locked more for safety than security, stood ajar by a couple of inches. "Who's there?" he repeated, pulling the door the rest of the way open.

Clarence appeared, a barking mass of fur, just as something, *somebody*, rammed into Luke. Because he wasn't prepared, he lost his footing and went down hard. Luke tried to grab the other guy's leg, but his hand hit empty air. Before he could get back on his feet, the figure disappeared into the northern tree line, Clarence yipping in hot pursuit.

Luke's first instinct was to chase his attacker down, but common sense told him it would be a waste of time. Whoever it was ran too fast; he was long gone. And he may not have been alone. Luke was around six-two and well-muscled from hard physical labor, but he wasn't strong enough to take on a group of men. Or weapons.

"Let's see what he was up to." Clarence reappeared, breathing hard. Even in the aftermath, Luke couldn't help but be surprised by his dog's courage. He slowly pulled the door open and reached in to hit the light switch.

"Oh, no." Somebody had been in there all right. And they used way more than the two cans of spray paint Luke saw lying on the ground. Obscene language was painted on nearly every surface of the building, and his equipment. Even the glass on the cab of his tractor had writing on it. Who would do something like this?

He pulled the phone out of his pocket and dialed. His buddy Mitch Landon picked up on the second ring.

"Sheriff Landon here."

"Mitch, this is Luke. I had a break-in and some vandalism out here in my machine shed this evening.

"You okay, Luke?"

"Yeah. I don't think anything is missing or damaged, but I figure I'll need a police report for insurance. Somebody emptied more than one can of spray paint in here."

"Did you see anything suspicious?" Luke could tell Mitch was already in motion as he spoke.

"You could say that." Clarence's front feet landed on Luke's chest, and a rough tongue slathered across his nose. "Knock it off, Clarence." Luke shoved the dog's face away.

"Beg your pardon?"

"Nothing." Clarence's close-up panting told Luke it was time for a doggy breath treat. "I got bum rushed when I opened the door."

"You're sure you weren't injured?"

"I'll have some bruises, but nothing to worry about. Mitch, he mowed me over. I don't think many men in Shadow could do that." In fact, he was speaking to one of the few who could.

"Well, sit tight. Try not to touch anything. I'd like to see it just like the vandal left it."

"Okay." Thankfully, Clarence had finished "kissing" Luke, and was back on all fours. He could hear his mom now.

"I'll be there in about ten minutes." Mitch disconnected the call.

Luke turned and walked out of the machine shed, Clarence on his heels. He didn't want to do anything to mess up Mitch's investigation. He just couldn't figure out why anybody would do this to him. As far as he knew, he didn't have any enemies. He didn't even know of anybody angry with him.

The dog nuzzled Luke's leg. "I know, Clarence. You tried to get him, didn't you?"

He looked around the yard, lit by security lights. Nothing else seemed out of place. How had his attacker got out here? Luke's lane was over a quarter of a mile long; he would've noticed if a vehicle was parked on it. And it was a good two-mile trek through the woods to reach a road. The intruder must either know the area very well or be extremely desperate.

"Come on, boy. Let's go check the barn before Mitch gets here." He was fairly certain nobody had been in the house. The door was securely locked when he opened it to let Clarence out. Still, he'd check it too, after the barn.

He was just on his way back to the machine shed after discovering both his house and barn undisturbed when Mitch's squad car pulled up. The big, ex-football linebacker got out and reached back in for a flashlight.

"You sure you're not hurt, Luke? You're limping." Mitch looked questioningly at him.

Luke hadn't realized he was favoring his left hip. Still, he had suffered broken bones and torn ligaments before; this was different. "I may have a bruise or two, but I'm all right."

Mitch appeared ready to argue, but then just shook his head. "Stand still for a few minutes, please." Luke's friend was replaced by the sheriff, now headed to the machine shed. "I want to have a look at the ground around the building. Which side did he take off on?"

"He ran to my right and disappeared into the tree line just north of the shed."

"And there was only one person involved?"

Luke had wondered about that as he checked his other buildings. "I only saw one, and I think if somebody else was here, there would be more damage."

Mitch hunkered down, flashlight pointed at the ground beside the machine shed. "What shoes do you have on?"

He felt silly, but he had to look. With all that was going on, he couldn't remember what he wore. "Hiking boots. I was with the youth group at Willis' Preserve all afternoon."

"This guy was wearing tennis shoes." Mitch stood back up. "I'd guess a size twelve or bigger. Not many men around here with feet that size."

Luke started to walk toward him. "Is it okay for me to come over there now?"

In the glow of the security light, what little of Mitch's hair not covered by his hat looked even redder than Luke knew it to be. "Come on, and we'll check out the inside. You say it's been spray painted?"

"With foul language." Luke stood beside him at the door. "I didn't stay inside and do any serious reading after I called. I didn't want to mess anything up."

Mitch stepped through the door and let out a low whistle. "Somebody needs their mouth washed out with soap. That's what my grandma would say."

Luke grimaced as he looked around. There was even more than he first thought. "I just don't know who would do this, Mitch. I can't think of anybody who's angry with me, let alone set up to do something this malicious."

Mitch's flashlight shone in the corners where the overhead lights didn't quite reach. There was even painting back there. Suddenly, the beam of his flashlight froze—aimed at the glass-encased cab of the tractor.

"Mean anything to you, Luke?"

Luke focused on the sloppily painted words. *She's mine.* He shook his head. "No idea."

"Let's go inside, and I'll write a report. At least, your insurance should pay for the clean-up." Mitch turned and headed out the door.

"I hope this was a one-time thing. Maybe the guy didn't even know whose place this is." Surely, that was the case.

"Could very well be true."

As he led the way into his house, Luke silently said a prayer of thanks that nobody—not even Clarence—was hurt. What a bizarre ending to an otherwise pleasant day.

Chapter 5

Holly arrived at school to find Amy Brock sitting on the bench outside her office, tears streaming down the girl's lovely face. As usual, the young lady wore too short of a skirt and a very tight blouse. Holly quickly unlocked her door and ushered the teenager into the room.

"Miss Morris, why'd you make me change my clothes yesterday?" were the first words out of the girl's mouth.

"I told you, Amy." It seemed like the prudent way to handle the situation. "Dresses are impractical for fishing, and if you had left those shoes on, you might have fallen off the dock. My clothes weren't that bad, were they?" A pair of jeans and plain pink T-shirt may not be the height of fashion, but they weren't sackcloth. Besides the truth of Holly's words, Luke had a valid point about the boys' reaction to Amy's clothing. It was a church-sponsored event, after all.

"But now the boys are saying I'm a…not a nice girl." Amy took a tissue from the box Holly held out. "They never said anything about me before, but since they saw me in your clothes, they say I dress like a … I can't even say the word, Miss Morris." More tears fell.

Holly sat on a chair beside her and spoke quietly. "Amy, do you like the way you dress?"

The girl didn't hesitate. She vehemently shook her head side to side. "My mom wants me to look like her, but I don't want to. I want to look like other girls my age."

"Have you ever told your mom that?" May as well charge through the drones, straight to the queen bee of the problem.

Amy looked at her through tears. "I can't. She works hard to buy my clothes. I can't tell her I don't like them."

Please, give me the right words. "I know your mom doesn't have anybody to help take care of you and your little brother. She's working hard to do it alone, and she must love you very much. Right?"

31

"She loves me and Ryan more than anything."

"Well, then, don't you think she wants you to be happy?" Holly sent another prayer out; dealing with parental issues was tricky.

Amy nodded.

"Maybe you need to tell her your clothes are making you unhappy. I believe if you tell her you'd rather dress like the other girls your age, she'll listen. And do you know what?" The young lady looked expectantly at Holly. "I'm pretty sure the clothes you'd like to wear cost less than the ones she's been buying you. Maybe she's been buying them because she thinks they're what you want. If you're not honest with her, she'll never know the truth." It didn't take a fashion maven to know the outfit Amy wore at that moment probably cost more than a week's worth of clothes from Holly's wardrobe.

Hope appeared in Amy's eyes. "Do you think so? If she knew, she'd understand?"

"I do. I think your mom would want to know if something was making you unhappy. And the only way that can happen is if you tell her. Okay?"

A smile finally broke through on the teenager's face. "Okay. I'm going to talk to her as soon as she gets home from work this evening."

Holly patted Amy's hand before she stood and walked around her desk. "I'll write your pass with an extra five minutes thrown in. You can use the time to wash your face and dry those tears. I'll have a talk with the boys, too, so they'll leave you alone." She retrieved her pen and wrote Amy's pass before putting the pen to a separate sheet of paper. "Can I assume the same boys at the nature preserve yesterday are the ones giving you trouble today?"

"Especially Ronnie. He's the one who called me that awful name."

Well, a church-sponsored outing didn't seem to have affected that young man's behavior. "I'll take care of it. Head on back to class now. Stop in tomorrow, and let me know how it goes with your mom."

"Thank you, Miss Morris." Amy smiled gratefully as she turned, backpack over her shoulder, and walked out the door.

Holly's second round of excitement began twenty minutes later when she called the four boys from the youth outing into her office. At first, they all denied saying anything. Only after she picked up the phone to invite Luke to come join them, did they confess.

Not unexpectedly, Ronnie was the most belligerent. "But Miss Morris, she doesn't dress like a regular girl. She dresses like a—"

"Watch it, Ronnie." Holly would not tolerate language or name-calling. "Did you listen to Pastor Rollins at all yesterday?"

He had the grace to look ashamed as he stared at his feet. "Not really."

"Well, I wish you had, because he told us we needed to look at everybody and try to see them the way God does. It doesn't matter how they're dressed, or how they look." All she needed was a lectern. The boys' eyes were already starting to glaze over.

Fine. She'd speak their language.

"All four of you have earned detention for the rest of the week. You have your choice of lunchtime or after school."

"I can fix up your phone again." Ronnie's hopeful expression quickly vanished as he looked at her face.

"Lunchtime or after school?" If they didn't choose, she would.

"I can't stay after school. I have baseball practice." Troy Cotter protested.

Holly picked up her detention pad. "Lunch it is, then. What about the rest of you?"

After muttering and mumbling, all four boys ended up with lunch detentions, and an assurance that if they were caught name-calling or making fun of anybody again, their parents would be contacted.

She had barely ushered the boys out when Coach Hopper arrived with a sullen Billy Andrews beside him.

"Miss Morris, it seems Mr. Andrews slept in the locker room last night. The assistant principal told me to bring him to you; you'd know how to handle it."

Lord, give me strength. I don't understand how a parent can choose alcohol over her child's well-being.

"Thank you, Coach." Holly stood back and held the door open. "Go on in and have a seat, Billy. I'll be right in." She waited until he was inside before she turned back to Al Hopper. "Did Mr. Graham say whether he wants me to call Children's Services?" While Billy Andrews was a frequent topic of faculty meeting conversations, a plan of action had never actually been put in place.

Coach Hopper shrugged. "He just said you'd know what to do, so I guess it's up to you. I found him behind the lockers with a pallet made out of his gym clothes and towel. Couldn't have been very comfortable."

"Thanks again." She turned and walked into her office, softly closing the door behind her.

Deciding it was pointless to wish just once, Mr. Graham would step in and take care of more disciplinary matters, she sat behind her desk and focused on the slouching teenager.

"First of all, Billy, does your mom know where you're at? That you're all right?" Holly waited for him to answer.

His eyes peered defiantly from between locks of blond hair. "Don't matter to her. She's probably plastered again. She probably don't even know I was gone."

"Why did you stay at school?" What must his home life be like?

He shrugged. "Didn't wanna go home. Nothing there I care about."

"What about Gracie?" Holly was certain Billy loved and would do anything for his five-year-old sister.

"He doesn't hurt Gracie." It was obvious Billy wanted to take back the words as soon as he said them.

"Who doesn't hurt Gracie?" Was Cliff Andrews finally home?

For a minute, Holly didn't think Billy was going to answer. He finally looked into her eyes, trying to appear defiant, but a frightened child sat in front of her. "Mom's got a boyfriend."

Wait a minute. His *married* mother had a boyfriend? Well, that wasn't her primary concern at the moment. Billy's reference to this man not hurting Gracie led her to believe he *was* hurting Billy. This could get tricky. Holly needed another adult in here—a witness, preferably male.

"Billy, is there somebody here at school you trust? A teacher, I mean. Sometimes, it takes more than one person to give you the best help. Is there somebody I can have join us for a few minutes?" Now, if he didn't shy away.

The sad-looking teenager seemed to carefully consider his answer before speaking. "I guess Mr. Murdock is okay. He lets me use the computers in study hall if I have all my homework done."

Virgil Murdock. He was a jovial man in his early sixties, soft-spoken and easy-going. The kids liked him. He taught English and monitored study hall. Holly checked the master schedule and saw he was in the library that period. Well, Mr. Graham could just cover study hall for Virgil since he chose not to step up and help the boy himself.

"Let me make a couple of phone calls." Holly smiled encouragingly at Billy.

After explaining to the assistant principal how the situation warranted an adult male's presence and Billy had asked for Mr.

Murdock, it didn't take very long to get everything arranged. Within ten minutes, a soft knock sounded on Holly's office door.

"Come in."

Virgil Murdock, with his salt-and-pepper hair in its usual cacophony, and his ever-present cordial expression in place, stepped into the room.

"Good morning, Billy. Miss Morris." He greeted them before he sat beside the teenager.

"Mr. Murdock, Billy spent last night here at the school. It seems he slept in the locker room." She would have to start this conversation. "So, Billy, will you tell me again, and Mr. Murdock, why you spent the night here?"

Her question was met with complete silence. Was the presence of another grown-up, even one Billy claimed to trust, going to keep him from talking?

"You can tell us anything, Billy." Virgil Murdock's voice was steady. "You're not going to be in trouble. We know you wouldn't have stayed here and slept in that smelly locker room unless something was wrong. Please let us help you."

Billy's lips quivered for a moment, but then he turned to his teacher with a look of determination. "My mom's got a boyfriend. She doesn't care if my dad gets hurt, or even killed while he's fighting in the war."

Holly was relieved to hear him open up, but afraid this was only the tip of the iceberg. "You said your mom's boyfriend doesn't hurt Gracie. What did you mean?"

Billy didn't take his eyes off Mr. Murdock. "Jack. That's his name, Jack Wallace. He doesn't like me. He likes Gracie. He's nice to her and brings her toys and candy."

"Is Jack ever alone with her?" Her stomach churned.

"He ain't like that." Billy turned his attention to Holly, and for a moment, an angry man stared from the frightened boy's eyes. "I'd kill anyone who touched my sister like that." Just as quickly as his fury came, it disappeared. "He really likes her. He even wants to be her dad."

"What about how he treats you?" It was Virgil asking the question.

For the first time since Holly had known the boy, she saw tears in his eyes. He looked blindly toward his feet. "He hates me. He calls me names and says I'm worthless."

"Is that all he does?" was Mr. Murdock's quiet inquiry.

Billy looked into his teacher's eyes for a moment before wordlessly raising the sleeve of his T-shirt. Holly couldn't stop her gasp when she saw the livid marks left so unquestionably by large fingers. There were circular bruises and what appeared to be small burn marks above them, on Billy's upper arm. Unbidden tears came to her eyes as she ached for the young man, still a child, in front of her.

"That ain't all." Billy, seeming almost embarrassed now, pulled his sleeve back down. "I got more bruises, but I can't show them to you, Miss Morris."

Holly exchanged a look with Mr. Murdock before speaking. "Billy, what Jack did to you isn't just being mean. It's against the law. I don't want to scare or upset you, but I have to call the police."

The teenager's eyes were perfect circles. "The police?"

Holly rushed to reassure him. "You won't be in any kind of trouble; I promise, but they'll want to see your bruises."

"All of them?" Billy's voice was shaking.

"Yes." Holly tried to smile encouragingly at him. "You'll have to tell them what happened. It'll be okay. Mr. Murdock can stay with you if you'd like." Mr. Graham could just try to teach English today. Maybe next time he'd step up and help his student.

Billy looked at his teacher again. "Will they put Jack in jail?"

The compassionate man nodded. "They'll fix it so he can never hurt you again. And Billy, you're doing a very brave thing. I know he likes your sister now, but if she ever makes him mad…think how easily he hurt you."

"He likes it." Billy studied his hands. Holly wasn't certain what was going through his mind, but the boy who looked up at Holly was a determined young man. "Okay." He took a deep breath and sat straighter. "I'll show my bruises to the police and tell them everything."

"All right." Holly stood up. "You stay here with Mr. Murdock while I go make some phone calls. Get yourself a can of root beer out of my mini-fridge if you'd like." She waited until he made eye contact with her. "I'm very proud of you, Billy."

Holly turned and walked out of the office as Virgil stood to get a soft drink for the boy. As soon as she closed the door, she leaned against the wall, thankful the hall was empty, and shook. A man put his hands on that child and hurt him. This was part of her job; she was trained for it. The reality was nearly her undoing, though. After taking a deep breath, she stiffened her spine and headed toward the library.

After she had informed Mr. Graham of the situation, she called the police and Department of Children and Family Services. Somebody had to protect the Andrews children since their mother obviously wasn't.

Finally, after a heartbreaking interview with an emergency caseworker, Billy and Virgil Murdock headed to the hospital with Deputy Hank Stone.

Once alone, the emotional strength she held onto for Billy's sake vanished. There was only one thing she knew would help. She picked up the phone on her desk and dialed a familiar number. Hopefully,

Luke would be in from the fields for lunch or somewhere he could hear his cell phone. She needed the comfort of his voice.

Chapter 6

Luke ound himself humming while he pulled the disk through his field. Holly had called him. She was upset, and chose him, of all people, to reach out to for support and comfort. Could she finally feel something more than friendship?

Father, you know how much I love Holly. I know it's your will and not mine, but I'm asking for her to love me back. Please open her eyes, so she can see the love I'm offering her. Give me the courage to show her. Amen

The tractor was one of his favorite places to pray. He found it comforting to talk to his Savior in the midst of God's blessing of bounty. He started the practice while he was a teenager working on his dad's farm. It helped him through those adolescent years when it was a struggle to pray and be a "real man" at the same time. Now he understood praying was what made him a real man.

The sunlight flashing off the old silo caught his attention. The original home site of the farm was located between what was now the northwest corner of his field and the woods he owned. Unoccupied after the new house was built, the old one had fallen into a state of disrepair. Soon after Luke bought the farm, his dad helped him tear down the one wall still standing, and they used a backhoe to clean the place off. Even though it was too far from his barn to be of use, he didn't have the heart to tear down the sturdy silo. Of course, Luke hadn't checked it for structural soundness in quite a while. He'd never gotten around to filling in the cellar, either, come to think of it. Both those tasks would go at the top of his to-do list as soon as his bean field was finished. All he needed was a trespasser to get himself hurt out there. The person would break the law, and then sue Luke for everything he owned.

Thinking of a trespasser reminded him of the machine shed. He felt a twinge of guilt because he hadn't told Holly about the vandalism.

Mitch advised him to keep it quiet so they could both keep their ears open. If anybody around town started talking about it, they'd most likely have their intruder. It was just that he and Holly didn't keep things from each other. She told him everything about her job. He always kept it to himself, too. She would be hurt if—*when*—she found out what happened.

She's mine. He had gone over those words many times. Among the expletives and suggestions for physically impossible bodily actions, they were the only words not filth printed in the shed. It just didn't make any sense to him, though. The only "she" Luke could imagine was Holly, and as far as he knew, nobody else had set his cap for her. And, since he always acted appropriately with women, there was no way he could have angered one of their significant others. It just didn't make sense.

He forced his thoughts elsewhere. The class reunion was coming up. Holly already asked him if they could go together. He could tell while she was excited about seeing some of their old classmates, she was also nervous. Luke remembered how some of them, especially the "cool" kids, treated her. Only a few were downright cruel; the majority paid no attention to her at all.

He'd done all he could, though. If Luke Walker was invited, Holly Morris was coming too. Of course, it hadn't helped her with female get-togethers. She had been left out of many sleepovers and parties, especially when they were thrown by Lucy Phillips or Sally Young. Those two seemed to thrive on Holly's misery.

At least, since her arrival in Shadow at the beginning of fifth grade, Tessa was there. She stepped in and threw her own party on the same night Lucy or Sally had hers. Only a few girls showed up for Tessa's, but Holly always talked about the fun they had. Luke was glad Holly had Tessa in her life. He was doubly glad when the two of them went to college together.

Seeing Holly leave for a school way out in Massachusetts was one of the hardest things Luke had ever done. Because he helped his dad on the farm and planned on buying his grandparents' place as soon as he graduated, he studied agriculture at a college only an hour's drive from Shadow. Holly would probably never know it, but he actually skipped a few classes to be home when she was back in town for visits. He took advantage of every opportunity to spend time with her during those four years.

Unfortunately, also during those years, Luke managed to develop a false sense of security and courage. He told himself as soon as they were both out of college and back home, he'd ask her to marry him, and they would live happily ever after. He never pictured their relationship remaining the same; he wanted it to grow. It took the better part of a year for him to accept the reality of the situation.

He thought of the ring his grandparents had given him. What would Holly think of it? Would there be anything to gain by showing the heirloom to her and telling her the story? Or would she just think it was an interesting tale about her friend's family? It was something to consider, at least. The ring may provide him with an opportunity.

Holly didn't see it the same way, but for all intents and purposes, they had been steadily and exclusively dating for over five years. He wanted her to realize how good they were together. She fit not only into his heart; she fit into his life. They shared the same beliefs and values. She knew what living on a farm was like, and he'd never ask her to give up her career unless she wanted to. They would have beautiful children with her big, brown eyes. If only she could see it.

He started praying again.

Chapter 7

"Wake up, sleepyhead." Luke's soft voice roused Holly from her nap. She sat straight up.

"I'm sorry." Oh, my. Had she really been snuggled against him like that? "I was drowsy during Bible study, but I didn't mean to nod off on you. Why didn't you wake me?" The poor man only came in for a piece of the pie she therapeutically baked the night before.

"You're obviously exhausted." Holly felt Luke reach from where his hand rested behind her and gently capture a strand of her hair. "Any word on Billy?"

"The doctor said the cigarette burns will leave scars." Holly blinked tears away. "And, I guess with such dark bruises on Billy's lower back and stomach, the doctor feared he might have sustained internal injuries." When he confessed to her and Virgil, the teenager had minimized the beatings he received from that monster. "He's going to be in the hospital a couple more days, and then he'll live with his grandmother. The judge granted her temporary custody of both Andrews children."

"I'm sorry you had to deal with it." What was Luke doing? A brief tug, and then her unclipped hair tumbled onto her shoulders. "It had to be one of the most difficult things you've ever handled."

"Except for the ..." She stopped. Her tired mind almost let her blurt out the news of a long year spent in constant terror. And even though she'd been repeatedly assured it wasn't her fault, she still had a tiny niggle of doubt. What if she did something to cause it? "Yes, it was."

"And Amy?"

The thought of Amy brought a smile to her face. "You should see her. I don't think the jeans she wore to school today were even a name brand. Her hair was in a ponytail, and not a trace of makeup. She looks like any girl her age."

Tingles rushed through her as his fingers dove deeper through her tresses. "You gave her great advice. Just think, Holly. Her mom bought those clothes because she thought it was what Amy wanted, and Amy wore them because she thought it was what her mom wanted. All they had to do was be honest with each other." His tender caresses had her so relaxed, she was disappointed when Luke's hand dropped to her shoulder. "You're good at your job, Holly. God called you to an important task and gave you the skills to accomplish it."

"You're good at your job, too." Holly momentarily rested her cheek against Luke's hand before she stood. "And not just farming. You're wonderful with our youth group. If I hadn't told those boys they could explain things to you, I doubt they would have given in quite so quickly."

"But doesn't the fact they behaved that way right after spending time with me prove I'm not getting through to them?" Luke's eyes were filled with doubt.

"You're missing the point, Luke. They respect you, or they wouldn't have cared a lick about having to tell you what they did. And respect is the hardest thing to earn when it comes to their age group. I know that for a fact."

"I hope you're right." Luke's long day must have caught up with him because he yawned widely. "I'd better go so you can get some proper sleep. We can't have an exhausted guidance counselor at school, can we?"

"You—" A vociferous "Er, er-er, er-er" rudely interrupted Holly. Okay. The rooster ringtone wasn't much more pleasant than the scream. "Excuse me. I'd better get it." After nine-thirty on a weeknight, it better be that Publishers Clearing House guy telling her she'd won. "Hello."

"You think you're real smart, don't you?" An unfamiliar male voice came across the line.

"I beg your pardon." He probably wasn't the sweepstakes guy. "I think you must have the wrong number."

"Miss Smarty Guidance Counselor." Hatred could have flown from the phone in a cloud of red dust. "Think you fixed everything, don't you? Well, I'm out, honey. And maybe you need to learn a lesson just like that snot-nosed brat did."

Holly suddenly realized who she was listening to. "All right, Mr. Wallace. It's not wise to make threats when you're already in trouble. Would you like for me to share this call with my friend, *Sheriff* Mitch Landon?"

"You think that scares me?" Laughter worthy of a late-night horror movie resounded. "Well, it don't. You'll be begging me to finish you off before I'm through with you."

"Any man who would hurt a child is nothing but a coward." Holly mustered up every last bit of courage to reply.

"I'll see you soon." The coldly spoken words were followed by the sound of the phone being disconnected.

Forgetting Luke was there, Holly sank onto a chair and covered her face. Jack Wallace's call brought the horror of her past back, in spades.

"Holly?" Gentle hands pulled hers down to show Luke knelt before her. "Hey, it's okay. He was just trying to scare you, and you set him straight. He won't bother you again."

She looked into Luke's compassionate eyes. "I-I may have only made him angrier. He says he's going to hurt me."

Luke gently took her hands in his. "Okay, then we'll call Mitch. He'll tell us what we need to do."

Maybe it was because of Saturday's prank call or the stress of helping Billy, but Jack Wallace's threat was just too much. "Will you call him for me?"

"Sure." Luke stood and pulled his phone out of his pocket. After pushing a couple of buttons, he began to speak.

"Hey, Ray, it's Luke Walker. Can you patch me through to Mitch?" He was talking to one of the dispatchers.

"Mitch, it's Luke." He frowned as he listened to the sheriff.

"No, nothing has happened to me. I'm calling for Holly." His frown deepened.

"We didn't know that, but we knew he was out on bail. He just called and threatened Holly." Luke's eyes focused on her, deep concern etched on his brow.

"Well, no, we didn't tape it. We didn't know he was going to call." Luke seemed a little irate with the sheriff.

"Okay. I'll tell her. How long before a trial?" A look of incredulity appeared on his face before he masked it.

"Our legal system needs some overhauling, doesn't it?" Luke shook his head when he heard the other man's response.

"I agree. Thank you, Mitch."

Luke disconnected the call and turned back to Holly. "Billy's mom must be a piece of work, Holly. She managed to scrape up enough money to pay Jack Wallace's bail. The man who beat her son."

Holly knew without asking. "Threatening me can't get his bail revoked because there's no proof."

"Mitch doesn't like it any better than we do, but it looks like he's out on bail until his case goes to trial. I guess that could take several months."

"So, he's free to hurt Billy again?" The boy may not survive another beating.

"No." Luke pulled her to her feet and put his hands on her shoulders. "They took out a restraining order. If he comes within five hundred feet of either Billy or his sister, his bail will be revoked, and he'll stay in jail until his trial. Mitch thinks you should get the same kind of order set up."

She was all too familiar with the definitions of restraining orders, orders of protection, and no-contact orders. Unfortunately, her circumstances hadn't allowed her to take advantage of any of them. Maybe this time would be different. "I'll stop by and take one out after school tomorrow."

Holly was totally unprepared for what happened next. Luke's hands gently framed her face before his warm, firm lips met hers. It was a short, chaste kiss, but he most definitely kissed her.

"Why did you do that?" And why did her knees suddenly feel weak?

Luke answered with a small smile. "Just be careful, Holly. Call Mitch or me if anything spooks you. Promise?"

Still stunned by his kiss, she silently nodded.

"Lock the door behind me."

She was still staring at it long after he left.

Chapter 8

"So, I'm putting you and Holly both down on the RSVP list." Jennifer Ewing was talking ninety miles an hour. Luke could probably lay his phone down and not miss a thing while he fetched the bottle of water calling his name.

"We'll be there." Thank goodness. That kiss could have ended everything. Friday evening, things had been the same as always, though. It had probably been unreasonable to hope she'd answer the door with a passionate kiss and declaration of undying love.

"I've spoken to so many people. I can't believe it. Melody Appleby, only she's Melody Newton now. Brent Dasher, Seth Murphy, Natalie Beason, Cal Fultz, and you'll never guess, Luke."

Dare he ask? "What?"

"Tom Dwer and Kevin Tripp both called. Remember how much trouble those big lugs were always in? Tom always had the bright ideas, and Kevin always carried them out. I tell you, I don't think I've ever heard Kevin string a complete sentence together."

The infamous Tom and Kevin. Luke wasn't the right kind of kid to hang with those two. He refused to stuff the toilets full of paper or use shoe polish to black out the windows on every staff member's vehicle.

"Melody lives in New York City. Can you believe it? A person from Shadow, Illinois living in the Big Apple?" What a surprise. She actually paused to take a breath. "And I think Tom and Kevin both live out east somewhere, too, but not in the same place."

"It sounds like there's going to be a good turnout." He would have asked Holly to call with their RSVPs, but she'd been out-of-sorts since the threatening phone call from Jack Wallace. At least there hadn't been another one.

"Oh my, yes. I have twenty-one responses, and with spouses or dates, we'll have even more people here. You know, it was my idea to put 'plus one' on the invitations. I pointed out to Rob and Annie, some people were just dating. Like you and Holly. You're dating. If we stated it like Rob suggested, you two might not feel right about coming together." She giggled breathlessly. "Unless you two are getting engaged within the next three weeks."

I wish. "Plus one was a good idea." If she didn't let him go soon, he was going to risk insulting her by chugging a bottle of water. The sun was unusually hot for April, and he was sweating. The next time, he'd remember to hit the fridge before he called Jennifer. Not that he intended to make a habit of calling the chatty woman.

He swiped his hand down his face. Surely, she would run out of steam any moment.

"You know, I heard Joe is going to propose to Missy. Have you heard that? I mean, you men don't talk to each other like we women do, but you and Joe are friends. Has he told you anything about it? I promise I can keep a secret."

Okay. This was beginning to sound too much like gossip. "If Joe told me something like that, I wouldn't be free to share it with anybody, Jen." The sun's rays picked that moment to shine through the window and land on his shiny, stainless steel refrigerator—like a beacon pointing his way to bliss. "I'm sorry, but I just came in from the fields, and I really need to get cleaned up. Are we supposed to send in the questionnaires before the reunion, or just bring them with us?"

"I'd like to have them at least a week before the event. Dennis is very skilled on the computer, you know." How convenient, since he was the school district's technology manager. "He's putting together a presentation. We'll show it on the big drop-down screen they have on the stage now. Wouldn't it have been nice if that had been there when we graduated? Why, that block wall made us all look like zit-covered children."

Leave it to Jennifer Ewing to worry about acne on baby pictures. "Okay. I'll let Holly know, and we'll get them to you soon. Thanks for organizing this, Jen. It'll be fun."

"You're welcome. I said somebody needed to do it. You know, we should have had a five-year reunion, but nobody—"

"I really need to go, Jen. Thanks again." Luke quickly disconnected the call. Clarence looked at him like he was seriously concerned about his master's sanity while Luke rushed over to the refrigerator and finally grabbed the bottle of water he'd been longing for. He had just taken his first gulp when the phone rang.

"She is not calling me back." Hmmm. Clarence was closer to the phone. "I'll tell you what. You can listen to her this time, boy. Just make a noise every so often. She'll never know the difference."

His dog snorted before turning and plodding out of the room. Oh, well. Maybe Jennifer had something important to say—like hadn't their graduation gowns made them look fat?

"She's mine," a low, guttural male voice hissed.

"Who is yours? I don't even know who *you* are!" This had to be a scene from a really cheesy old movie.

"She's mine," the voice repeated. "Stay away from her, or you won't like what happens." The line went dead.

Luke sat in the chair closest to him. None of this made any sense. There was only one woman he was ever really with—Holly. And with a population of less than ten thousand, Shadow wasn't a big town. He was positive he'd know if another man were interested in her.

He decided to call Mitch.

"Sheriff Landon," Mitch answered.

"Mitch, it's Luke again."

"Another break-in?" Mitch's concern was evident in his voice.

"No." Luke was quick to respond. He quickly summarized the phone call.

"Any idea what woman he's warning you away from?" Mitch sounded as perplexed as Luke felt.

He only had one answer. "It doesn't make any sense, Mitch, but Holly is the only woman I spend time with. Don't you think I'd know if another man were interested in her?"

"You'd think so. You two are together enough." Mitch paused for a moment. "Have you asked Holly if she has any ideas?"

Luke sighed. "She's had a lot on her plate with some stuff happening at work, so she doesn't need any more stress in her life. I didn't tell her about the machine shed."

"Oh, boy." A low whistle came from Luke's phone. "When I told you to keep it quiet, I figured you'd still tell Holly. If she's anything like my sister, she's going to give you a buzz cut with a weed whacker when she finds out."

"I know." Maybe after church the next day he'd tell her. "I'll talk to her tomorrow afternoon. We're going to Tony and Susan's for lunch, so we'll have plenty of time."

"I think I would," Mitch advised. "Besides, she might have an idea who it could be. You never know."

After the two men had said their goodbyes, Luke stood and paced around the table. Was it possible? Someone else was interested in Holly, and she hadn't told Luke? Okay. He didn't have any real claim on her, but she'd tell him if there was another man. Wouldn't she?

"I have enough of a battle just convincing her we can be more than friends." Clarence had returned and was once again Luke's confidant. "I don't think I can compete with another man, too. Besides, just because there might be someone interested in her doesn't mean it's mutual, does it, boy?"

Clarence angled his head and looked up at his owner. Not for the first time, Luke wished his dog could contribute to their conversation. He'd heard of horse sense. Maybe there was such a thing as dog sense. And he would take all the sense he could get right now.

Chapter 9

"Remember when you tied your wagon behind the pony?" Susan was laughing so hard, she barely got the words out as she addressed her daughter.

"Not one of my brightest ideas." And heaven knew she came up with a lot of them.

"I thought it was." Luke patted her shoulder. "I'm the one who tried it out. Remember?"

As if she could forget. After watching an exciting horse race on *Little House on the Prairie*, she decided her pony, Ferdinand, could pull her little wagon just like the televised horses did the big ones. So, with Luke's help, she tied Ferdie's bridle to the handle—with jump ropes of all things. Then, because she was a good friend and wanted Luke to experience the daring adventure, she let him have the first ride.

It started out just fine with Ferdie pulling Luke up a slight rise in the pasture. Then, they started downhill. Of course, the wagon rolled faster than the pony was walking and smacked into his legs. That sent him into a full-out gallop with Luke holding on for dear life. They made it all the way to the pond where Ferdie circled it twice before unceremoniously dumping Luke right into a nice patch of gooey mud. When he stood up, his eyes were the only thing not covered with the dark goop, and Holly ended up rolling on the ground laughing so hard she couldn't talk.

"We were only ten." Surely, that had to count for something.

"That's as good as the breaking vine." Tony chuckled.

Luke's eyebrows rose as he gave her a questioning look. "Remind me why I was always the one who had the privilege of trying out your projects."

"How was I supposed to know the thing was going to break while you were right over the creek?" Luke ended up covered in a lot of mud that day, too.

"That's okay, Luke." Susan smiled warmly at him. "You never climbed a tree and sat in it for two hours because you were afraid to come down and nobody was there to help you."

"Mom," Holly protested. "I was only seven or eight then."

"And I thought you were in the pasture with your dad while he thought you were in the kitchen with me. We should all just be thankful he came in early that day, or you may still be sitting in that tree crying your eyes out." Susan clearly enjoyed the memory.

"Too bad Luke wasn't with you." Tony's speculative glance shifted to the younger man. "He always rescued you, didn't he?"

Luke's green eyes were so dark, they looked black. He had been her champion...her hero. How had she not realized it before? He was the one who climbed onto a tree branch and sat with her until her dad's cranky old bull wandered to greener grass. He pulled her off the electric fence when she slipped in the mud and flopped across it, unable to regain her footing. He gave Seth Murphy a black eye for calling Holly a porker and making her cry. On his sixteenth birthday, he missed his own party and made use of his brand new license to drive a heartbroken Holly and her old, rapidly failing dog to the vet. There, he sat and held her hand while Twink went to sleep for the final time. When they got home and her dog didn't run out to greet them, she cried harder than ever. Luke held her tightly and used his shirttail to wipe the tears from her eyes.

"You've been there for me more times than I can count." She impulsively hugged him. "Thank you for being such a good friend."

Something strange appeared in Luke's eyes for a brief moment before he returned her smile. "I can't imagine my life any other way."

"Why don't you two walk out to the pond? The snow geese will be moving on soon. You don't want to miss seeing them." Susan was already standing up. "Tony, you can come help me with the dishes."

Before Holly even knew quite what was happening, she found herself walking beside Luke as they traversed the field between the barn and pond.

"Holly, there's something I need to tell you." Luke sounded more nervous than she had ever known him to be. "You're not going to like it, and I probably should have told you sooner, but you've been dealing with the Billy Andrews situation."

"What?" His demeanor put her on edge.

He stopped walking and turned to face her. "Last Sunday, after I got home from the youth group outing, somebody was in my machine shed. He vandalized it with spray paint."

"Luke." She felt sick at the thought of someone destroying what Luke worked so hard for. "What happened?"

He seemed even more reluctant to talk. "I let Clarence out of the house, and then I thought I saw movement. It was too big to be an animal, so I walked out to see what it was."

"By yourself? With only Clarence to help you?" Without thinking, she grasped his hands.

A crooked grin appeared on his face. "You'd have been proud of Clarence. When I checked the machine shed door, somebody plowed me over on his way out. Clarence chased the guy all the way to the tree line."

He had been attacked. Forget propriety. She couldn't get close enough. Her arms slid around his shoulders, and she buried her face against his neck. "Were you hurt?"

His arms wrapped snugly around her waist. "See? This is why I didn't tell you. I have a bruise. That's all."

She pulled back and looked into his face. "Who was he?"

"I have no idea. I just know from the way he ran me down he has to be pretty good-sized."

"You said he used spray paint. What did he do?" She could only imagine.

"He sprayed obscenities on just about every surface in the place." He appeared more uncomfortable for a moment before he spoke again. "There's something else you need to know."

What could be worse than what he already described? "Please, just tell me."

She could see the hesitation in his eyes before he finally spoke. "A man called me. Mitch and I both think it's the same man who vandalized my machine shed."

"Why?"

"He said the same thing he painted on my tractor."

Holly was afraid to ask, but she had to know. "What was it?"

"It's probably nothing, Holly. Just somebody being foolish." He didn't meet her eyes.

"Lucas Ryan Walker, if you don't tell me right now, I'll ... I'll ..." She was at a loss for words.

"He told me 'she's mine' and to leave her alone, or I won't like what will happen." He tilted her chin up and looked directly into her eyes. "You're the only woman I'm ever with." He visibly made a valiant attempt to smile but didn't quite succeed. "Holly, have you...?" Long eyelashes touched his cheeks as his lids closed for a moment. Then, clouded green eyes met hers. "Have you met someone—a man?"

Words. Luke was right in front of her, but she couldn't hear him. She slapped her hands over her ears as another voice—harsh and angry—grew louder and louder. "You're mine. *You are mine!* "

Luke's hands covered hers. "Holly?"

His eyes—so dark—now suddenly white. His face disappeared in a blinding light.

"Honey, wake up. You're okay. Come on." How had she ended up in bed? Why was her mom in her bedroom?

"She's opening her eyes, Susan." That was Luke speaking.

"Luke?" She was even more puzzled when she opened her eyes and saw him kneeling beside the sofa on which she lay.

"I'm right here." His face was pale under his tan as he looked worriedly at her.

"What happened?" Holly could remember walking with Luke. They were going to look at the snow geese.

He reached over and gently brushed the hair off her forehead. "You passed out. It's my fault. I upset you, and you passed out."

"You, how did you—" Suddenly, she remembered— everything. She tried to sit up, only to be met with a throbbing in her head.

"Slow and easy there, Holly." Her dad appeared at the end of the sofa and placed his hands on her shoulders. "Sit up slowly, or you'll be right back down."

She took her time and finally managed to make it to an upright position. She looked into Luke's eyes and saw the guilt there. "It's not your fault, Luke." She couldn't stop the tears from running down her face. She couldn't pretend this wasn't happening. It wouldn't do any good. "We need to call Mitch. I need to tell all of you something, and I can only do it once." She looked at her parents' worried faces. "Mom, will you call Tessa? I could use her help."

It was written all over their faces; they wanted to ask her more questions. She silently begged them not to. Finally, her mom nodded and stood while Luke pulled his phone out of his pocket.

"I'll call Mitch."

Holly closed her eyes to shut out the deep concern in Luke's.

Chapter 10

What was going on? Tessa had just arrived at Holly's parents', and Mitch should be there any moment. Something about what Luke told Holly terrified her. So much she fainted. He was thankful his arms were around her; he kept her from falling and being injured.

"Is it finally time?" Tessa asked Holly as she sat beside her on the sofa.

Holly silently nodded, her tear-streaked face still too pale.

Time for what? Luke wanted to ask. Somehow he held onto his tongue. She would tell them when she could.

"Sorry it took me so long. I was celebrating with Missy and Joe." Mitch spoke as he entered the room behind Tony. "I guess I can tell all of you. Joe popped the question yesterday."

It looked like Jennifer Ewing's Intel had been correct.

"So, what's going on?" Mitch asked Holly.

"Tell him everything, Holly." Tessa's blond curls shook with her dictatorial command. "You have to tell him everything, or he won't be able to help."

The hope that appeared on Holly's face was quickly replaced by despair. "He won't be able to anyway, Tess. Nobody can, remember?" She looked at her friend. "He's found me."

"Who?" Luke had to ask. No way was it a new boyfriend; Holly was afraid.

Tessa put her arm around Holly's shoulders. "Do you want me to tell them?"

"Yes," was Holly's whispered answer.

Tessa's gaze scanned the group standing in front of her before landing on Mitch. "During the first week of our senior year of college, we received a phone call. Neither of us thought too much about it since it was a hang-up. We figured it was a wrong number or something."

Her arm tightened around Holly. "But then we started getting more of them, as many as ten times a day. At first, we didn't know whether it was both, or just one of us, being harassed."

"Then he said my name." Holly's breath hitched. "He called me 'my Holly.' I asked him to please stop calling me. I thought he'd just go away."

Tessa resumed speaking. "He just became worse. He called and told her she was his, and they were going to be together."

Mitch spoke up. "Did you have your number changed?"

Holly looked guiltily at her parents. "That's when I told you I was only going to use my cell phone from then on. I got rid of the land line, remember?"

Susan's eyes widened. "That's why you did that?"

"I'm sorry, Mom." Holly's gaze dropped to her lap. "I thought if he didn't have a phone to call me on, it would stop."

"Why didn't you tell us?" Frustration warred with concern in Tony's expression.

"Mom didn't want me to go to Tullen in the first place, Dad." The agony in her eyes as she turned to Susan tore Luke's heart out. "I'm sorry, Mom, but it's true. You didn't make it very easy for me. If you'd have known about him, it would have been more challenging for me to stay there. And I didn't want to give up my life because a man was frightening me."

"I take it he somehow managed to get your cell phone number." Mitch made the observation.

Holly visibly shuddered. "The house phone hadn't even been disconnected for a week when the calls started coming to my cell phone. I don't know how he managed to get the number. I never gave it to anybody except my study groups and administration. But he got it anyway."

"You changed your cell number when you got a better deal with another carrier," her dad said flatly. "You were trying to get away from him then, too, weren't you?"

"I'm so sorry, Dad." Holly's tears were falling again. "I didn't mean to lie to you and Mom. I was just trying to handle it on my own. To be an adult."

"Is he the reason you've never wanted a computer of your own?" Susan shared a look of comprehension with her husband. "You were afraid he'd send you e-mails?"

Holly's sad eyes met Tessa's for a moment before she turned to her mom. "He's never contacted me on my e-mail account at school. It sounds silly, but I'm afraid that might change if the computer is in my house."

"I don't think it's silly." As always, Tony had chosen to support his daughter. "You have every reason to feel that way."

"Did you call the police?" Luke could no longer remain silent.

Tessa answered him. "Campus security tried helping first, but they soon turned it over to the Tullen City Police. They told us Holly was doing everything right; ignoring him, and changing her number. They said there wasn't anything that could be done unless—" Her cheeks flushed red, and steam was bound to rise any time as Tessa spit the words out. "She had to wait until he made physical contact. If he got his hands on her and did who knows what, *then* they would do something. Cretins."

Holly gently patted her friend's leg. "It wasn't their fault. They didn't know who he was, either."

Mitch pulled his pad and ink pen out of his shirt pocket. "What happened to make you think he's found you, Holly?"

"I received a call last week. I tried to tell myself it was just laughter, but it wasn't. He said my name. He called me 'my Holly.'"

Holly didn't quite meet Tessa's gaze. "I've also been receiving hang-ups for the past two weeks."

"Holly." Tessa's voice was a mixture of shock and dismay.

"I'm sorry. I chose to pretend everything was okay." Holly's eyes were begging Tessa for understanding. "I wanted it to not be true, but I'm sure it was him now."

"What makes you sure?" Mitch asked.

Holly's gaze shifted to Luke. "One of the things he told me over and over." She drew a ragged breath. "He'd say 'you are mine.' And he would never allow any other man to be with me."

Luke's breath caught in his throat. "The vandalism."

"He's close, Luke. He's close enough he knows I spend a lot of time with you. He's warning you away from me. Don't you see?" Holly's tears were falling faster. "He's going to hurt you, and it will be my fault."

Forget what kind of relationship she thought they had. He knelt and held the woman he loved as tightly as he could.

"None of this is your fault." She wasn't going to blame herself. "It's that twisted man's fault. Mitch will help us, and we'll find him. Do you hear me?"

"Holly." Mitch sounded hesitant. "Are you sure this couldn't be Jack Wallace trying to frighten you? You made him pretty angry when you helped Billy."

Holly seemed unaware of leaning toward Luke as he released her and dropped to his knees. "Jack Wallace didn't try to disguise his voice when he called me. He wanted me to know who he was so he could make sure I understood his threats. This other man, my stalker, just wants to torment me."

Susan stepped toward her daughter. "Well, that does it. You are packing your things and moving home until this is all over."

"I can't, Mom." Holly's eyes begged for understanding. "If I give up my house, he's taking something away from me. It's enough he's able to call and threaten me. Let alone damage Luke's shed. I can't let him take my life away from me. I can't let him win."

"But honey, if he's brazen enough to attack somebody Luke's size, what might he do if he managed to get his hands on you?" Tony questioned his daughter.

The phone's ringing saved Holly from having to answer her father.

Susan walked over to the table and answered it.

"Hello."

The genteel woman Luke had known most of his life abruptly became a fierce Amazon warrior. "You, listen to me." Her grip on the phone tightened. "You will never...and I mean, *never* so much as breathe on my daughter. I don't even want you to *look* at her! Who do you think you are, anyway? Skulking around town like some James Bond wannabe."

Her frown grew as she listened. "Don't you even say her name. You leave her alone, you...you—"

Mitch managed to pull the phone from her hand. "This is the Shadow County Sheriff. I am telling you right now to stop harassing Holly Morris. This isn't some big town where you can slither around like the cowardly snake you are. Holly has many, many friends in Shadow, and we'll find you. And when we do, believe me, *you'll* be the one who doesn't like what happens."

Luke had never heard Mitch use that tone of voice before, and he was impressed. He sure wouldn't want to be on the receiving end.

Mitch was silent for a moment before he returned the phone to its cradle. "He hung up, but it wasn't until after I finished talking. He heard everything I said."

"What can we do to protect our daughter?" Susan asked Mitch. "Please tell us what we should do."

Mitch gave Holly a concerned look. "Holly, I understand what you're saying about giving in to him. I really do. The fact remains, if this is the same man who wasn't afraid to tackle Luke, you're in danger. I just can't advise you to stay at your house. Not alone."

"What if I move in with her?" Tessa asked. "He never approached her physically while we were together in Tullen."

"You can't put yourself in danger," Holly protested.

"Please!" Tessa let out an unladylike snort. "If he's seen you with Luke, you can bet your pretty little petunia basket he's seen you with me."

Holly shook her head. "But—"

"Listen, Holly Morris, I wasn't his tar...I wasn't the one he called, but he has to recognize me. He's called Luke and your parents; he'll call me, and you know it. And since I'm not about to sit down and have a friendly chat about your blissful future together, he won't like me. You and I will be safer together." Blonde curls shook as she turned to the sheriff. "Tell her, Mitch. It's an ideal solution."

"It would be better than being there alone," While he definitely wasn't enthused, Mitch seemed satisfied with Tessa's suggestion.

Luke looked at the women—Holly, slender and, although at five-seven, considered tall for a woman, seemed petite to him. Tessa was about the same height as Holly, but not quite as slim. While both women were healthy and in good physical shape, he couldn't see the two of them-even together-confronting the giant who ran him over. Just as he was about to voice his concerns, an idea popped into his head.

"I can arrange for them to have an overnight guest to keep them safe."

"Luke!" Holly's puritanical mother was back. "I know you would be a perfect gentleman, but it's still inappropriate for you to stay there."

Luke laughed in spite of himself. "Not me. Clarence."

He grinned at the look on Holly's face. "You know how he feels about you, Holly. He won't even let Dad get close." The idea was growing on him. "I'll bring him after dinner every evening, and pick him up before I do morning chores. You won't have to worry about him during the day, and he'll sleep all night unless he's needed."

Holly slowly smiled. "I like the idea, Luke." She turned to Mitch. "Is that safe enough, do you think? I mean, he called my parents' number, so he knows this place. It'd be just as safe in my house as out at the farm, wouldn't it? Tessa and me…and Clarence."

"I guess." The sheriff still wasn't one hundred percent on board.

Displeased looks appeared on her parents' faces. Luke may just have fallen out of favor with them, but he had a feeling Holly was going to stay in her house one way or another. At least, Clarence would offer some protection.

"Thank you, Luke," Holly murmured.

His voice was just as hushed. "Don't you know by now I would do anything for you?"

His heart leaped as he saw the light in her eyes. That was as close as he'd ever come to telling her how he really felt, and she looked pleased. He wanted to kiss her very much, but this was neither the time nor place. However, he knew now he was going to kiss her again. It was worth the risk. She was worth the risk.

Chapter 11

"Clarence, get off my bed right now, or I'll tie your legs together and use you as a footstool!" Holly hid a smile behind her hand as Tessa scolded the dog for at least the third time since Luke dropped him off.

"I guess we didn't really consider where Clarence would sleep when Luke told us he'd sleep all night." It was all Holly could do not to laugh at her friend's frustrated expression as Tess chased the dog into the living room again.

"Well, I don't know why he likes my bed so much. It's not even a full size, for the love of Einstein. He hangs off both sides when he stretches out on it." Tessa glared at Clarence.

Holly couldn't hold back her laughter. "Well, it is the guest room after all. And Clarence is a guest."

"What am I?" Tessa was trying to look indignant, but Holly could see the amusement in her friend's eyes. "Maybe I should go make a pallet out of blankets and curl up on the floor next to your bed."

"No. You snore." It felt good to joke around with Tessa. Normal.

Clarence took advantage of Tessa's inattention and slipped back past her into her bedroom. Holly bit her lip to keep from laughing harder. She wondered which one of them would win this battle.

"Luke loves you, you know." Tessa made the observation out of the blue.

Holly's laughter died. "We're good friends, Tess. He loves me like that. I love him the same way. You, of all people, know that."

Tessa shook her head. "He loves you like a man loves a woman, Holly. You have to see it. You just don't want to acknowledge it, because then you'd have a decision to make."

"He can't—I can't." Holly closed her eyes for a moment. "I just can't deal with this right now. Please don't ask me to. Things are fine the way they are. Right now, I have to get through this stalker trouble again." She would think positive. "At least, being here, I feel like I have a chance of him being caught. Mitch is right that a new person will stand out, and somebody is bound to notice if he's paying too close of attention to Luke or me."

"I pray you're right." Tessa walked over and gave Holly a hug. "I agree it's better we're home this time. You have many people around here who care about you; you're much safer than when it was just you and me."

Tessa's words made Holly realize something. "You know what, Tess?" Her friend looked questioningly at her. "There's one thing I need to do I haven't done. I need to call Pastor Rollins and ask for my problem to be added to the prayer chain. I can't keep this a secret if I expect people to be on the lookout for him, and I need God's help more than ever. How could I forget the most important One to go to?"

"I know what you mean." Tessa smiled gently. "I've been praying, but the more people who pray, the better. And between our Lord and Clarence, I feel safer already." She suddenly looked around. "Where is Clarence? He'd better not have..." She turned and headed to her room.

Holly laughed softly as she dug the phone out of her purse and punched in the pastor's number. Hopefully, he wouldn't be able to hear the one-woman tirade coming from her guest room.

"Pastor Rollins here."

"Pastor, this is Holly. I'm sorry to be calling at this time of the evening, but I have an urgent request for the prayer chain."

The pastor's cheerful demeanor didn't seem fazed. "You can call at any time of the day or night for the prayer chain, Holly. You know that. What do we need to add?"

Holly took a deep breath and began talking. Pastor Rollins listened silently as she told him everything, starting with the first call in Tullen.

He was assuring her the chain members would both pray and keep their eyes open, when suddenly, a howl erupted from the guest room.

"What was that?" the pastor asked.

"Luke is letting Clarence spend nights with Tessa and me. I'd say that was him getting kicked out of Tessa's bed for the last time."

She could hear Pastor Rollins chuckle. "Clarence is your watchdog?"

"He always stays close to me when I'm out at Luke's, and he nearly attacked Richard once, for trying to hug me." She couldn't believe she was defending the dog. "Luke is pretty confident Clarence would do his best to take care of me if I were threatened."

"Well, from my experience, he might lick the guy half to death." The minister was outright laughing.

Clarence chose that moment to appear in Tessa's open bedroom door. One of his ears was standing straight up like it was stuck that way, and his typical unkempt hairdo looked even wilder than usual. It appeared he and Tessa had gotten into a wrestling match. Holly wondered what Tessa looked like.

"Thank you for listening to my problems, Pastor Rollins." Holly had a feeling she better get off the phone before her friend made an appearance.

"I'll start the prayer chain as soon as we hang up, dear." His voice was full of kindness. "And please let me know if you require some extra help. There isn't any shame in needing to talk about things. Sometimes it helps more than we can imagine."

"I'll do that."

"Goodnight, Holly."

"Goodnight, Pastor."

Tessa emerged from the bedroom just as Holly placed her phone on the end table. Holly promptly burst into laughter. Tessa's blond hair, which usually framed her face, was in complete chaos, sticking out in every imaginable direction. Holly laughed even harder when her friend stuck out her lower lip and blew several unruly curls out of her eyes.

"I won!" Tessa was proud of herself.

Clarence turned his head and looked over his flanks at her before marching resolutely into Holly's room. Holly just hoped he made himself comfortable on the bed she fixed on the floor. Otherwise, she'd be wallowing around with him next.

Her phone rang.

"Pastor Rollins must need to tell me something." She picked it up and answered.

"You'd better stay away from Walker, my Holly. I'll have to show him he can't have you. Nobody can have you." It was the voice she dreaded the most. "You're mine. *All* mine. Don't forget it."

Before Holly could respond, the caller disconnected.

"Holly? Are you all right?" Tessa rushed over to her. "Was it him?"

Holly nodded wordlessly.

"Sit down before you pass out again." Tessa helped Holly onto the sofa. "What did he say?"

The realization hit her. "It's really him, Tessa. Doing all this." Holly shuddered. "Just like he told Luke to stay away from me, he told me to stay away from him. That Luke...he will show Luke he can't have me." She looked at her friend with fear in her eyes. "Maybe it would be safer for Luke if I stayed away from him for a while."

"That's not going to happen, Holly." Tessa's lips formed a firm line. "You talk about this man taking something away from you. You can't let him take one of the most important relationships in your life. Got it?"

Holly considered her words and slowly nodded. "You're right. I just couldn't bear it if Luke were hurt because of me. It's bad enough he's exposed to this mess."

Tessa gave her a hug. "Believe me, Luke wouldn't have it any other way."

Holly remembered Luke's words. He would do anything for her. While she couldn't allow herself to consider exactly what he meant, Holly knew Tessa spoke the truth.

Chapter 12

"Is there any news about Holly's case?" The older-than-dirt, wooden chair creaked ominously as Luke lowered his large frame onto it.

The sheriff set the can of soda he'd been drinking on his desk and looked across it. "It's only Tuesday, but thanks to Pastor Rollins and his prayer chain, I think at least half of Shadow already knows she has a stalker."

"Yeah. Besides praying, Pastor asked people to keep their eyes open for a stranger." Luke was worried about Holly, though. She looked incredibly tired that morning when he picked Clarence up.

"Are we so sure it's a stranger?" Mitch asked.

"It has to be." Luke surely misunderstood the other man. "You can't think one of our friends or neighbors would be doing this. Everybody likes Holly." His seat tottered as he thought of another reason Mitch was wrong. "They wouldn't have been in Massachusetts when she was there."

"I don't know." Mitch pulled a file folder out of his desk drawer. "This is all the paperwork from the Tullen Police Department. They wondered why he never physically approached her. There was not one reported sighting." He pulled what Luke could see was a campus map out of the folder, and indicated a blue circle. "The girls lived here, in a busy apartment building on the edge of campus. According to the officer I spoke with, it's a heavily trafficked area, and a lurker would have drawn attention." Mitch slid a full-page photograph of Holly out of the folder. "The guy was coming on too strong not to have wanted to be around Holly, don't you think? If he was there."

This was opening up and entirely new line of possibilities, none of which seemed desirable, to Luke.

"Just suppose," Mitch continued, "the stalker knows Holly because they're both from Shadow. He could have been making those calls from anywhere, Luke."

"Then why the time gap? She's been home from Massachusetts for nearly six years, and he's just now starting to do this again." None of this—nothing— made sense.

Mitch sat back in his chair and sighed. "I don't know. Maybe he saw something that made him think your friendship was deepening into something else, and it set him off."

It was true Luke was finding it more and more difficult to hide his feelings for Holly. Might somebody close to them have noticed? "This man would have to fit in our environment."

Mitch nodded. "It would explain how he knows where you live. That Tony and Susan are Holly's parents."

Then Luke remembered the phone call. "But I didn't recognize his voice. If he were somebody I knew, wouldn't it be familiar, even though he tried to disguise it?"

"Let me show you something." Mitch reached into another desk drawer and pulled out a small object resembling a tape recorder. "Hank picked this up at the last convention he went to. He thought it looked like a trouble-causing gadget."

He pushed a button and spoke. "My name is Mitch Landon. I'm the sheriff of Shadow."

Then he set the machine down and pushed another button. Mitch's recorded voice came out. Next he adjusted a dial on the edge of the device. This time, when he pressed play, the voice it produced sounded like an elderly woman. The speech was clear and intelligible, but it wasn't Mitch's voice anymore. He adjusted the dial and repeated the play process. A child spoke this time.

"I can make my voice sound like just about anything I want with this thing." Mitch picked it up and held it out to Luke. "The device costs less than a hundred dollars, and you can order it from a thousand places on the Internet. Maybe our guy has one of these or something like it. Hank said there's some that alter your voice when you speak directly through them."

Luke turned the small recorder over in his hands. "Who thinks of things like this?"

"People who are smarter and have a lot more extra time time than me." Mitch returned the two sheets of paper to the folder from Tullen and slid it back in a drawer. "What's the latest on Holly's calls?"

"I know she's gotten one every night this week." Luke handed the device back to Mitch.

"I wish I had the manpower to set up a watch around her house. I don't like that she lives on the edge of town. It would be safer if she had neighbors who would notice if anything strange was going on." Mitch returned the recorder to his desk.

"She would skin me alive if I tried to sleep in my Jeep outside her house." Luke knew that for a fact. "Or else I'd do it, just so she could feel safe enough to sleep."

"Sheriff?" Haley Johnson, the dispatcher, was speaking over the intercom.

Mitch pushed a button on a dust-covered electronic device. "What do you need, Haley?"

"A call just came in that Jack Wallace showed up at the high school. One of the teachers caught him on the ball diamond, asking students where Billy Andrews was. He has the restraining order, so Hank went to arrest him. Wallace is nowhere to be found. What do you want Hank to do?"

Luke's heart leaped into his throat as he came to his feet. "Did he get to Holly?"

Mitch stood and held his hand in a "stop" gesture. "Hank is aware of the entire situation. If Holly were involved in any way, he'd have let me know. I promise." He pushed his intercom button again. "Tell Hank to go to Gina Andrews' house and sit tight. I'm on my way. Call the state dispatcher and have a BOLO put out on him so the state guys know we're looking for him."

"Will do."

"Sorry to run, Luke, but I can stick the guy back in jail now. One less thing for Holly to worry about." Mitch waited for Luke to walk to the door. "I figured he'd break the order. I'm just glad he did it while Billy was safe at school. Now the creep will be behind bars until his trial."

Luke followed Mitch out of the building and made his way to his Jeep. Just as he was about to get in, Dennis Ewing pulled up beside him.

"Looks like I can save myself a phone call." Dennis pushed back the goofy looking, purple fedora he always wore, releasing a few blond curls.

"How's that?"

Dennis rolled his eyes. "Jen is bugging the daylights out of me. She's on the warpath about those questionnaires. I know we still have a couple of weeks before the reunion, but I guess she has just about everybody's. She's worried about yours and Holly's."

In all honesty, with all that was going on, the reunion and questionnaires were just about the last thing on Luke's mind. He didn't imagine they were very high on Holly's list of priorities at the moment, either. "I'll get mine to her tomorrow, and remind Holly. Good enough?"

"Thank you." Nearly white eyebrows met in the middle of his forehead as Dennis frowned. "I was sorry to hear about someone harassing Holly. Did Mitch make any progress yet?"

Luke leaned against the cab of his vehicle. "He's afraid now it may not be a stranger. That's worse, since nobody will suspect one of our own."

"Jen and I are praying for her, and I told all the employees at the store to be on the lookout for any strangers. I'll change it to unusual behavior from anybody."

"That's a big help. Thank you." Besides his job with the school district, Dennis owned one of the busiest places in town, a convenience store next to the interstate. It gave Luke hope to think the people who worked there had their eyes open.

"Give Holly my best." Dennis waved and pulled away.

Luke slid behind the steering wheel of his Jeep. The stalker may not be a stranger. He might be one of the people Luke saw on a regular basis. Somebody he would never suspect. Somebody who could get close to Holly without raising any red flags. He didn't like that idea. He didn't like that idea at all.

Chapter 13

"I don't know what my favorite memory of high school is." Holly was about ready to wad the silly questionnaire up and pitch it in the trash can. Jen could just make one up for her. It wasn't like very many would know the difference anyway.

"I know what your favorite memory of school is." From across the kitchen table, Tessa looked up from the papers she was grading.

"I'm glad one of us does." Holly had no idea what her friend might be referring to.

"It was our adult living class. Remember?" Tessa waited expectantly.

Holly thought about the class. It was set up so all the important aspects of adulthood were covered. The curriculum included handling money and necessary household chores. Her favorite though had been...

"When I finally changed a tire on my car." She shared a smile with Tessa.

"You were the only one left who hadn't managed it." Tessa clicked her tongue. "And you had to do it to pass the class that quarter. Remember?"

Holly remembered quite well. "I still think somebody sneaked my car in and tightened the lug nuts with some kind of machine. I liked to never get those silly things off."

Tessa giggled. "You finally climbed up and balanced on the four-way wrench and jumped up and down. What I would have given for a video camera."

"Well, I got my tire changed." Holly mustered up a little indignity.

"In forty-five minutes." Tessa's eyes watered as her laughter grew.

"There was no time limit, was there?" Holly harrumphed. What she never told anybody, nor would she ever, was before she pulled out of her parking space, Luke insisted on tightening her lug nuts. He was afraid she wasn't strong enough to do it very well, and it worried him. He turned them several times before they stayed put, so he probably had good reason to be concerned. Yet another "rescue" from him.

"Would you look at this?" Tessa had gotten distracted by the paper she was grading. She shoved it across the table to Holly.

Holly looked at it. "What am I supposed to see?"

"Look at question number nine." Holly wouldn't have been surprised to see steam coming from Tessa's ears.

She looked at the question. *In the above triangle, which is the right angle?* The student had written *the one that isn't wrong.*

Holly chuckled. "Whose paper is this? You ought to give partial credit for originality. At least, it's not blank."

"Ronnie Chambers. I never know what to expect from him." Tessa glared at the offending paper as she accepted it. "According to him, acute angles are better looking than ugly ones."

Her little darling cell phone programmer. Why wasn't she surprised? "Do you want me to talk to him?"

"It probably wouldn't hurt." Tessa scribbled his grade at the top of the paper and went on to the next one in her pile. "He tells his pals he's going to college. I shudder to think of him set loose on college math courses."

That knowledge would help Holly. "I'll just tell him he'd better start taking his grades seriously if he wants to go to college, then."

"Thanks, Holly."

Holly's phone rang—a nice normal bell sound. She looked at the clock. It wasn't even seven o'clock yet.

"It's probably Luke. We haven't made plans for Bible study tomorrow. It's at Annie Sanders' house, so it's not out of his way to pick us up."

"Holly, don't forget to check—"

"Hello." The word was out of Holly's mouth before Tessa's warning soaked in. She immediately regretted it.

"You'll be my wife soon. Mine, not his." After Dennis Ewing so graciously set it up, she hadn't even thought of using Caller ID.

"Just leave me alone." Holly tried to sound forceful.

"You're going to marry me, and have my babies. You'll never be with anybody else. You better tell Walker before he gets hurt. You're mine. You've been mine for a long time. Don't forget it."

The line went dead before Holly could say anything. She set her phone down with shaking hands.

"It was him, wasn't it?" Tessa was out of her chair and next to Holly in a flash.

She drew a shuddering breath. "He said we were going to get married and have babies, and I'll never be with anybody besides him." Her eyes welled with tears. "He said I'd better tell Luke before he gets hurt. Tessa, he's going to do something awful to Luke if I don't stay away from him."

"And we've had this conversation before." Tessa picked up her own phone and dialed a number.

"Mitch, this is Tessa. That creep just called Holly again, and he's getting more precise in his threats."

Her hand on her hip, Tessa barely left enough time for a response.

"He told her she was going to marry him and have his children, that's what." Tessa turned and nodded reassuringly to Holly; she had this under control. Holly would have laughed at her haphazard friend if she wasn't so frightened.

"Well, then, he told her if she didn't stay away from Luke, he was going to get hurt. Mitch, you've got to find this guy and take him down. D-o-w-n, down. Before he actually does someth—what?"

Now, Mitch was receiving her nod, telepathically—no, telephonically. Holly slapped a hand over her mouth to stop hysterical giggles from erupting.

"Just a minute and I'll ask."

Tessa pulled the phone away from her mouth and, seemingly unaware of Holly's oncoming meltdown, spoke calmly. "Mitch wants to know two things. Did he seem to respond directly to anything you said, and what exactly did he call Luke?"

Any last urge to laugh disappeared as Holly mentally replayed the conversation. "He acted like he didn't hear a word I said. And he referred to Luke by his last name."

Tessa passed the information on to Mitch. There was a longer silence while she listened to his response.

"Okay. We'll come straight there after school tomorrow. But what about tonight, Mitch? Am I supposed to tell him to go away because I told on him? Or maybe throw my hairdryer at the cr—" Tessa frowned as she listened to him.

"Well, let's hope he's such an idiot he tries to get us during the three minutes of an hour when Hank's driving by. My worst student will tell you those odds stink." Then, whatever Mitch said softened Tessa's features. With rosy red cheeks, she turned away from Holly and murmured too low to be overheard.

Just as Holly was about to ask if they were sharing naughty jokes, Tessa placed her phone back on the table.

"He wants us to come to the station after school tomorrow to hear about a theory he has. He made sure we had Clarence tonight and said to double check all the doors and windows. He's going to have Hank drive by at least once an hour all night, too, just to be safe."

Shelving her curiosity about blushing whispers, Holly returned to the nightmare her life seemed to have once more become. "Did he say what his theory is?"

Clearly back in the real world with Holly, Tessa started nervously wringing her hands. "He wants to tell us in person, but Holly, he's worried enough to have Hank watching us. And, he'd have him parked across the street if there were more officers on the force. M...maybe we need to think about going to your parents' place."

Holly stood and began to pace back and forth in her small dining area. Whatever Mitch's theory was, it obviously had him on edge. Was it fair to ask others to go out of their way, just so she could stay in her own house?

"How about this?" Tessa stepped away from the table and walked over to her. "How about if we go ahead and stay here, but only during the week?"

Holly waited for her to elaborate.

"Clarence will be with us at night, and we'll be sure to double-check the doors and windows. We can even see about putting new deadbolts on both doors and sturdier locks on the windows."

That was a reasonable suggestion. "Do you think your dad could help mine install them, or is he too busy at the factory?"

Tessa's blush returned. "Mitch is off Thursday evening. We were planning to go out for dinner, but I can bribe him with home cooking in return for installing the locks. We'll get Luke here to help him."

Holly was surprised by her friend's demeanor. Tessa and Mitch had been dating since the women returned from Massachusetts, but they had always been platonic as far as Holly knew. "Has something changed between you and Mitch?"

If Tessa blushed any harder, they could do without electric lights. "Yes. He told me...we told each other...we're in love."

"Wow." Holly was happy for her friend, who, like her, didn't take romantic dating lightly. "When did this happen?" Hopefully, their first declarations of love hadn't been whispered over Tessa's phone a few moments ago.

"He stopped by the school this afternoon. You knew Jack Wallace tried to get to Billy?"

Holly had wanted to go find the boy and lock him safely in her office until that animal was in custody. "Thank heavens Al Hopper came along when he did."

"Well, when Mitch came to talk to the boys Wallace approached, he stopped by my room. At first, I thought he was there to discuss your situation." Her eyes glowed, and a soft smile appeared. "Then, he sat down in one of the student desks and started talking."

"So that's when he told you?" As outgoing as Mitch was, Holly still had trouble imagining him blurting those sacred three words.

Tessa took Holly's hands in hers. "He explained he doesn't believe in romance unless he feels like it could lead to something more serious—permanent. God has to be front and center in the equation."

Holly couldn't contain her smile as her friend brought a mathematical term into their dialog.

"He wanted to be sure I understand where he plans on going with our relationship before we changed things." Tessa squeezed Holly's hands and smiled beautifully. "Then, when I told him I wanted the same thing, he...he said he couldn't wait until we were somewhere romantic to tell me he loves me. And, for the first time in my life, I said 'I love you' to a man—besides Dad."

"That's wonderful." Holly pulled her hands free and gave Tessa a hug. "You two share so many values; you're meant to be."

"I know." Suddenly, Tessa pulled away and sobered. "I'm sorry, Holly. Here I am going all hearts and flowers while you're being stalked."

Holly shook her head. "It feels good to talk about happy, normal things. Please don't apologize."

Tessa's lower lip popped out in a cute little-girl pout. "So, is my plan to bribe Mitch and Luke with my homemade lasagna okay with you?"

"Not only is it okay with me, I think we should let Clarence stay home, and spend our weekends at my parents' house. It will give everybody involved a chance to relax." The idea grew on Holly and eased her guilt over all the trouble people were going to for her.

"Okay. I'm going to check the locks right now. We can stop at the hardware store on our way home tomorrow and buy whatever we need. I'll even pay half." It was all too apparent Holly's answer relieved her friend.

"We'll do that, but this is my house, so I'm paying for everything." That wasn't up for discussion. "You can buy dinner for us, though. We won't have time to cook between shopping and Bible study."

"You've got yourself a deal."

Holly watched as Tessa walked to the back door and checked the lock. She better check and see where Clarence had bedded down. He slept very soundly, and if he had taken up residence on her bed, it would be a challenge to get him off it.

Thank You, Father, for giving me my friends and family. I know you never give us more than we can handle...with your help. And, I see the help you're giving me through the people you've blessed my life with. I am truly grateful.

She felt a peace settle on her as she went to try to relocate a dog.

Chapter 14

Luke pulled on a denim jacket as he stepped out of the house, Clarence right in front of him. His day had started off rough and failed to improve. He was looking forward to picking Holly and Tessa up and taking them to Rob Sanders' for Bible study.

Clarence was going with him now so he didn't have to make a second trip after the study was over. The dog could stay in the Sanders' fenced-in backyard and turn up his nose at their purebred Labradors.

Luke was nearly to his Jeep when he noticed it was sitting strangely. "What's going on, Clarence?" He walked closer to the vehicle and saw the problem.

"We have a flat tire, boy." He walked to the back of the Jeep to get the jack and spare. As he walked past the right rear tire, he realized something else. "Two flat tires?" What was going on? With a feeling of dread, he circled the Jeep. All four tires were flat.

He rubbed his hand down his face. "Okay, Clarence. The tractor not wanting to start and cutting out badly all morning can be explained. I can even accept the fence on the south property line being down, and Mrs. Pickler's goats making themselves at home in my field. But there is no way on earth all four of my tires went flat at the same time." He suddenly had a terrible thought. The truck. He headed toward the lean-to he kept his pickup parked under. He could see before he got there the back two tires were flat, so he wasn't surprised to find the other two in the same shape.

Luke nearly dropped his phone when it rang before he had it all the way out of his pocket. He quickly checked caller ID, hoping Mitch was calling him for some reason. The caller was unknown.

"Hello."

"You won't take my Holly anywhere tonight, will you? I told you to leave her alone. Stay away from *my* Holly, or your tires won't be the only thing slashed."

The line went dead.

That wasn't a vague "you'll be sorry," but the threat of physical harm.

"I have to call Mitch, but I'd better call Holly first." Clarence nodded in agreement. Luke thought for a moment. He wouldn't tell her what happened yet. He'd wait at least until after she was home from Bible study. She'd be safe there while Mitch helped him deal with this mess. Then he would borrow one of his dad's vehicles to take Clarence to her house. "That'll work."

Holly answered on the second ring.

"You sound happy." It was nice to hear a smile in her voice.

"I'll be happier after you get here and agree to do me a favor." Was she teasing? It seemed like forever since she'd done that.

"What favor are you asking?" He decided to join in on the fun. "Because I'm not giving Clarence a bath. He's not due for one for at least another week."

Her laughter was beautiful. "You can at least brush his teeth. I woke up this morning with his face hanging over mine, and he adds a whole new dimension to the idea of morning breath."

"At least he didn't kiss you." Luke had gotten into the daily habit of just pulling into the driveway and opening the door for Clarence to get in. Holly and Tessa were busy getting ready for work, and he needed to get started on his day, so it quickly became a routine. The only bad thing was the missed opportunity to talk to Holly.

"He'd better not, either!" Another giggle came across the phone. "He's not my type, you know."

"So, what do you need me to do?" As much as he wanted to continue their conversation, he needed to call Mitch and deal with his vehicles.

"Can I just ask you when you get here? It'll be harder for you to tell me no in person."

Luke was beyond disappointed. "I'm sorry, Holly. That's why I called. I'm going to have to miss Bible study this evening." He hesitated. "I have a flat tire." Plus seven.

"That's okay." She was still in a good mood. "Tessa and I can fit in your truck with you."

Oh, what a tangled web...Luke sighed. "It has a flat tire, too."

The line went silent for a moment before Holly's soft voice spoke.

"What happened, Luke? Please tell me the truth."

He had no choice. "All the tires on both my Jeep and pickup are flat." At least, he could spare her the horror of the stalker's threat of slashing for now.

"He did it, didn't he?" The happiness disappeared from her voice, replaced now by despondency. "He let the air out of your tires."

"Yes." He tried to sound reassuring. "They're just tires, Holly. You and Tessa go ahead to Rob's. I'll borrow Dad's truck and run Clarence to town after Mitch leaves. Okay?"

"Why don't we come out and get him?" He could hear the guilt in her voice.

"You don't need to be out at that time of the night. I don't mind bringing him." He realized something and lightened his tone of voice. "What favor do you need?"

"It's okay. You have enough trouble."

"I want to help you," he insisted. "Now, what's the favor?"

He heard her shaky breath and wondered if she was trying not to cry. "Tess is fixing homemade lasagna tomorrow evening. We wanted you and Mitch to come for supper, and install new locks on my doors and windows."

Luke didn't hesitate. "I'll be there. What time?"

"Is five too early?"

He would have rearranged his entire day if it meant helping her. "I'll be there."

There was still a tremor in her voice as she spoke. "Thank you, Luke. For everything."

"I told you, Holly, I would do anything for you. I meant it."

Her voice was so soft he barely heard her. "Goodbye, Luke."

He said good-bye to an empty line.

"Well, I'm pretty sure she's crying." Clarence, who was sniffing a deflated tire on the truck, turned and looked at him. "I wish at least one of us was there to comfort her." Not that he could imagine Holly cuddling with his dog.

He dialed Mitch's number. At this rate, he was going to have to put his friend on speed dial.

Within twenty minutes of his call to Mitch, the squad car pulled in behind the Jeep.

"He seems bent on making your life miserable." Mitch made the observation as he walked around the Jeep, using his flashlight to inspect the tires. "I don't know what he used to slash these with, but it has a big blade. You won't be able to patch them."

Luke had only told Mitch about the tires. He had to tell him the rest.

"Mitch, he called again."

Mitch looked up sharply. "Another threat?"

Luke nodded. "Pretty specific this time. If I don't stay away from 'his' Holly, my tires won't be the only thing he slashes."

Mitch stuck his flashlight in his pocket before pulling out his pad and pen. "Can you tell me, as accurately as possible, his exact words?"

Luke tried to repeat the caller's words verbatim. Mitch wrote them down.

"Whether it's a recorder or more like a microphone, I really think he's using one of those voice altering devices." Even with his face only half-lit by a security light, Mitch's determination was visible. "Luke, we really have to face the probability this is not a stranger."

"I know." Luke had reached the same conclusion, unpleasant though it was. "The girls are safe at Rob and Annie's this evening, but do you think it's a good idea for them to stay at Holly's house anymore? The guy knew I was picking Holly up, and he's threatening me. What if he decides to blame her for not staying away from me?"

"I've been giving this a lot of thought." Mitch returned his pad and pen to his pocket. "I think they're as safe at Holly's as they would be at Tony and Susan's. I don't know if you've talked to Holly today, but they've come up with a sensible plan."

"Holly asked me about installing new locks tomorrow night."

"Yes, they're having us do that." Mitch absent-mindedly scratched behind Clarence's ears. "But they've decided to spend weekends at the Morris farm. Holly figures it will ease everybody's minds. Safety in numbers, plus Tony is there."

Luke thought of Holly's plan. "At least with those Coonhounds, nobody will get close to the house without Tony knowing it." Biscuit and Lemon were probably the most idiotic animals the good Lord put on the face of the earth, but they liked to bark and howl at anything that moved. "I think it's a good idea."

"Don't tell Holly, but it'll help out a lot. I have Hank driving by her place on the hour every night. You know with budget cuts, we're stretched thin the way it is. If the county board finds out I'm focusing that much attention on one person, I'll be raked over the coals."

Luke felt a deep gratitude for his friend. "Thank you. I know Holly wouldn't want you to risk your job for her, though."

"I won't be if I don't have to send Hank out on weekends. He can make it part of his cruising pattern on weeknights without it being a big deal. If he comes in on weekends to do it, we're looking at overtime, which is a big fat 'no' in the boss's book." Mitch patted Clarence's head and stepped away from him.

"Thanks just the same, Mitch. I appreciate it." It encouraged Luke to know others were looking out for Holly.

Mitch straightened. "Tell you what. You aren't going to be able to do anything about these tires tonight. I'll write up a report for your insurance, and then I'll take Clarence to town with me."

"Are you sure you don't mind?" Clarence was liable to develop an attitude if all this attention kept up much longer. He'd feel important riding in the squad car.

"I don't mind a bit." A growl came from deep in Clarence's throat, and something thudded behind the lean-to. Mitch went into action. "Stay put, Luke." He unsnapped his holster and grasped the flashlight in his other hand as he slowly walked toward the back of the lean-to.

"Who's back there?" Mitch's deep voice echoed off the aluminum siding.

A loud rustle was followed by the sound of running feet. Luke grabbed for Clarence's collar, but he wasn't fast enough. His dog tore around the structure and took off in hot pursuit of the runner. Mitch ran after the figure, too, the beam of his flashlight bouncing with each step. Luke started after them but slowed to a stop and surveyed the direction they were headed. If he ran fast enough, and the trespasser stuck to the treeline, Luke might be able to head him off.

Luke hadn't made it more than a few yards when, to his right, Clarence's barks became louder and more rapid. Mitch shouted, and then there it was—another voice, yelling obscenities. At the sound of his dog's growls, Luke took off at a dead run.

"Shadow County Sheriff–stop or I will shoot."

Brush rustled and a mixture of men's grunts and a dog's growls led Luke to the scuffle. Just as he ran through the brush, Mitch seemed to fly into him, as though launched. The two men went down hard.

"Where's my gun?" Mitch's elbow caught Luke in his solar plexus as the giant managed to get on his feet.

At the sound of his dog's yelp, Luke scrambled to his feet. "Clarence!"

Mitch straightened with his gun in hand and even in the moonlight, relief was visible on his face. Clarence came bounding straight to Luke and nearly knocked him over with an enthusiastic jump.

Instead of taking off, Mitch shook his head. "Too dark out here. I could walk right past him."

Not feeling any wounds on Clarence, Luke gently pulled the dog off him and back to all fours. "Did you recognize him?"

"No." The sheriff sounded disappointed. "He was wearing something over his face, and his voice was…weird. I should have at least managed to get some kind of identifying feature."

Luke didn't like seeing his friend blame himself. "Mitch, that guy sent you flying. He must be a giant."

"'Bout my size, but he's strong—our guy works out, Luke. A lot." Mitch reached down to scratch behind the dog's ears. "Good job, Clarence. You nearly had him."

"What now?"

"Now, we get back to the squad car and I call for every kind of help I can find. The guy's on foot in these woods. If I can get some manpower out here, we may be able to pen him in. We may have Holly's stalker in custody before the night is over. "Mitch was already shoving branches aside and walking toward the farmhouse.

Luke stayed close behind him.

As soon as they reached the edge of Luke's yard, Mitch turned to him.

"I'll need you to stay at the house, Luke. Hopefully, we'll either hem the guy in or flush him out in this direction. If he shows up," Mitch hesitated, "do you still have your shotgun?"

"Yes." Then Luke realized what Mitch was telling him. "But I could never shoot a human being—any human being."

Mitch patted his shoulder. "I know that, and you know that, but hopefully our giant friend doesn't. Remember, he's stronger than me, Luke, so you have to use something. Just hold it up and tell him to freeze. You don't even have to load it. He wasn't armed when I tackled him."

It was then Luke noticed Mitch's rapidly swelling eye and a darkening discoloration on his jaw. "Are you okay, Mitch? Did he hurt you?"

Mitch grimaced. "I've taken worse spills on the football field. Don't worry about me. I've got to get going, though. Just watch, and call me if you see anything. Okay?"

"Okay."

When Luke went inside a few minutes later, he had to force himself to pull his gun off the rack. He and his dad liked to tag a deer or two every year, but game hunting was much different than aiming at a man. Even though he knew it wasn't loaded, he still double checked before taking it outside.

Leaving Clarence inside the house, out of harm's way, he sat in the shadows on his wide porch rail. Then, he prayed fervently the stalker would either take off in a different direction or pass out cold at the sight of a gun. Because Luke was pretty sure he'd automatically fall back on the routine his grandpa once used to get rid of an angry nine-point buck. He'd just stand there, shout like a madman, and shake his weapon at the criminal. Somehow, he doubted that would be enough.

Chapter 15

"He just disappeared?" Tessa was once more examining Mitch's black eye. "How did he get past all of you?"

"I told you, Tess." Mitch reached up and placed his hand over hers. "It was just three of us. He could have come out of the woods in a hundred different places. Or he could have hunkered down and hid. Tomorrow morning, when we do a sweep of Luke's place with the state police, maybe we'll find him."

"I can't believe he was that close to you." Holly had a strong urge to wrap her arms around Luke and hold on tightly just to make sure he was really there and unhurt. "At least, he only wanted to ruin your tires."

She didn't miss the look the two men exchanged. Mitch subtly nodded before Luke spoke.

"I didn't tell you last night because I didn't want to frighten you any more than you already were." He reached across the table and took her hand in his. "He called me. The stalker, I mean."

Holly couldn't stop the shiver that ran through her. "What did he say this time?"

"Holly..." His reluctance to tell her was written all over his face. "He told me if I don't stay away from his Holly, my tires won't be the only thing he slashes."

Tears came unbidden to Holly's eyes. "You have to stay away from me, Luke. I can't let you get hurt."

He was on his feet, pulling her up into his arms before she was barely finished speaking. "No. I'm not staying away from you. We're not going to let him dictate our actions, Holly. I'm careful, and so are you. So far, he's all talk and vandalism."

Holly buried her face against Luke's neck. "I'm afraid for you, Luke."

"Well, don't be." He pulled away from her and tilted her chin so she was looking into his dark green eyes. "I can take care of myself. You just need to make sure you're safe. And we are not changing our habits. Understand?"

She reached up and wiped away her tears. "I'm still going to stay at Mom and Dad's on the weekends. It'll give you and Mitch at least a couple of days not to worry about me."

Luke smiled encouragingly at her. "Biscuit and Lemon can fill in for Clarence."

Holly felt her fear lessen as she shakily returned Luke's smile. "They can jump on my stalker and slobber all over him, I guess." Her dad's Blue ticks were good for hunting, but not much else. Her mom routinely threatened to enroll them in a class for mentally challenged dogs. Lemon's favorite nocturnal pastime was lying under the pole light closest to the house and howling. At least, they barked like crazy if anything disturbed them. Her dad may find himself confronting a squirrel or raccoon, but no prowler would sneak around the house undetected.

"Better?" Luke gave her a brief hug.

"Better." She returned his embrace before sitting back down.

"So, I guess we should get to work on these locks unless you ladies need us to help clean up." Mitch smiled at Tessa.

Tessa's cheeks reddened. "Cooking a meal and cleaning up afterward is the least we can do in exchange for having new locks installed. Thank you for the offer, though."

The couple exchanged an emotion-filled look. It appeared Holly's friend had found love. And they had been right there in front of each other for years. How had they gone so long without realizing they were meant to be together?

She stood and began to stack plates. "I'll go ahead and start washing, Tess."

Tessa looked up from the pan of lasagna. "Okay. I'm going to put this in a container so Mitch can eat it later."

"Give him the rest of the garlic bread, too," Holly suggested.

She earned a smile in response to her offer.

Several minutes later Holly found herself relaxing during the everyday routine of washing dishes while Tessa dried.

"So, how did your day go?" It was the first time the two women really had a chance to talk all day. Deciding there would be more time, they'd saved their shopping for today. Then, they were both a bit overwhelmed by the myriad lock choices. If a patient salesman hadn't appeared to help them, the two of them may very well still be standing there trying to figure out the difference between a regular deadbolt and something called a mortise. Even now, Holly wasn't sure if she understood. She was satisfied with the salesman's assurance nobody would be able to break through the ones she bought. At least not without busting down the full door.

Tessa smiled at Holly. "I gave my freshmen a pop quiz today. I should have brought Ronnie's home to show you."

"Did my talk have any effect on his efforts?" It didn't seem like a very productive meeting to her.

"Not exactly." Tessa picked up another plate and began drying it. "One of the problems was calculating the area of the sides of a cube. Do you know what his answer was?"

Holly placed a handful of clean silver in the drain tray. "I wouldn't hazard a guess."

"He wrote *it depends on how fast it's melting*." Tessa slid a freshly dried plate onto the stack on the counter. "You know, if he gave half as much effort to studying as he does to smarting off, he would be a genius."

"Did you know you're one lock short, Holly?" Luke had appeared at her elbow, his hands full of hardware.

She looked at the locks he held. "I didn't think I needed one in the bathroom. That window is too small for even a child to fit through." His frown told her he didn't agree. "You think I need a lock on it?"

"Might not be a bad idea. The window's small, but that wouldn't stop somebody from putting something through it."

"What do you mean?" Holly was confused.

"Like he could put a wild animal or rodent of some sort through it?" Tessa asked him.

Luke nodded. "Or trash."

"Say no more." Holly had heard enough. "I'll run to Amok and pick up another lock, as soon as I'm finished with the dishes. Okay?"

"I think you should," Luke advised her.

So it was that she found herself once more perusing locks at the hardware store thirty minutes later. Thankfully, she knew what she wanted this time. It was a good thing since Tessa had received an urgent call from a parent. She'd motioned for Holly to wait, but the hardware store closed early on weeknights. Besides, Tessa shouldn't have to suffer every discomfort or inconvenience with her.

"Good lock there, honey." The older man at the register nodded as he placed her purchase in a sack. "Take a bulldozer to bust through one of these."

"Then, I'm glad I bought them for my house." Suddenly filled with an irrational sense of urgency, Holly grabbed her credit card rather than count out cash. The rest of the clerk's sage comments flew past her as she quickly signed her name and grabbed the bag.

"You forgot your receipt!" The man held the slip of yellow paper out.

"It's okay." She practically ran through the door, toward her car. At least she had parked under a light.

Her heart kicked into high gear when she noticed the driver's door was ajar. Just as she cautiously tried to see through the reflected pole light into the backseat, the sound of heavy, running footsteps echoed across the parking lot and seemed to be headed her way.

"Jack Wallace." Holly quickly slid behind the wheel and hit the autolock button as she tossed the small sack onto the passenger seat. The shadowy image of a large man hovered in her peripheral vision as she finally found her keys and managed to start her car. She should have taken a good look in the rearview mirror—she might have been able to identify Jack Wallace for certain. But, she was scared. And, what if it wasn't the irate fugitive, and instead was her stalker? A man large enough to mow Mitch over.

Her breath finally slowed enough to talk, so she reached for her phone. If she could find the right button, she could use it hands-free.

A strange noise behind her was all the warning Holly had before something flew down her face and tugged tightly against her neck. She lifted a hand and pulled at the unyielding strap, now digging into the flesh of her neck.

"You'll learn now, lady." A hate-filled voice snarled in her ear. "Pull over and stop."

"No!" She dug at the band, trying to get at least a finger under it. If anything, he pulled tighter.

"Then, I'll finish you here."

His words echoed through her fogged brain and terrified her. He was going to kill her. All sense of logic left Holly; she wanted to breathe. She *had* to breathe. Her hand flew from the steering wheel to her neck, digging and grasping at the ever-tightening constraint. "Stop!" Her effort at a yell resulted in a gasp.

This was surely a nightmare. *Please, God, let this be a nightmare. I don't want to die. Not yet. Not like this.*

Even though a part of her knew this was happening quickly, it seemed to be taking forever. The pain around her neck was so intense, a hard blow to the side of her head barely registered.

A string of profanity unlike any she'd ever heard was produced by her ear as she felt someone leaning up over the seat and reaching for the steering wheel. Somehow, the action tightened the band around her neck even farther.

Her feet reflexively pushed against the floor, and she felt the person hanging over the seat beside her seem to be thrust backward. An intense roaring filled her ears before the world exploded.

Chapter 16

Luke was just finishing the last window when he saw Tessa alone at the table.

"Holly in the bedroom?" He must have walked right past her.

Tessa frowned as she looked at him. "No. I didn't go with her. I thought you did."

She'd gone alone. Luke looked at his watch, and his heart immediately went into overdrive. "She's been gone more than long enough."

Mitch rushed into the room. "I have to run. There's been a car accident over on Biltway. The driver is injured."

"Wait." Luke stopped him. "Holly isn't back from the hardware store. What if it's her?" Before Mitch could respond, Luke decided. "I'll follow you."

"I'm coming." Tessa was uncharacteristically somber.

Mitch gave a little nod. "Okay, but you need to stay back when we get there."

"I will." Luke didn't know how or why, but in his heart, he knew it was Holly in that accident.

Within minutes, his fears were confirmed when he saw Holly's small car sitting cockeyed across the wide sidewalk, the front crumpled around a pole. He was parked on the side of the road, and out of his Jeep while Tessa was still unfastening her seat belt.

"Holly!" He yelled as he ran toward the car.

"Luke. You need to wait here." Deputy Jeff Fielding stepped forward from the squad car.

"I'm not waiting anywhere. I need to get to Holly RIGHT NOW!!" Nothing was going to keep him away from her. Nothing.

"Let him through, Jeff." Mitch's authoritative voice sounded over Luke's growing panic. "She's right here, Luke."

Luke started shaking when he saw her lying on the ground beside the car. She was so pale. And she wasn't moving.

"She isn't..."

"She's breathing fine, and her heartbeat is strong and steady. The airbag probably hit her pretty hard and knocked her out. We're waiting for the ambulance now."

Luke dropped to his knees beside her and picked up her hand. "Let me stay with her, Mitch. I need to be with her."

Mitch grimly nodded. "Just stay out of the EMTs' way and let them do their job. I'll have Jeff fill Tessa in, and she can follow the ambulance to the hospital."

Luke looked up at the car, the hood crumpled like an accordion. "What happened? Did she have a blowout, or did something cause her to swerve?"

"We'll talk later. There's the ambulance."

Luke followed Mitch's directions and stayed back while Barney Nettles and Tillie Carter did their job. He lost all sense of time as they finally made it to the hospital. The next hour or so seemed like a nightmare, with an unconscious Holly being transported from the emergency room to radiology for X-rays, and then off for a CT scan. Somewhere in there, her parents arrived, Tony stoic and Susan in tears.

They were finally in the emergency examination room with Holly and the doctor.

"Okay, folks, the good news is Holly doesn't have anything too seriously wrong with her. She has a concussion and some pretty nasty bruising on her neck and face, but there are no broken bones or internal injuries." Dr. Potter peered over the top of his glasses at Tony and Susan. "Your daughter had an angel in that car with her. When they first brought her in, I fully expected to find some broken bones or more significant damage to her head. She'll probably have a case of whiplash from her seatbelt holding her back, too, but that's impossible to diagnose without her being awake to tell me if it hurts." He indicated a continuous strip of reddened skin, almost welt-like in appearance, across the front and sides of her neck. "I am puzzled about this mark. I don't know how her seat belt or the air bag could have left it. We'll have to see what Holly can tell us."

"Why isn't she waking up?" Tony didn't take his eyes off his daughter.

Dr. Potter leaned over and lifted Holly's eyelid to shine his penlight. "I expect she will any time now, and she's going to have one whopper of a headache. She'll probably feel like a giant bruise, too, so I'm going to order some pain relievers for her. I'll be at the nurses' station. One of them will be in to administer her medication. Please let me know when she wakes up."

Luke sank into the chair next to her bed, her hand in both of his. He leaned down and rested his head on their hands.

Thank you, Lord, for saving her. Thank you for not taking her away from us...from me. Please continue your Healing Touch and be with the medical staff as they tend to her.

"Amen." It wasn't until Susan softly spoke the word he realized he prayed aloud.

He looked into Susan's bloodshot eyes and tried to return the smile she so bravely managed to produce. "She's going to be okay, Luke." She sat down on the other side of the bed and took Holly's other hand in hers. "Isn't she, Tony?"

"How is she?" Mitch's quietly spoken words announced his presence in the room.

Luke looked over his shoulder at his friend. "She has a concussion, and she's going to be sore, but Dr. Potter said she'll be okay. It could have been much worse." He smiled shakily. "The doctor said she had an angel with her."

"Good." Mitch looked decidedly uncomfortable. "Luke, can I have a word with you? I won't keep you more than a minute."

He didn't want to let go of Holly, but Luke knew she didn't need his touch to heal her. He leaned over and put his mouth close to her ear. "I'll be right back."

Mitch held the door for him, and they both stepped into the hall. Luke couldn't help but notice Mitch led him where they wouldn't be overheard.

"What's going on?"

"We got the floodlights out there and examined the scene." Mitch's brow was furrowed. "Luke, there are no skid marks. If she swerved to miss a dog, or tried to stop, there would have been skid marks."

Luke didn't understand. "What are you trying to say, Mitch?"

"She drove herself into that pole, at a pretty good speed. We won't know until the pros get out there and do their measurements, but I'm sure she was driving well over the speed limit. I need to talk to her as soon as possible. We need to find out what's going on."

Anger slowly started to build as Luke processed Mitch's words. "You can't seriously think Holly tried to hurt herself. She would never do that; you know it as well as I do."

Mitch put his hand on Luke's shoulder and spoke calmly. "I'm not saying any such thing. I'm saying something strange happened, and I need to talk to Holly as soon as possible to find out what it was."

Luke immediately calmed down. His brain had gone into overdrive, though. "Isn't there a chance she had a blowout, or her brakes failed?"

"Her tires look good as new, and the limited examination we could do tonight didn't show any problems with her brakes." Mitch gave Luke a commiserating look. "Just let me know as soon as she's awake and lucid. I need to talk to her. Okay?"

"Where will you be?" Luke now just wanted to be back in the room beside Holly.

Mitch gestured toward the entrance. "I'm going to let Tessa know what's going on, and then I'm going to sit with her until you come and get me. She's out of her mind with worry."

Tessa! "I'm sorry. Tell her how sorry I am. I just didn't think. I was so scared, and they kept taking Holly off for more tests. I should have made sure Tessa knew what was going on."

"She understands." Mitch touched Luke's arm. "She understands how much Holly means to you. We all do." With a sad smile, the sheriff patted Luke's shoulder before turning away.

Luke watched as Mitch walked through the door that would take him to the waiting room before he turned to go back to Holly. He could only pray *she* understood how much she meant to him. It could have been too late to tell her. It wasn't yet, though. He still had time.

Chapter 17

Holly's childhood pony, Ferdinand, was pulling her in the wagon, and they were going too fast. He kept going in circles, around and around, faster and faster. If he wasn't careful, they were going to crash into...

She moaned as the light hit her eyes. Maybe she'd just leave them closed a little longer.

"Holly?" Luke's gentle voice came from beside her.

She turned slightly toward him. "Did...did Ferdie dump you again?" Why did it feel like she'd gargled with salt water?

"Ferdie?" Luke seemed bewildered. "Holly, Ferdinand isn't here. You had an accident. Don't you remember?"

Holly tried to nod, but it hurt in too many places to count, so she gave up. "Ferdie drove us into a pole. He was going too fast to stop."

"She's still not completely awake." Her father's voice came from the other side of her bed.

She turned her head that way, but her eyes still only opened a slit before the light was too much. "Don't be mad at Ferdie, Dad. He's just a pony, and that thing was too tight around our necks."

"She's not making any sense at all." Her mom was closer to her than her dad. Maybe she could get her eyes open far enough to look at her mom.

"Mom?" She blinked once...twice...Finally, her eyes stayed open far enough she could see her mom.

"There you are." Susan smiled through her tears. "I was beginning to think you decided to go ahead and sleep all night, and let us sit here and watch you."

"Wh-Where am I?" This didn't make sense. She had just been behind Ferdie, with that rope or something choking them. And now, she was...

"You're in the hospital, Holly." Her mom answered her. "You had a car accident. You have a concussion, so everything is probably confusing right now. The important thing is you're okay."

"So, my patient is awake." Was that Dr. Potter with her dad? When had her dad gone to get the doctor? Since when did doctors make house calls, anyway?

"My insurance won't cover house calls." She looked confusedly at Dr. Potter. "Do you know how to help ponies? I think Ferdie hurt his neck. He was being choked, so he ran too fast, and we hit a pole."

"Is this normal?" Why would her mom be asking such a silly question? Of course, it wasn't normal for a horse to be choked, or for the doctor to come and take care of her like this.

Somebody had to do something, though. Someone had tried to hurt Ferdie. "Luke?"

"Right here, Holly."

She managed to focus on his worried face. "Will you call Mitch? Somebody tried to choke Ferdie while I was riding him. I want Mitch to help Ferdie."

"Holly, you had a car accident." Dr. Potter's voice was firm. "Right now everything is jumbled in your mind. Mitch is here, and he wants to talk to you as soon as things make sense to you again. Right now, I want you to try to understand you're in the hospital because you had a car accident. Nobody named Fergie was involved."

Holly frowned. "His name is Ferdie, not Fergie."

Dr. Potter sighed. "Very well. Ferdie wasn't involved. There are no ponies or horses of any kind here with you. Rest for a while and give your mind time to understand what happened."

Now, that sounded like a good idea. She let her eyes drift closed again, longing for sleep to take her away from this confusion.

"She hit her head pretty hard." Dr. Potter was still speaking. "I'm sure she'll understand everything once she's had some time to wake completely up."

"Doctor?" Luke's voice was still near, which comforted her— even if she wasn't sure what he meant. "She keeps saying somebody was choking Ferdie." He sounded troubled. "Could that mark on her neck be from having been choked?"

She felt fingers gently probe her neck. "You know, Luke, I believe that's exactly what it is." A searing pain struck where he touched her. "This looks like the leather loop of a belt. It will help greatly when Holly can tell us exactly what happened."

Wait a minute. Somebody had choked *her*, not Ferdie? Her mind began to assimilate memories. She had gone to get a lock for the bathroom window. Yes. That's what she had done. Then what happened? She had gotten into her car and driven home. Hadn't she?

No. She locked the car, but her door was open. She thought she was foolish for not being sure her car door was closed after she locked it. So, she looked in the back seat...Only, she hadn't. The man running behind her...she was scared of him, so she just got in and drove.

Suddenly, she felt a steel band wrapped tightly around her neck. A voice full of hatred; *I'll finish you here.*

"No!" She yelled and jerked her eyes open. "No! Don't let him strangle me! Luke, stop him! Don't let him do it!"

"Shhh." Luke's voice was close to her ear. "You're safe now. Nobody can hurt you. You're safe."

Her body shook as sobs overtook her. "L-Luke, he-he was going...to kill me." She felt him gently draw her into his arms and cradle her against his chest.

"Nobody is going to hurt you now. I promise." Luke's voice was tender, yet firm. He had never made a promise he didn't keep, not as long as Holly had known him. She began to relax.

"Holly, I know this is difficult, but the sheriff is waiting to speak with you." Dr. Potter was talking again. "You need to tell him what happened. He needs to get started right away so he can catch the man who tried to hurt you. Do you think you can do that now?"

She reached up and put her hand on Luke's shoulder. "Stay with me. Please."

"Try to make me leave."

Holly watched as the doctor spoke to her father before leaving the room, and soon Mitch was standing behind Luke.

"I'm going to lay you back down so you can talk to Mitch." Luke's voice was soothing. "But I'll be right here. I'm not going anywhere."

"We're here, too." Holly's mom spoke from the other side of the bed. Holly had almost forgotten her parents were there. She turned and tried to smile at them.

"Thank you."

Susan had tears in her eyes as she nodded. Holly shifted her gaze to Luke's steady, green gaze once more before turning her focus to Mitch.

"I'm sorry I have to ask you these questions right now," were the softly spoken words that came from the sheriff. "But the sooner I know what happened, the quicker I can take care of it."

"I know." Holly took a deep breath and felt it in a hundred different places. Was there not one molecule of her that didn't hurt?

"Okay. So you made it to the hardware store?"

"Amok." She started to nod and then thought better of it. "I went in and bought the window latch." She returned her gaze to Luke and found the strength to continue. "When I got back out to my car, the driver's door was open. I started to check the backseat…" Her heart pounded harder. "Someone…a man, I think, came running toward me, and I was scared." She fully expected Mitch to be disgusted. "I just jumped in and took off. I didn't look in the backseat at all."

"In that situation, anyone would have done that." Luke's gaze scanned the room and seemed to dare one of them to disagree.

"I was foolish." Holly could admit that. "I know I should have looked in the backseat before getting in the car. I just couldn't think."

"This is not your fault." Luke grasped her hand as he spoke firmly.

"No, it's not," Mitch agreed. "Can you tell me more?"

"Yes." Another deep breath and pain throbbing everywhere. "I was near the old park I think, when he put a band—like maybe a rope or something leather—around my neck." She was not going to cry. She refused to. She focused on Luke's steady gaze. "He kept pulling it tighter, and it hurt so bad. He kept telling me to pull over, but I wouldn't. He was so angry…I think he hit me." A fire blazed in Luke's eyes for a moment before he seemed to regain control. "He was trying to take control of the wheel and choking me at the same time. I remember pushing my feet on the floor. Then, everything exploded." She shifted her gaze to Mitch. "What did I do?"

"I think your foot must have still been on the gas pedal, because you had to have been going fast." The sheriff seemed to have it all figured out. "During the struggle, the car went off the road and hit a telephone pole."

Thank heavens she'd been wearing her seat belt, but… "What about the man who choked me? Was he hurt in the crash?"

Mitch looked hesitant to answer. "There was no sign of anybody else at the scene, Holly."

Holly's heart sped up, and her breathing became erratic. "He was there. I didn't imagine it, Mitch. He was in my backseat, and he tried to choke me."

"I know," Mitch said quickly. "I can see the mark on your neck, Holly. I believe you. I'm just telling you he got away. I have no idea who he was."

Suddenly, the cruel voice was as clear as day to Holly. "I do." She looked from Mitch to Luke. "It was Jack Wallace. I recognized his voice. Jack Wallace was in my car."

Mitch frowned. "Are you sure, Holly? Because Dr. Potter told me, you've been pretty confused."

"I'm sure." She had to convince him of her certainty. "I remember everything. I can still hear him. It was Jack Wallace."

Mitch exchanged a frustrated look with Luke. "That man is on my last nerve. I'm going to call state, and we're going to search aggressively for him. He left his pickup at the Andrews house, so I don't know how he's getting around, but he's not invisible. He can't hide forever."

"I'm sorry I was so careless." Holly felt the need to apologize again.

"Like Luke said, this is not your fault, Holly." Mitch looked at her parents. "I don't know what the doctor's orders will be, but I hope you can keep her and Tessa at your place for a while. Give me some time to catch this man."

"I'm going to play every parenting trick in the book," Tony assured him. "My daughter and her friend are going to be safe and sound at our house indefinitely."

Holly couldn't take her eyes off this suddenly domineering parent.

"You're coming home with your mother and me. That's not up for discussion, young lady." Though usually easygoing and supportive, Tony Morris seemed to have reached his limit. If for no other reason than respect for her father, Holly would not argue.

"Okay."

"Okay?" An exhalation that could have deflated a tire came from Luke. "Thank you. I was going to camp out in your driveway if you didn't. There's no way you can be alone anymore, Holly. Not right now."

Holly's mind whirled with the implications of Jack Wallace's attack. Mitch had shared his horribly possible theory of her stalker possibly being somebody local, with one of those voice-altering devices.

"Mitch, where did Jack Wallace come from?" A new idea was forming in her head.

Mitch frowned. "Out east—Connecticut, if I remember correctly. Why?"

"He just showed up here? He doesn't have any family around?" Holly hoped she was right because it would answer some questions.

Comprehension dawned on Mitch's and Luke's faces at the same time. "You wonder if he's your stalker?" It was Luke's question.

"I've wondered for a while why he only came after you." Mitch seemed ready to consider the possibility. "I mean, you got the ball rolling, but Virgil Murdock was with Billy through it all. And the Child Services caseworker or even my two deputies who brought him in— You'd think he'd be just as mad at those people."

"Unless he was already fixated on her." Luke leaned toward her as though the criminal might attack at any moment.

She looked at Mitch. "Could Jack Wallace be my stalker? Does the timeline work? When he got here—Where he lived?"

"Let me get somebody digging into his background. I'll have to assign it, though, because I am going to be out there hunting him down." Mitch's aggravation with the fugitive was evident.

"Thank you." Holly finally had a real glimmer of hope. Maybe when they caught Jack Wallace, they would have the man who seemed to thrive on making her miserable and vandalizing Luke's home. And now who had even tried to k—hurt her.

"I'm going to get on this." Mitch looked at Dr. Potter, who Holly hadn't even noticed walk back in. "Can I send Tessa back? She's beside herself—won't feel any better until she sees Holly with her own two eyes."

The doctor seemed apologetic when he answered. "There really should only be two visitors back here. I'm stretching it now because I know how close Luke and Holly are." He'd been doctoring both for years, and his grandson was Troy Potter, Holly's student and one of Luke's youth group boys.

Luke looked into Holly's eyes. "Is it okay if I leave long enough to let Tessa come back and sit with you for a while? I promise I won't go far."

Holly yearned to tell him she didn't want him to let go of her hand or move one inch farther away from her than he already was. She felt secure with him there. Nevertheless, she knew, rationally, she would still be safe if he left. And if it were Tessa back here, Holly would be equally worried. "Go ahead. I'll be okay."

"We're not leaving her," Tony said reassuringly.

Susan settled herself in her chair. "I'm planted."

"You can all leave for the night if you'd like," Dr. Potter advised them. "I'm admitting her just to be safe. I like to watch concussions for twenty-four hours, and I'm particularly concerned about the degree of confusion she experienced when she regained consciousness."

"We'll stay until you get ready to move her to her room." And that was that, Holly could have told the doctor. Susan had made up her mind, and nobody was changing it.

"I'll be back before I go home." Luke tenderly touched her cheek before he leaned down and softly kissed her forehead.

Holly watched him and Mitch follow the doctor out of the room.

"Luke loves you very much," her mother observed.

She was not up to this conversation. "Mom, he's the best friend I've ever had. We love each other like best friends do. Please stop trying to make it into something else."

"Don't upset her, Susan." Tony smiled at his daughter. "We'll not talk about it again."

The door flew open. "Oh, Holly!" Tessa practically ran to the bed. "Oh, Holly, I should have gone with you. I could have called Mrs. Turkin back. I'm so sorry. I should have gone with you."

Holly gingerly returned the light hug Tessa gave her. "Then we'd both be lying here. Do you think your being with me would have scared Jack Wallace off?"

Tessa sat on the chair Luke had just vacated. "I could have hit him over the head with my purse. You always tell me it weighs more than I do." Her smile wobbled, and unshed tears glistened in her eyes.

"You'd probably have missed and knocked me out." Holly tried to lighten the mood. She even managed what might pass for a laugh. "Besides, I should have kept my wits about me. Instead, I panicked and got into an unlocked car without checking the backseat."

"What about the man running toward you?" Tony quietly asked. "Mitch didn't even seem interested, but do you remember anything about him?"

Holly considered his question. "All I remember was a shadow—and the sound of footsteps—he ran like a man." The vision of an elderly man holding out a paper popped into Holly's mind. "I didn't take my charge slip. Maybe the clerk asked one of the workers to catch me." That made perfect sense—so why was Holly still unnerved by the memory?

"You couldn't know, Holly," Tessa consoled her. "I think even if you saw that monster in your backseat, he would have caught you and…" Tears trickled down Tessa's cheeks.

"Well, what's important is you're safe now." Susan sat up straight and spoke firmly.

"Sorry to interrupt, but our patient's bed is ready. I need to move her to her room." A smiling nurse spoke from the doorway.

"What room will she be in?" Tessa wanted to know.

The nurse looked at the clipboard she carried. "Two-fifteen, Bed A."

"I'll tell Luke. I think he wanted to come and say goodnight." Tessa explained why she had asked.

"Thank you." Holly still longed for the feeling of security she had with Luke next to her.

Her parents kissed her, and it was soon just the nurse and Holly on their way to the room. Holly hoped she could stay awake until Luke came to say goodnight. She thought maybe it would keep the bad dreams away if his face was the last thing she saw before she fell asleep.

Chapter 18

Luke stretched his aching back again before he drove his ATV out to the fence. He'd like to stay at the house and enjoy a long, hot shower, but if he didn't get the fence fixed, Mrs. Pickler's goats were going to clean out his bean field before it even grew.

Clarence jumped onto the box bed, beside the fencing and tools Luke needed. He liked to ride when Luke took the Gator. He probably figured it was his limo and Luke was his driver.

"You know, Clarence, those hospital chairs may be supposed to double as beds, but they aren't made for a man my size. I could have stuck two of them together, and I don't think I would have ever gotten comfortable."

Clarence yawned in response.

"Why are you sleepy? You were home. I was the one in the hospital all night." Luke hadn't planned on spending the night at Mercy General, but when he started to say good night, something in Holly's eyes wouldn't let him. No matter what she said, she was frightened. And for whatever reason, it seemed to make her feel safer when he was around. Besides, he had been too tired to think rationally himself, and couldn't get the image of Jack Wallace slipping into her room out of his head.

He started the motor and turned to make sure Clarence was situated before he took off for the field.

As bad as Holly having the accident was, it was still better than if she had given in to Wallace and stopped the car. Luke had no doubt the man had evil intentions toward Holly and would have acted on them. The fact he choked her like he did was proof of that.

Thank You, Lord, for telling Holly what to do. Without Your Presence, I know it would have been worse.

He had a lot of work to get done today. Susan had invited him for supper on Holly and Tessa's first night there. He meant what he said when he told Holly he would have camped in her driveway. He could kick himself thirty ways from Sunday for not running to the hardware store himself. They all knew there was a man out there who wanted Holly. And what had he done? Sent her into the night alone.

She was already talking about going back to work, elated that Dr. Potter told her, as long as she didn't lose consciousness or become disoriented again, she could resume her daily routine on Monday. Holly cared deeply for the students she counseled. Luke didn't know for certain, but he figured it was probably mutual.

Maybe with the class reunion coming up, they would be able to focus on something besides the stalker. Luke didn't think of him as only being Holly's stalker because he also felt like a target. He no longer went to bed without double checking the doors of all of his buildings and making sure the garage door was locked. He couldn't protect his truck tires from a knife, but at least the Jeep was safe.

Of course, there was no way he would share his perspective on the situation with Holly. It would only add to the guilt she couldn't seem to let go of. In her eyes, she had to have done something to attract this guy's attention in the first place. Then she was upset the stalker had turned his attention to Luke. And now she was beating herself up because she panicked and didn't check her backseat before she got into an unlocked car.

Like she didn't have a lot of stuff on her mind? Nobody was infallible, and she should realize Jack Wallace would have been able to overpower her right there in the parking lot if she discovered him.

Then there was the mystery man in the parking lot. Mitch brushed it off as Holly's fear causing an overreaction to someone walking or jogging by. Luke disagreed. He didn't know why, but he just had a feeling the other man was dangerous for Holly, too.

The thought of two men there, ready to attack, caused a burning sensation in Luke's chest. Holly was alone and virtually defenseless. He doubted if there would have been anyone around to help in the hardware store parking lot on a Thursday evening. He once more said a fervent prayer of thanksgiving before forcing his mind to his current task.

He stopped short of where the goats stood, munching merrily on their free smorgasbord. It surprised him when his dog stayed on the vehicle and watched as Luke circle around to the fence. Ordinarily, Clarence would be strutting around the farm animals like a general inspecting the ranks. "Clarence, get off there and help me chase these goats back home. Come on!"

Clarence looked at Luke like he had to be kidding and yawned again. Luke climbed on the ATV and gunned the engine. As soon as the first goat began to run, Clarence got the idea. He hopped out of the trailer and tore out after another one. Between the vehicle and yapping dog, they soon had the goats back on their own property.

"Now, would you mind keeping them over there while I fix this fence?" Clarence looked from Luke to the goats and flopped onto his stomach.

"Don't let me disturb your morning nap. You just lie there and sleep while I chase goats away and fix a fence at the same time." Luke seriously considered giving Clarence a little nudge under his hind end to see if he could get him up and going. It appeared the goats were content in the tall grass on Mrs. Pickler's property for the time being, so he spared his dog's posterior.

It took nearly two hours before he had the fence back up and sturdy enough to keep out the uninvited munchers.

"Are you really that tired?" Luke asked Clarence incredulously. While he wasn't a blue-ribbon farm dog by any stretch of the imagination, it wasn't like Clarence to be this lazy either. "Come on, Clarence, let's go home."

Clarence raised his head for a moment and then dropped it back to the ground.

"Clarence, I mean it. Get on." Luke couldn't believe his dog was just lying there looking at him.

Wait a minute. His dog was just lying there looking at him. He hopped back off the ATV and hurried over to Clarence.

"Come on, boy. Get up." Clarence only managed to raise his head again.

"Clarence!" Luke hurriedly pulled his phone out and dialed the vet as quickly as he could.

"Shadow County Animal Clinic." Tina, the vet's assistant answered the phone.

"Tina, this is Luke Walker. There's something wrong with Clarence. We're at the south edge of my farm, and he can't get up. I'm going to try to get him onto the ATV and back to the house. Is Doc Waters there?"

"He's out on a call at the Kitner farm. Let me see if he's almost done. It may be easier for him to come to you than for you to try to bring Clarence to the clinic." Tina was known for a calm head and efficiency.

There was silence for a few moments while he was placed on hold, and then Tina was back. "He said if you can get Clarence to the house, he'll be there shortly. I hope your dog is okay, Luke. I know how much he means to you."

"Thank you, Tina."

Luke pocketed his phone and went to the Gator. He wouldn't be able to carry the large dog very far, but he thought he could lift him to the box bed. At least, there were only the few tools left. He shoved them to the side before he climbed on and pulled the vehicle as close beside his dog as he could.

"Come on, Clarence. Help me out as much as you can." Luke's heart went into his throat when he felt Clarence try to get his legs under him, and they buckled. It took all of Luke's strength, but he finally managed to lift him into the trailer. "Lie still. I'm going to get us to the house as fast as I can."

Luke drove at the highest speed he thought possible without jarring Clarence off the vehicle. Dr. Waters' blue van was pulling into the lane when he parked the ATV in front of the house.

"Good morning, Luke." The friendly, ever cheerful vet in his bright blue bib overalls walked toward him. "What's going on with Clarence?"

"He's been drowsy all morning, and now he can't do more than lift his head."

"Let's have a listen." Dr. Waters set his bag on the bed beside Clarence and pulled out a stethoscope. After he had listened to his heart and lungs, the vet felt his ribcage and examined his eyes.

"What has Clarence eaten lately?" The doctor was prodding the dog's stomach.

"Dog food." That was one rule Luke never broke. Dogs might enjoy table scraps, but it wasn't healthy for them.

"Where do you keep his food?"

"On the back porch. His bowl is in the kitchen. Why?" Did Clarence have a food allergy or something?

"Is your porch locked?" Dr. Waters rubbed Clarence's head between his ears and murmured to him.

"Yes. It's part of the house, my mud room."" Luke couldn't wait any longer. "What's the matter with him? Why are you asking about his food?"

The vet's kind eyes met Luke's. "I'll have to get him to the clinic and run some blood work, but I'm ninety-nine percent certain your dog has been poisoned."

"Poisoned?" Luke's mind raced as the grim reality hit him. "How?"

"Somebody could have left Clarence what he thought was a treat, when, in reality, it was laced with something. I need to get him to the clinic and run some tests so I can get him on the right medicine." Dr. Waters returned the equipment to his bag.

Luke put his hand on Clarence's back. "He's going to be okay, isn't he, Doc?"

"I think so." The vet smiled kindly. "I don't think he was fed a lethal dose. He just ate enough to make him good and sick. We need to get it out of his system, though. Let's get him into the back of my van."

Luke shook his head. "I'll put him in the backseat of my Jeep. He likes to ride there."

Dr. Waters looked like he was going to object, but thought better of it. "Pull your Jeep as close as you can get, and between the two of us, we should be able to transfer him."

Within minutes, Luke and Clarence were following the vet to the clinic.

"I'm sorry I got mad at you, boy. I thought you were lazy. I didn't know you were sick."

Who would have poisoned his dog? Why...Luke's fists clenched on the steering wheel. He barely controlled this never-before-experienced, intense rage when Holly told them Wallace hit her, and now it was back. The stalker or Jack Wallace—maybe one and the same—poisoned his dog. A defenseless animal that had done nothing to deserve this.

Please, Lord, help me stay in control. You don't ever give us trials that you don't give us the means to deal with, but Father, I don't know how much more I can take. The woman I love has been hurt and is still in danger. And I don't care about my things. They can all be replaced. But Clarence—he can't be. Please help me know what to do...How to deal with the anger inside me.

He'd call Mitch as soon as he got to the clinic. This had to stop. Please, God, it had to stop.

Chapter 19

"I like blue, but that shade of pink looks fantastic with your complexion." Tessa scrutinized the garments Holly held.

Are you sure we have to wear dresses to the reunion? Maybe it's casual." She could hope so, anyway.

"I asked Jennifer, and it's semi-formal. Dresses and suits. Now, pick one of those. They both fit like they were made for you." Wow. Tessa was pulling out her teacher's voice.

Holly looked from one to the other. "You're buying the powder blue, right?"

"You told me it made my eyes light up." Tessa seemed quite pleased by the compliment.

"It does," Holly assured her. "If you're going with blue, I'll go with pink. We don't need to be wearing the same color."

Tessa nodded. "Good choice. Now let's look at shoes. Our men are both more than tall enough we can wear high heels."

The men. Luke. Clarence. Holly lowered the dress she was still holding as tears filled her eyes.

"How can we be shopping like nothing is wrong when Clarence is in the animal clinic because somebody poisoned him?" She should have known better than to leave home.

"Stop it, Holly." Tessa walked over and took the dress out of her hand. "Luke said he wanted you to have an ordinary day. The reunion is two weeks away. We need new dresses so we can stun our classmates. Now, please do what Luke asked, and relax and enjoy yourself."

Holly gestured toward the red-haired man standing in the entry. "How can I relax when I know Hank is following us everywhere?"

"That's exactly why you can relax. Besides, Hank is enjoying himself. He's young and unattached. He's been standing there checking out every female in the mall." Tessa grinned. "And getting paid to do it."

That finally brought a smile to Holly's face. "You're right. Mitch went to the trouble of putting Hank on plainclothes protection detail, and Luke did ask me to have a good day. So, lead the way to the shoe department."

Nearly an hour later, Holly sank gratefully into a chair in the mall's small food court. She placed her bags on an empty chair next to her before she looked at her friend.

"I still can't believe I let you talk me into buying those pink shoes. Do you know how impractical pink shoes are? You can only wear them with pink clothes." While Holly had protested, the shoes actually looked good on her, and the insole was soft enough, even with three-inch heels, they were comfortable.

"Oh, phooey." Tessa set her own packages down. "People wear pink shoes with all kinds of colors. I've even seen women wear bright green clothes with pink shoes."

"Well, I'm not that daring." Holly was self-conscious enough, without fearing she resembled a clown. "I wear colors I think should go together."

"Then, I guess we'll have to look for some more pink dresses." Tessa's eyes sparkled with humor. "We can get you a pink negligee, and you can walk around the house in your heels. We'll let you answer the door in it a few times, and before you know it, you'll be the talk of the town."

"Right. Me and Hubert Belton. He got picked up for indecent exposure again, you know. It was in this morning's paper."

Tessa nodded. "Maybe the man is afraid of bathtubs." Mr. Belton let anybody who'd listen know he liked to air dry as he bathed, hence the practice of outdoor sponge baths.

"I wonder why he keeps doing it when they arrest him nearly every week." They were joking, but she actually felt sorry for the elderly man.

Hank seemed to appear from nowhere. "Would you ladies like me to watch your packages while you get your lunch?"

"Will you answer a police-related question for us first?" Tessa asked him.

"Tess, that's not the kind of—"

"Why do the police keep arresting Hubert Belton for indecent exposure when you know he's going to do the same thing the next time he needs a bath?" Holly wanted to crawl under her chair and hide as she watched Hank's ears turn red before his face flushed to the color of a beet.

"Uh, we only arrest him when somebody complains. You have to look behind his bushes to see him, but every so often one of his neighbors complains, so we have to do something." If Hank turned any redder, he would make a nice six-foot-tall flare.

"I apologize for my friend's impolite question when you so nicely offered to watch our packages." Holly kept her tone light so her words wouldn't be taken as criticism. "And we'll take you up on your kind offer because I'm starving, and I don't want to try to juggle three sacks and a tray of food."

"Can we get you anything?" Tessa, having embarrassed the poor young man beyond words, was considerate enough to offer.

Hank's easy-going grin was back in place, even if his face was still a little pinkish. "No, thank you. I'll wait until you're both situated, and then I'll get my own lunch."

Holly stood up to leave, but then she had a question she simply had to ask.

"Hank, if we do run into Jack Wallace, what are you going to do? He's a big man." Hank was lean and muscular, but a match for the man who sent Mitch flying? Luke had told her about the fugitive's size, but she knew his strength firsthand.

The young police officer turned sideways so nobody except the women could see what he showed them. Then he lifted his jacket to display a stun gun strapped to his waist. "I'm going to arrest him."

His quiet confidence spoke volumes and impressed Holly. Luke had wished for her to have a normal, happy, safe day, and Mitch made sure to keep it that way. She was grateful to all three men.

"Mitch wants to take me out this weekend," Tessa said, once they were in line at the Chinese restaurant.

Holly looked quizzically at her friend. "Isn't he going to?"

Tessa solemnly shook her head. "He's not going to have any spare time until Jack Wallace is safely behind bars." She didn't give Holly time to so much as draw a breath. "You can't feel bad, either, because you're not the only one in danger from him now. He's tried to hurt Billy again, and probably poisoned Clarence. Face it, Holly. He sees any of us around you as fair game."

Once again, Holly couldn't help but feel like this was somehow all her fault. It seemed like everybody who cared about her was in danger. At least, the worst that had happened to her parents was the one phone call. She was thankful for that blessing.

"I'm sorry, Holly." Tessa gave her a gentle hug. "Here you are all sore and bruised, and I'm making you feel bad again, aren't I?"

Holly managed to push her aches away but hadn't been able to completely ignore the looks her bruised face garnered. A couple of times she had the urge to wink at the gaping people and say, "You should see the other gal." At least the scarf she wore covered the fading welt on her neck. It would have to be gone in order for her to wear her new dress to the reunion. "It's okay, Tess. You have every right to feel disappointed. I know how excited you are to be in love, and now you can't do anything about it." Her friend must be longing for a flowers and candy kind of date.

Tessa smiled bravely. "This won't go on forever, though. And then Mitch and I will have all the time in the world."

"Do you think you'll like being a sheriff's wife?" Holly, herself, couldn't picture living with the knowledge her husband was in danger every day.

"He hasn't proposed yet." A hint of color highlighted Tess's cheeks.

"But he pretty much laid it on the line," Holly reminded her. "He's ready for romance because he sees a future together."

"I know." Tessa seemed to consider her words carefully. "And the answer to your question is if I'm meant to be Mitch's wife, God will give me the strength to accept his job. Don't you agree?"

Holly was moved by her friend's quiet conviction. "I think that's a wonderful way to look at it."

They finally reached the counter and were able to order their lunches. Hank smiled broadly at them when they returned to the table.

He eyeballed Holly's lunch. "I was going to get a burger and fries, but your sweet and sour chicken looks mighty good."

It was her turn to be embarrassed. "It's about the only thing I know to order at a Chinese restaurant. I like it, so I stick with it."

"I tell her all the time to broaden her horizons and try something new, but alas!" Tessa dramatically placed the back of her hand on her brow and tilted her head. "She is but a creature of habit, my good friend Holly is."

Her "good friend" Holly groaned. "Please don't go all Shakespearean on me, Tess. I haven't eaten yet."

Hank grinned at the two friends' silliness before he sobered. "Ladies, please don't move from this table while I get my lunch. I need you where I have a clear line of vision."

"We'll sit still," Tessa assured him. "We're both starving. Shopping works up a girl's appetite."

Holly had just taken a bite of her chicken when Hank ran back past their table. Her first thought was he shouldn't be running so fast inside a public building.

"What's going on?" Tessa turned completely around just in time for Hank to disappear around the corner.

"I don't know." Holly looked around the food court. Other than a few people still looking curiously in the direction Hank had run, she didn't see anything out of the ordinary. "Let's just sit here like we promised and eat. He'll be back."

Tessa looked at her food. "I'm not sure if my stomach can settle enough for me to eat now."

"Excuse me, ladies."

"Yeee!" Tess jumped out of her chair, and Holly nearly fell off hers as the unfamiliar voice came from close behind them.

"Ladies, I'm a police officer. It's okay."

Holly accepted the hand Tessa offered, and the two of them slowly turned to face their threat. Relief was a tidal wave when Holly saw his uniform.

"Miss Morris and Miss Lincoln, right?"

"Yes." Holly's stomach rolled. What was going on?

"I apologize for startling you. I'm Officer Clark Bentley, with the State Police. We're helping out in Shadow County until the fugitive is caught."

"We're aware the state police are involved," Holly acknowledged.

"Deputy Hank Stone just reported he is in foot pursuit of Wallace. He didn't want to leave you ladies unprotected in case the fugitive circles back around."

Holly wanted to ask him exactly what they were expected to do now, but he continued before she had the chance.

"I'm just going to stand over there by the concourse so I can have a clear line of vision to you, and keep my eyes on anybody entering the food court. Please go ahead and continue your day as you were. I've been told you could use it." The officer, probably in his late forties, smiled stiffly before he turned and walked to the place he indicated.

"Well." Tessa seemed at a loss for words.

If Luke asked Holly how her day went, she wanted to tell him honestly she enjoyed herself, so she resolutely sat back down. "I'm going to eat this food before it gets cold. I doubt it would be tasty that way."

Tessa gave her a measuring look before she returned to her chair. "Good idea. Let's eat. We need to replenish our energy after the hard day of shopping we've put in."

"Yes, we do." Holly dug into her sweet and sour chicken.

Chapter 20

Luke had to once more fight the urge to put his arm around Holly. While some couples sat that way during church, he somehow didn't think Holly would appreciate it.

He tried to focus on Pastor Rollins' undoubtedly excellent sermon. He was just so frustrated. Hank saw Jack Wallace in the mall yesterday, headed toward Holly and Tessa. Instead of using the women as bait and further endangering them, he made a split-second decision to pursue the fugitive.

Wallace led Hank on a mad spree through Shadow Central Mall, with the wanted man knocking mannequins and other paraphernalia over in the stores, not caring what, or whom, he might hurt. Hank, on the other hand, had to remember other people were present, so he couldn't move at the same breakneck speed as Wallace. He was able to tail him to the east parking lot, where the fugitive appeared to have vanished.

One good thing seemed to have come from all this. With Wallace on the run, the phone calls had stopped. That further supported the idea Jack Wallace was Holly's stalker all along. They wouldn't have any way of knowing why until he was caught and persuaded to confess.

He felt Holly shift in her seat next to him. She must still be sore. Why hadn't he thought to bring a cushion for her? The wooden pews weren't comfortable at the best of times. In fact, when the church council considered padding them, Pastor Rollins asked them not to. He claimed the hard pews kept people from falling asleep during his sermon.

Sermon. He needed to listen to the sermon.

"Our plans aren't always God's plans. One man I know had his future perfectly planned. He studied psychology. He was going to enter the ministry and put that psychology to work as a pastor. And then, if he felt called to, he'd find a wife." Pastor Rollins chuckled. "I won't go into all the details, but suffice it to say he is a Christian psychologist in his own clinic. He's also married with two precious children. And he'll be the first to tell you the plans God had for him were far better than the ones he had for himself."

For just a moment, Luke's eyes met Pastor Rollins.' The minister continued. "And sometimes, God calls us to something with a voice so forceful we can't ignore him. That doesn't mean we can sit back and wait for him to hand it over on a silver platter. He expects us to use what he has blessed us with to accomplish goals."

"So, you ask, how am I supposed to know the difference between the plans I've made and the ones God has for me? The answer is prayer and meditation. The Holy Spirit will guide us if we but listen. Too often when we pray, we talk to God, but we don't stop talking long enough to listen to his answers. It is my firm belief he lets us know when something is wrong, just as he lets us know when it's right. It's difficult to acknowledge his judgment sometimes, especially if it's not the way we want it to be, but it's there brother and sisters. It's there."

This time, Luke could see the pastor's eyes were focused on Holly. He began to speak again.

"Most of you know what one member of our own church family is going through right now. I'm sorry if I'm embarrassing you, Holly, but I want you to remember you're not alone. The misguided individual tormenting you is not listening to God, but we are. We're praying for his intervention in this situation. We're praying for the man in question to be caught so he can be helped, and our sister can live a free and happy life again. Please, precious children of God, don't stop praying. For according to the fifth chapter of first John—the fourteenth verse, *And this is the confidence that we have in him, that, if we ask any thing according to his will, he heareth us.* Amen."

Luke felt Holly shift again, only this time it was to lean closer to him. And then he felt her hand slip into his. When he looked at her face, it was to see an expression of peace that hadn't been there for quite a while. Maybe her world wasn't set right yet, but she was okay with it now. Somehow, Luke knew that just as well as he knew his own name.

His hand felt empty when she pulled hers away to accept the collection plate a few minutes later. But then she returned it, lacing her fingers with his. Luke didn't know what this meant. As she seemed inclined to do lately, she may just be seeking the comfort his presence brought her. Or hopefully, she was starting to open her heart to his love. He'd keep praying for the latter until there was no hope left.

Twenty minutes later, he found himself standing behind Holly as she spoke to the minister.

"I'm sorry I put you on the spot." Pastor Rollins smiled ruefully. "I just don't want us to get stagnant in our prayers for this situation, and it went with the sermon material."

Holly gave him a quick hug. "You didn't embarrass me. You reminded me I'm part of a family with a Father nobody can defeat. It was just the message I needed to hear. Thank you."

"I enjoyed your sermon too, Pastor Rollins." At least he had after he started listening to it. "You hit the nail on the head with some truths I needed to hear."

"Bless you both."

Luke placed his hand on the small of Holly's back and led her out of the church. The warmth of sunlight felt good on this spring day, so he steered them away from the shade. As usual, they stopped to socialize with their friends.

After participating in several conversations, mostly centered either on Holly's stalker or the class reunion, Luke found himself alone with Holly.

"You're coming to Mom and Dad's for lunch, aren't you?" Holly's head tilted as she looked questioningly at him.

He hadn't known what to expect today. "If your parents don't mind, and they have enough food. I don't want to put them to any trouble."

Her hair glistened in the sunlight as she shook her head. "Luke, don't you know by now how much my parents love you? Mom would skin me alive if I didn't have you come."

"Well, then, let me run home and check on Clarence. I'll be there as soon as I change clothes."

"Why don't you bring Clarence with you? I miss him, and he hasn't spent a day with Biscuit and Lemon in ages."

Luke thought of the last time his dog paid Holly's parents a visit. After being stuck with two excited animals who seemed intent on rubbing against him, and then circling him like horses on a high speed merry-go-round, Clarence had refused to so much as look at his owner for nearly an entire day. "I just hope those two's habits never rub off on Clarence."

"Why?" There was a teasing glint in her eyes. "Afraid Clarence will sit under a pole light and think he's baying at the moon?"

"My dog already has a unique personality, thank you. He doesn't need any new habits." Since she was in such a good mood, he would play along. "Maybe I better have a talk with him before we get there. I don't want him to think he's spending the night with you."

Tessa walked up beside Holly, covering a wide yawn with her hand. "Excuse me. That silly Lemon sat outside my bedroom window last night and auditioned for the lead role in *The Hounds of Baskerville*."

Her words sent Holly into a fit of giggles, and Luke couldn't stop a chuckle. "We were just discussing my bringing Clarence to lunch with me. I don't want Lemon's habits to rub off on him."

"How about if we give you Lemon and keep Clarence with us for a few days?" The hopeful expression on Tessa's face was comical. "Maybe he'll teach Biscuit how to act like a real dog, and then when Lemon gets back, it'll rub off on him."

Holly's eyebrows shot up. "Are you referring to the ugly footstool you have to wrestle off your bed as a real dog?"

An unladylike snort erupted from Tessa. "Clarence seems like a Westminster champion after a couple of nights with those...Why, I'm not even sure what to call them."

"Isn't it exciting?" Jennifer Ewing's voice was close enough to Luke's ear he jumped.

"Hi, Jen." Holly greeted her warmly. "You're excited about our reunion?"

"Oh, yes." Jennifer linked her arm through her husband's. "Dennis spoke with Tyler Brady last night. And Wes Stevens is coming. He's been married three times! We've only been out of school ten years, and he's been married three times."

There she went with the gossip again. Luke began to think of a way to excuse himself.

"And Chris Howard is coming. Remember little Kim Feldhake?" She didn't wait for an answer. "She sent a photo, and I bet she weighs nearly two-hundred pounds. As short as she is. Nina Grant and Doug Markham have responded, too. And who else?" She frowned at her husband.

"You have a list at home, honey." He patted her arm as though to calm her. Luke wished him luck with that. "It's not even two weeks away now. Let the rest of them be surprises."

"Okay." Jennifer suddenly produced the sappiest smile Luke had ever seen, and he was less than thrilled when she aimed it in his direction. "Your favorite high school memory is just precious. Does H—"

"Surprises, Jen!" Dennis admonished her. "We need to get going. Our reservations are for noon."

After rushed goodbyes, Luke wondered if the women were as relieved as he was.

"I sure hope Jennifer isn't planning on giving any speeches," Tessa stated blandly. "Because if she does, we're liable to be sitting there until our twentieth reunion."

"I think I'll ride home with Luke." Holly's announcement was certainly fine with him. "I can visit with Clarence while he changes clothes, and then we'll all three be at Mom and Dad's in a short while."

Tessa looked surprised for a moment before a satisfied smile appeared. "That's a great idea. You need to get out, and you'll be safe with Luke and Clarence."

"You're sure in a good mood." He made the observation as they watched Tess walk away.

"It's a warm, sunny day. The police are out en masse looking for the man whose name I won't say today. Nothing else can be done, and worrying isn't going to help one single thing. So, I'm going to have a spectacular Sunday afternoon with my two best friends and family."

Luke's soaring heart thumped as it landed hard on the ground. He was still classified as a friend. Granted, it was a best friend, but a friend just wasn't what he hoped for. Oh, well. He wasn't going to ruin the day Holly had planned.

They had a pleasant conversation during the drive from the church to his farm. Luke laughed as Clarence nearly floated with delight at the first sight of Holly. It looked like master and dog both had it bad for the lady.

He left Holly sitting in the living room conversing with Clarence while he went upstairs to change clothes.

When he went to put his good watch away, he noticed the sparkling ring. Impulsively, he picked it up and took it with him as he headed downstairs.

"I want to show you something." He sat down beside Holly, glad she was in the middle of the sofa with Clarence on the other end.

"What?" She looked at him curiously.

He held out his hand and opened it, hoping she wouldn't notice it shaking. "This is my grandma's ring. It belonged to her mother. Dad told me it's been in my family for over four generations now."

Holly reached over and took it to closely examine. "Look how dainty it is. The band looks almost like lace." Her beautiful brown eyes were glued to the ring. "What kind of stone is it, Luke? It's not a diamond, but it doesn't look like any other stone I've ever seen."

"I don't know. My dad doesn't know either."

"So, you inherited the family ring." She turned it over to examine the setting. "What are you going to do with it?"

Luke decided to go for broke. "I'm going to give it to the woman I marry. It'll be her engagement ring. What do you think?"

Holly looked from the ring to his face, a strange light in her eyes. "I think she would be happy to have a family heirloom on her finger."

"Let's see how it looks on you." Before she could voice a protest, Luke took the ring out of her hand and slid it onto her ring finger. "It fits perfectly, like it was made for you."

"It's beautiful." Holly looked at the ring on her hand and then back at Luke.

"Holly." He spoke her name before he leaned toward her and gently kissed her lips, mindful of the bruises on her face.

At first, he felt her return his kiss, but slowly she pulled away. She had a sad look on her face.

"Luke, I...I'm..."

"I love you, Holly." There. He had just gone and said it.

"Well, I love you, too. Best friends are supposed to love—"

"That's not the only way I love you." This was it. "I'm *in* love with you. The kind of love a man feels for the woman he wants to marry."

Her face crumpled, and tears began to fall.

"Holly? I didn't mean to upset you. I'm sorry. I just had to tell you how I feel."

She buried her face in her hands. "It's just, I don't know how *I* feel. Please don't get mad and stop being my friend, Luke. I need you right now more than ever."

He sighed deeply. "I told you I'd do anything for you. But I want you to know the truth. I've been in love with you for a very long time, and I want you to be my wife."

She lifted her head and looked at him through her tears. "That means a lot to me, Luke, but it's too much right now." She slid the ring off her finger and placed it in his hand. "Please, give me time. Can we just go on like this—at least for now?"

"If you'll honestly tell me one thing."

"I will if I can."

The answer to this question meant everything. "Is there even a chance your answer will ever be yes?"

The look she gave him caused his heart to go into overdrive. "There is."

"Can I kiss you one more time before we have to go back to being strictly friends?" One to tide him over.

"Okay." His hands shook as he carefully cradled her face. This was their first real kiss. He prayed it wouldn't be the last. His lips met hers, and they shared a soft, sweet kiss he would remember for the rest of his life. No matter what.

"Thank you," he said as he pulled away. Then he stood up. "I need to go put this ring away so it doesn't get lost. I'm going to pray it ends up right where it was a few minutes ago."

Even though she hadn't said yes, she hadn't said no either. And there was no more pretending on his part. She knew the truth. He loved and wanted to marry her. With that in mind, he could meet the challenge of remaining her friend. For as long as he had to.

Chapter 21

Holly crossed her arms on her desk and laid her head on them. Maybe she should have accepted the doctor's offer and taken a few more days off work. The longer she was on her feet, the worse she felt.

Yesterday was one of the best days she had experienced in weeks. The only troubling spot was when Luke confessed his love. He would never know how much she wished she could have told him what he wanted to hear. But too much was going on. Right now, all her feelings for him were entwined too deeply with the comfort and security their friendship provided. What if she agreed to marry him only to realize, after the stalker was caught, her feelings were just friendship mixed with profound gratitude? It wouldn't be fair to either of them.

A knock on her office door brought her out of her reverie. "Come in."

"Miss Morris?" Billy Andrews walked hesitantly into the room.

"Hi, Billy." She was surprised to see him. "Come on in and sit down."

He sank into a chair and looked at Holly. She watched his eyes grow larger as he took in her appearance, finally focusing on the scarf draped around her neck.

"What can I do for you?" She would keep this meeting as positive as she could.

"I'm not skipping class or anything." He placed a familiar pink slip of paper on her desk. "Mr. Murdock gave me a pass out of study hall."

Holly smiled at him. "That's good." Maybe if she gave him a few minutes, he'd start talking.

Billy looked at her face again before fixing his gaze on the desk between them. "Miss Morris, do you hate me now?"

"Hate you?" She was stunned. "Why on earth would I hate you, Billy?"

Holly nearly rubbed her eyes to make sure she was seeing what she thought she was. A tear trickled down the young man's face.

"It's all my fault. Jack wouldn't have hurt you if you hadn't helped me." He quickly wiped his face with his shirtsleeve. "I didn't know he'd do that. Honest."

Her heart broke as she stood up and walked over to sit in the chair next to his. "Billy, I want you to listen to me." She waited until he met her gaze. "Jack is a very troubled man. I would much rather he be angry with me than you. What he did is not your fault." She searched her mind for the right words. "Just like it wasn't my fault."

"No way was it your fault!" Billy exclaimed vehemently.

"You're right." She placed her hand on his arm. "But I was careless. I got into an unlocked car without checking the backseat. That made me think it was my fault, just like you feel like it's yours."

"Jack did it! It wasn't your fault!"

Holly kept her voice calm and steady. "And it's not yours either. Let's make a deal."

The teenager appeared cautiously hopeful. "What?"

"I won't blame myself if you won't blame yourself. We'll both remember who's really responsible." She held out her hand to shake. "Deal?"

She could see the wheels turning as Billy considered her words. Finally, with a determined look on his face, he shook her hand. "Deal."

"So, do you feel ready to get back to study hall and hit those books?" It wasn't difficult to smile at the young man beside her.

He stood up. "I better. Miss Lincoln gave us a big math assignment, and I didn't get it all done last night. I think I had too much on my mind."

Holly stood and signed his pass before handing it back to him. "You just do as much of your math as you can. I'll speak with Miss Lincoln. She'll let you make up anything you don't turn in today."

"Thank you, Miss Morris." Billy clutched the piece of paper. "For everything."

Her heart warmed. "That's what I'm here for, Billy."

He had only been gone fifteen minutes, and Holly was trying to motivate herself into getting caught up on paperwork, when the intercom on her desk buzzed.

"Yes?"

"Miss Morris, can you come to my office at your earliest convenience?" It was Mr. Graham.

"Is now all right?"

"That would be fine."

Holly sighed deeply as she stood and headed out of the office. What new duty had Mr. Graham gone and decided would be better taken care of by the guidance counselor than the assistant principal? If he tried to force her to accept more disciplinary matters than she already had, she would be speaking with the principal. And if he didn't help, by golly, she'd go all the way to the superintendent. Maybe the board. Holly didn't mind shouldering a little extra weight, but she wasn't there to assume all of Mr. Graham's responsibilities.

By the time she sat down in his office, she had worked herself up enough to argue about anything he might say. The sky was blue? It looked green to her today. She was in such a tizzy she almost didn't catch what he said.

"I'm glad to see you here, Miss Morris. I was sorry to hear that Mr. Wallace caused you bodily harm."

Talk about taking the wind out of her sails. "Thank you."

"The administration and board are aware that you placed the needs of young Mr. Andrews over your own. You are to be commended for that."

"I just did my job." Holly couldn't quite believe he was complimenting her. Where were the hidden camera and guy who jumped out and yelled surprise?

"Of course, that's not the only reason I asked you here." Mr. Graham peered over the top of his wire-rim glasses, a look of uneasiness on his face.

She almost felt relieved. This was more like it. Now, they would get down to business.

"You see, the junior and senior classes have received permission to hold what they're calling a Spring Fling."

Okey-dokey. "I'm aware of their plans." It was to be a carnival of sorts, with games and prizes. The Parent-Teacher Organization were helping them prepare for it, and the students were very excited.

"Well, it seems a problem—a rather large one, actually—has developed, and I would appreciate your assistance in solving it." Holly realized she had never seen Mr. Graham in quite such a state before. He seemed unaware of the long lock of hair he usually arranged to cover his bald spot now poised precariously over his ear.

She swallowed laughter as the image of a lopsided Gerber baby popped into her head. He was her boss, and she would be respectful if it killed her. "What would you like me to do?"

"You are probably aware Diana Dowden and Walter Chantmeier are going to be the chaperones. Strictly in a supervisory capacity." She didn't like his obsequious tone of voice nor the direction he was headed. "It seems we need two more adult chaperones in order to meet our insurance company's requirements for coverage on an event of this size. I would deeply appreciate it if you and your friend Mr. Walker would be kind enough to help out."

He had to be joking. "It's this coming Saturday."

"I realize it's very short notice. I have exhausted all other options, or I wouldn't be bothering you." He smiled stiffly. "I would be indebted to you."

She closed her eyes and sighed. "There really is nobody else?"

"All other qualified staff members have plans."

She was going to have a talk with Tessa. What plans were keeping her from doing this? "And if I don't agree, what will happen?"

"I guess we'll have to cancel the event." What was *he* doing on Saturday? Maybe he and Tessa should "volunteer."

Holly said a quick prayer for patience and guidance. "Okay. I'll do it. I can't promise Luke will help, but I'll ask."

"Thank you." The assistant principal stood. "While we can't imagine Jack Wallace showing up at such a public event, the other administrators and I agree Mr. Walker would serve as protection for you. Being your friend, he will be more committed than someone else may be."

"I'll try." She repeated the assurance as she stood and turned to the door.

It wasn't until she reached her office she remembered the class reunion. Wonderful. She would spend this Saturday with a group of sixteen and seventeen-year-olds, and next Saturday she would spend the day reminiscing about when she was that age herself.

Lord, you have a sense of humor, don't you?

Chapter 22

Tessa's car was parked in front of his garage when Luke drove the tractor in from the field and around the barn. Tessa was visible behind the wheel, talking on her phone. Holly was sitting on his back porch step with Clarence. As he watched, Clarence stuck his nose right up against her neck and nuzzled her. The dog was crazy about Holly. That made two of them.

Holly and Clarence joined him as he shut the barn door.

"This is a nice surprise." He smiled at Holly and would have scratched behind Clarence's ears if the mutt were paying the least bit of attention to him. As it was, he'd have to chase the dog around Holly's legs to get close to him.

Holly's answering smile lit a flame in his heart. "Wait until you see the rest of it."

They walked together to Tessa's car, where Holly opened the back passenger door and pulled out a large, plastic container.

"I brought you some homemade, cinnamon-raisin cookies." She held the gift out for him to take.

"My favorite." Luke gladly accepted it before looking from Holly to Tessa, wondering who she was talking to so animatedly.

"Mitch," Holly whispered.

"Oh." He was happy that his friends realized how they felt about each other. "Can you come in and have some cookies and milk with me?"

"I can come in." Holly walked beside him. "But if I eat one more cookie, I'll explode."

Luke chuckled. "Still sampling while you bake?"

"Is there any other way to do it?" Her eyes twinkled as she asked him the question.

He washed up once they were in the mud room, and they were soon seated at the kitchen table.

Luke moaned when he took his first bite. "This is good, Holly. I haven't had these in ages. Thank you."

"You're welcome." There was something different in her expression now—guilt?

"So, what did I do to deserve my favorite cookies?" She had to know he didn't want to be repaid for trying to help her with the stalker situation.

There it was again. It *was* guilt on her face.

"I'll make you cookies whenever you want me to." Her eyes met his, and he was so captured by their beauty he almost didn't hear her next words. "But this time I have an ulterior motive."

He stopped with a cookie midway between the glass of milk and his mouth. "What? I don't think I heard you correctly. You don't have ulterior motives. It's not in your genetic makeup."

"Did you ask him yet?" Tessa swooped into the kitchen. "He said he would, didn't he? I told you there was nothing to worry about."

Holly turned and looked pointedly at her friend. "I was just about ready to, thank you."

Luke set his cookie down. He had a feeling he needed to brace himself. "What are you two talking about?"

"Could you make yourself available for four or five hours this Saturday?" The smile Holly produced definitely didn't make it to her eyes.

"I guess." He didn't have any plans beyond clearing what appeared to be remnants of an old beaver dam out of the creek. "What for?"

Holly stared at him for a long moment, and then the words gushed out. "The junior and senior classes are having a carnival. I have to chaperone it, and Mr. Graham told me I needed to find another adult to help me. You, to be exact."

Chaperone a carnival? Luke liked the idea of spending time with Holly, but watching that many kids? It would be very different than his small youth group.

"Isn't there somebody else? A staff member?" He had to ask.

A sad smile and small shake of her head accompanied the answer. "Mr. Graham told me I was the only qualified staff member available."

Qualified. "I'm not qualified, am I? I mean, supervising eight teenagers for church activities doesn't qualify me for something like this."

"I'm pretty sure in this case, just being you is enough." Her eyes pleaded with him. "The administration wants you there to keep me safe. I asked Mitch, just in case you didn't want to, and he can't spare an officer to watch me this Saturday. Hank has been working twelve days straight and has to have this weekend off. If you don't go with me, I don't think my bosses will allow me to be there. Then the kids will have to cancel it."

"They've been working hard, Luke," Tessa chipped in. "I would do it if I hadn't signed up for a webinar. I'll be online for two hours."

Luke looked into Holly's incredible brown eyes and knew he was a goner. "Okay. What time should I pick you up?"

Relief flooded her face. "The Spring Fling officially begins at two o'clock, but we're supposed to be there at one. Then, it will be open to the public for three hours, and we'll have to stay while they close up. Is that too long?"

He had a feeling a much shorter period of time was going to be too long in this situation, but he would do it for her. "It's fine."

"Thank you, Luke." Who was he trying to fool? He would volunteer for diaper duty in the church nursery to earn that smile.

"You're welcome." A day watching Holly and supervising fifty or sixty teenagers. What could possibly go wrong?

Chapter 23

Straightening the *Shadow High Staff* T-shirt tucked into her jeans, Holly gazed around the football field. The students had really outdone themselves, and the community was turning out in full force to support them. At this rate, they would raise plenty of money for next year's senior trip. The senior's practice of "paying it forward" always touched her. Five years ago, the seniors voted to help that year's juniors raise the money they would need the following year. They gained nothing from their efforts other than knowing their underclassmen would be able to afford a good senior trip. The tradition had continued, and now she doubted if any of them would even consider changing it.

Looking for Luke, her guilt eased when she saw him laughing as he helped a few of the boys brace the backboard for the dart game. Something hadn't been attached properly, and when the first balloon popped, the entire wall toppled over backward. Luke had gone right over and taken charge. He caught her eye and winked.

"Can you believe this?" Holly hadn't noticed Diana Dowden standing next to her. "I'm surprised by how well it's going."

Holly turned to her. "I know. It's only been open for a little over a half hour and look at this crowd. If it keeps up at this pace, the students will raise more than enough money."

Diana didn't say anything, and when Holly looked at her, she saw the attractive blond had focused her gaze on the dart game.

Not taking her eyes off it, she spoke again. "I see Luke Walker is helping out today."

So that's what—or more like whom—Diana was ogling. "Yes. He was nice enough to pitch in."

Diana turned her gaze back to Holly. "He's single, isn't he?"

"He's not married if that's what you mean." Holly felt uncomfortable with this conversation.

"He's not in a committed relationship either, is he?" The look in Diana's eyes told Holly she already knew the answer. "Would you mind if I go talk to him? I mean, he's not your boyfriend or anything."

"Uh...I..." But Diana was already on her way to Luke.

As Holly watched, the two of them started talking. Then Diana laughed, and Luke smiled. An unpleasant sensation began in the pit of Holly's stomach and built until she felt like screaming. What was this emotion? It was something entirely foreign to her. Then, as she saw Luke laugh, she knew. Holly was jealous.

While she was still processing that knowledge, she saw Luke look her way and then say something to Diana. He headed toward Holly. Did that mean he'd rather be with her? Or was he fulfilling his guard duty?

"Are you okay, Holly?" Luke's anxious voice penetrated her foggy brain. "You're awfully pale. Are you sure you're not overdoing it too soon after the crash?"

"I'm-I'm fine," she managed to say. This new feeling was both powerful and confusing. "I think I need to sit down for a few minutes, though. I'll go down to the tiny-tot games and sit where I can watch all of them."

His frown deepened. "Then I'll stay there with you."

She needed to be away from him to try to sort things out. "I'll be fine there, Luke. I'll be right in the middle of a crowded area. He won't dare do anything with all these people around. You go ahead and make the rounds."

"I don't like leaving you alone." He took her elbow and started walking. "I'll walk you there and make sure you're situated. Then we'll see how everything looks."

They paused at the cake walk and watched as an elderly man ended up on the winning circle.

"Grandpa, you won!" The teenage girl was talking loudly enough it was apparent he was hard of hearing. "Come pick out a cake!"

Something about the young lady's interaction with her grandfather was touching. Holly watched as the girl led the older man to the prize table, which was laden with all sorts of baked delights. It wasn't until after he picked up a tray of cookies when Holly turned to resume their trek.

"Do you remember your grandma's apple pie?" Luke asked.

"Of course." Holly would never forget the incident he was referring to. "We got off the bus at her house because our parents were all at a farm bureau something-or-other. She offered us an after-school snack."

"She meant cookies or an apple." Luke's smile grew. "But I could only see that hot apple pie sitting on the counter."

"So, when Grandma asked you what you wanted, you told her you usually had apple pie when you got home from school. Like your mom kept a steady flow of them coming just for your after-school snack."

"Your grandma didn't care if I was windy." Luke chuckled. "I still say it was the best piece of pie I've ever had, or will have, in my life."

"I miss Grandma." Holly's grandmother passed away shortly after Holly's high school graduation, from complications due to pneumonia. Her grandfather had succumbed to heart disease before Holly was even born. Her maternal grandparents were missionaries in Haiti, and she saw them so seldom she didn't feel close to them at all.

"She would be proud of you," Luke said with conviction. "You're doing what she always told us to do—walking with Jesus."

The thought Grandma would be proud of her brought tears to Holly's eyes, but she fought them back. The Spring Fling was not the place to sit and cry. "Thank you for saying that, Luke."

They finally arrived at the end of the field, where the students set up what they designated tiny-tot amusements. Holly headed for a chair conveniently placed between the duck pond and winner's wheel game. From there, she would be able to see the entire area.

"See?" she asked once she sat down. "I can sit here and supervise this whole section. And I'm in plain sight, as long as you don't go behind any of the other amusements."

Luke stood beside her chair for a few minutes, looking down the football field at the rest of the carnival. Finally, he stepped around in front of her.

"Okay. I should have a fairly clear line of vision to you from almost everywhere. When you get ready to walk again, just stand up and wait until I come get you. Agreed?"

"Agreed." Holly smiled at him before he turned and headed away from her. He strolled, stopping to speak with the students running various games.

"I wanna ducky, Mommy! I wanna ducky!"

Holly was distracted by a chubby little boy pulling his mom to the small, water-filled swimming pool with plastic ducks bobbing around in it. When the player chose a duck, he won the prize that corresponded with the number written on its bottom.

The harried mother handed Joey Snowdon a ticket and followed the little boy to the pool. He was already bent over, naturally trying to reach the farthest duck. Joey saw what was going on, so he leaned down and stirred the water, causing the duck the little boy was after to float closer to him.

The toddler finally picked up the duck he'd set his sights on. When Joey took it to see which prize he won, the little boy burst into tears.

"I wanna ducky!" He looked at his mom as though his broken heart would never mend. "He taked my ducky! I wanna ducky!"

Joey gave Holly a helpless look. She stood and walked over to the trio.

"Look, honey." She turned the duck over to see the number eight. "Joey is going to give you a number eight prize. See?"

Joey quickly went to the tubs and retrieved a bright sparkling pinwheel.

The little boy was having none of that.

"I wanna ducky!"

Holly looked at the pool, where at least three dozen ducks remained. "Let him have the duck, Joey."

It wasn't like the child was unreasonable. In his eyes, he won a duck, and they were trying to take his prize away from him.

"Thank you." His mother looked relieved. "He would never have understood. I'd have to take him home."

"Little kids are weird," Joey proclaimed as soon as they left.

Holly patted his shoulder. "They just think differently than we do. You used to be that age, too, you know. I imagine if you were to ask your parents, they would have some stories to share."

Joey looked skeptical. "I don't think I'd have ever wanted a wet plastic duck instead of a neat pinwheel."

"You'd be surprised." Holly smiled as the memory of one of many shared holidays came to her. "A good friend of mine used to sit and play with the Christmas paper more than he did the presents he unwrapped."

Anita claimed she even had to fish Luke out of an extra-large plastic bag of discarded Christmas paper once. Thankfully, he was making enough noise there had been no danger of him being left to suffocate.

Holly left Joey to take care of the next customers and returned to her chair. The duck loving child was now spinning the winner's wheel. He was happy when Sylvia Tanner handed him a small, plastic slinky. Holly chuckled when she saw him try to push the slinky onto the duck's head like a crown.

She sat, relaxed, watching the toddlers play the various games. The students did a good job setting things up for them, and arranging an area specifically for the younger children was a smart idea.

While she watched, her thoughts returned to Luke. Why had she felt jealous when Diana asked about him, and even more so when Luke appeared to enjoy the attention? He had declared his love for Holly. She knew he would have never made the statement lightly. He meant what he said.

At least for now. She couldn't delude herself. If she put him off too long, she wouldn't have a choice whether or not to become more than friends. He wanted to be married with a family. He deserved to be married and have a family. And if she couldn't commit to him, she would have to give him up. She couldn't have it both ways.

The whole thing still came back to her uncertainty as to exactly what her feelings were. She felt closer to Luke than any other human being. But, how much of those feelings were brought on by the stability he offered in her otherwise off-kilter world? No. She could not commit to a romantic relationship with him until she knew it was sincerely love she felt. But, maybe...maybe Holly should show him even though she couldn't know with certainty she was in love with him, she wanted to be. He was the only man in her life, and she would give him no reason to doubt her dedication. She already felt better.

Lord, I'm asking again, please help me through this situation. Please help Mitch and the other officers catch Jack Wallace. Then, I pray the stalking will stop for good. Please do this so I can go on in my life. You know what's best, and I'll try to accept it, but you know what's in my heart better than even I do. Thank you for keeping me safe. And thank you for the past few days with no communication from the stalker. You are a magnificent God. Amen.

Holly brought her focus back to the children around her. Time passed quickly until she realized she was going to have to visit the ladies' room. Remembering her agreement with Luke, she stood and began to look for him. There was no sight of him anywhere, however.

Standing hadn't helped her situation any, and if she didn't take care of business soon, she was going to embarrass herself.

"Joey?" She waited until the teenager looked at her. "Please tell Mr. Walker I've gone to the restroom. I'll be right back."

The boy blushed at the concept of his guidance counselor requiring the use of a bathroom. It always amazed Holly when she realized kids of all ages had set ideas about the adults in their lives.

Right now, she was in a hurry. There were portable toilets placed both ends of the field, or she could go through the gates, to the concessions' building and use the restrooms there. While she didn't want to leave the field, a line of at least five children was at the facilities near her, and she wasn't sure if trying to make it the length of the carnival was a good idea. Her decision made; she headed for the gate.

She met several people heading in to enjoy the Spring Fling but didn't see anybody else headed toward the building she was going to. A drumbeat began in her heart. Going to the concessions' building wasn't a good idea. She was alone and putting herself in danger. What was she thinking?

Holly immediately turned and headed back toward the gate, determined to make it to the portable toilets where she would be surrounded by people.

She breathed a sigh of relief after she entered the gate and turned to her right. Suddenly, her hair was yanked hard enough to pull her around. The breath left her body when she saw a giant of a man with anger unlike Holly had ever seen pulsing from him. He grabbed her by her upper arms before she could move. Though she struggled with all her strength, he effortlessly pulled her off the path.

"You ruined everything." Her feet left the ground as he shook her like a rag doll. "My life was fine until you came along. You ruined everything."

"Let me go." His grip was so painful, it was all she could do to speak without screaming.

He didn't say anything. Instead, he began to drag her farther behind the amusements, toward the fence.

"I said, let me go!" She pushed against his chest as hard as she could, but all it served to do was earn her a second round of shaking. Her head felt like it was going to bounce off this time.

"Help! Help me!" She screamed at the top of her lungs. "Help!"

"Shut your mouth before I shut it for you." He yanked her to him and put his face right in front of hers. "Guess your giant hero man can't be everywhere you are, can he?"

His mouth was so close to hers, she tasted his breath. She jerked her head back. "No!"

He sneered. "Don't you worry about me kissing on you, lady. It's not my lips that are gonna land on your face."

What was she going to do? They were between the amusements and fence, and the crowd was making too much noise for her screams to be heard. "Just let me go." She tried to keep the tremors out of her voice.

He had evidently drag-carried her far enough away from the gate to suit himself. He released her arms so abruptly she nearly crumpled. Before she could take even one step, he had her by one arm.

"This is gonna feel good." She watched in horror, frozen, as he drew back his arm. Then, she closed her eyes, braced to feel the impact of his fist. *Help me, Lord.*

"Let her go!" A familiar voice sounded just before somebody rushed past, and Jack Wallace was jerked away from her. She stumbled and nearly fell, but managed to regain her footing.

"Billy!" Billy Andrews had tackled Jack Wallace with enough force, the giant lost his balance and went to the ground. As though he were glued on, Billy followed, hitting and kicking with all his might.

"You hurt Miss Morris!" He screamed at Jack.

A group of five or six boys appeared, Ronnie Chambers among them. "That's the guy who hurt Miss Morris?" Ronnie seemed as angry as Billy.

Holly heard her name while the boys, as a whole, swarmed over the prone man. It looked as if a quarterback had just been tackled, and now lay buried under a mound of players.

Then she heard a woman's voice. "Call the police! Somebody, call the police!"

The world began to spin, and all light disappeared.

Chapter 24

After fixing the rickety dartboard game again, Luke looked down the field, expecting to see Holly, only to see an empty chair. She must have gotten up to help one of the students. He took a deep breath and searched the area around the chair. No Holly.

He was on the verge of panicking when a couple of boys ran past him.

"Andrews took him down! The guy was hurting Miss Morris, and Andrews took him down."

The teenager's words sank in, and Luke spun to follow the boys. He heard a siren and saw the flashing lights of a squad car, just as he reached a mob of people.

"Let me through." This was not the time for good manners. He shoved his way past people until he saw Holly. She was lying on the ground, pale and lifeless. A few yards away, a mass of teenage boys was piled on top of something. Luke didn't care. He had to make sure Holly was okay.

He didn't notice the woman knelt beside her until he dropped to his knees.

"Your girlfriend's okay." She spoke reassuringly. "I'm a nurse. She was probably terrified and passed out. Her heartbeat is strong and steady, and her respiration is fine. An ambulance is on the way, but she's all right."

"Okay! What's going on?" Mitch and a couple of state police officers had forced their way through the crowd from the opposite direction. "What are you boys doing? You need to get up."

One of the boys on top lifted his head. "If we get up, the guy who hurt Miss Morris will get away."

"The guy who hurt..." Mitch's mouth dropped open. "You mean to tell me you boys have got Jack Wallace under there?"

"I don't know his name, but he's the guy who hurt her." The boy answered him.

Astonishment still on his face, the sheriff looked at his fellow officers, who were equally stunned. One of the state police officers pulled sturdy looking hand cuffs off his belt . The other officer stood beside Mitch.

He spoke to the teenagers again. "We'll handle it from here, boys. You can get up now."

It didn't look like the young men were going to respond for a minute, but finally, one by one, they unsnarled themselves and stood up. Soon, only one boy remained on top of the prone man.

Mitch leaned down close to the teenager. "Billy, it's Sheriff Landon. We're here now. He won't get away. You can get up."

The boy who Luke now knew had to be Billy Andrews—the boy Jack Wallace abused—looked up at Mitch. His voice shook when he spoke.

"You have to keep him in jail this time, Sheriff. He was gonna hurt Miss Morris again. Bad."

Mitch smiled grimly. "Don't worry, Billy. It's going to be a long time before he gets out of jail. Now, please get up so we can put these cuffs on him."

Luke held on to Holly's hand as he watched the disheveled teenager unsteadily stand up. He didn't know exactly what had happened, but he was sure of one thing. Somehow, that boy rescued Holly. Luke wouldn't forget it.

"Luke?" Holly's weak voice came from in front of him.

Relief flooded him as he looked into her open eyes. "You're going to have to stop this. I'm going to have gray hair before I hit thirty."

"Is Billy okay?" She tried to turn her head in that direction.

"He's more than okay," Luke assured her. "He's a hero in my book. Jack Wallace is still unconscious. They're going to have to put him in the ambulance they called for you."

"Billy got him?" Her voice sounded weak.

Luke nodded. "He sure did. He and some other boys."

"Does she need medical attention?" Having left the cuffed, still unconscious man under the watchful eye of the state officers, Mitch knelt beside the nurse.

The nurse spoke to Holly. "Are you hurt anywhere?"

"My arms hurt." Holly moved them slightly and grimaced. "But I'm okay."

"You're still recovering from the car wreck, Holly," Luke reminded her.

"I didn't know that." Blue eyes looked accusingly at Luke. "Her vitals are all good, and she seems to be recovering fine. But if she's just had an accident, I highly recommend she be examined in an emergency room."

"Okay." He watched the kind lady walk away before turning back to Holly.

"Can I lie here a few more minutes?" Holly winced. "And, can you drive me? I don't want an ambulance ride."

"Sure." When Luke saw her arm twitch, he silently lifted the sleeve of Holly's shirt. There were bright red, vivid marks left by the fingers of the man lying on the ground a few yards away. Pure, unadulterated rage poured through him. He started to stand, intent on making Jack Wallace sorry he ever laid a finger on Holly. That sorry excuse for a man would know— Holly's hand on his arm drew his attention back to her. It was in her eyes. She knew what he was going to do. A soft smile and slight shake of her head brought him back down to his knees.

He exhaled and relaxed. *Thank You, God, for Holly's calming influence.*

"Is Miss Morris okay?" Luke looked up to see Billy standing there.

Luke squeezed Holly's hand before he rose to his feet. "She's fine." He extended his hand. "I'd like to shake the hand of the young man who rescued her."

Billy's dirty face turned red, but he stood tall and shook Luke's hand.

"Will you introduce me to the fellows who helped you?" Luke looked at the motley group of boys and recognized Ronnie and Adam among them. "I only know a couple of them."

Billy introduced each boy to Luke, who solemnly shook their hands.

"He's our youth group leader," Ronnie proudly announced. "You guys oughtta come next time. He's cool. He took us fishing already, and we're going bowling in a few weeks."

Luke looked down at Holly, who smiled as best she could. Maybe he wasn't so bad with kids after all.

Mitch stood and turned around as Jack Wallace began to stir. The ambulance arrived and backed up as close as they could get to the scene.

Luke knelt beside Holly again and watched as an EMT examined a now awake, cursing man, and then pronounced him in good enough health to be taken to jail. He had just gotten the wind knocked out of him and lost consciousness. His bruises and scrapes were superficial.

"Looks like it's going to be an empty ambulance," Luke observed. He stood, and then leaned down to scoop Holly into his arms.

"I'll be able to walk in a few minutes," she protested.

"I'm able to carry you right now." He turned around and looked until he saw the other female chaperone. Donna, he thought her name was. "I'm sorry, but we can't finish our duty. Is there somebody we need to call?"

She shook her head. "Ronnie Chambers' parents agreed to complete the day. Just make sure Holly is okay."

"I will." He turned to walk to the gate, Holly cradled gently against his chest.

Mitch stopped him with a hand on his shoulder. "This has got to be one for the record books. Trained police officers have spent days and nights looking for this man, and half a dozen fourteen-year-old boys took him down and caught him for us."

Luke thought of the boost this would be to those boys' self-esteem, and how Ronnie was already responding more positively to Luke's role in his life. "God always has his hand in it, and he's a lot better at the job than we are."

"Amen." Mitch agreed.

Luke clutched Holly a little tighter. "Can you come to her parents' house to get her statement? I think she needs to stay home and rest."

Mitch nodded. "I'll be out as soon as we get our new guest behind bars. The district attorney has added attempted murder to his charges because of what he did in her car. Now he'll undoubtedly talk about assault and attempted kidnapping as well. I think Jack Wallace is looking at some hard time."

"I just hope he gets some help in the process." Holly's voice was stronger. "And I hope he was the one responsible for everything—so it will stop."

"I hope so, too," Mitch agreed.

"We'll see you later." Luke nodded at the group of boys and parents as he headed for the parking lot. It sure hadn't worked out in any way he would have imagined, but it worked out, all the same. God was in control.

Chapter 25

Holly turned over in bed, still sore in a few places. At least, she was in her own bed, in her own house. Mitch agreed with her, as long as she and Tessa went back to keeping Clarence at night, it was just as safe for her there as it was with her parents. Her dad understood, but her mom was unhappy.

Jack Wallace swore he knew nothing about stalking or slashed tires, but he came right out and bragged about what he did to Holly. There were even close calls she was unaware of. He almost had her one day at her mailbox, and another time when she was pumping gas. Something always got in his way. When questioned about Tessa, he laughed and said something about two for the price of one. Mitch told Holly speaking to him was an exercise in self-control; he nearly went across the table more than once.

Even without his confession, what the police had turned up in the investigation supported the theory he had been her stalker all along. He was not only living in Connecticut during Holly's senior year, his last-known address was less than ten miles from the Massachusetts campus. Then, he relocated to Illinois approximately three weeks before the harassment resumed. Mitch figured it would have taken him that long to get situated.

Tessa pointed out how coincidental his timing was to the stalker showing up.

Holly turned again, only to feel a sloppy wet tongue slather across her face.

"Yuck!" She sat up, wiping her face with the sheet. "Clarence, I've told you I don't like your morning kisses. Go kiss Tessa awake."

Luke claimed Clarence now considered himself as much Holly's dog as his. Even after they knew for sure this was over, the two of them were going to work out joint custody. Luke said Clarence didn't sleep well the entire time she stayed with her parents, instead roaming the house and whimpering. He even howled a few times. He seemed to think he lived with her during the night.

She looked at the clock. "I'd better get up or I'm going to be late for work."

Clarence used his front leg to signal he needed to be let out. "Just a minute. Let me get my housecoat."

A housecoat was probably unnecessary. She didn't have any neighbors close enough to see her inside the front door. It just made her feel strange to traipse around in her nightshirt. Besides, the world didn't need to see she slept in a Charley Brown shirt. She had Peanuts pajamas, too. So, if a man ever wanted to marry her, he better be ready to accept sleeping with a Snoopy-clad wife.

Her breath caught. A man did want to marry her. Maybe the stalking was permanently in her past. Maybe she would be able to focus on her feelings for Luke. Explore them. Give him a real answer.

She let Clarence out and stood behind the screen door, so she could let him back in. The sun was already peeking over the horizon. The world felt full of possibilities.

Thank You. I'm sorry I don't say that enough. I come to you with pleas so often, but I forget to thank you when you answer them. Thank you for keeping me safe. Thank you for even the possibility that my life will be stalker-free. Thank you for my family. Thank you for my students. Thank you especially for giving Billy the courage to do what he did. Thank you for my friends. And thank you for Luke. I don't know what part he will play in my life, but I can't imagine it without him in it somewhere. A paw scratching the screen door caught her attention. She smiled. *And thank you for Clarence's love and loyalty. Amen*

"Are you up already?" Tessa walked out of her bedroom, stretching as Clarence and Holly entered the room.

"Already?" Holly looked pointedly at her. "You better check the clock. If we don't get going, we'll be late for school." Then she thought of something that made her giggle. "I can be late without it being a problem, but if you're late, Mr. Graham will have to cover your first-period class. It's trigonometry, isn't it?"

Tessa's eyes opened wide. "Oh, no. The time he taught my pre-algebra class it took me two weeks to un-teach the students the completely incorrect way he showed them to work equations." She snorted. "Telling them they could ignore a number if it were taken to the zero power. Any number, no matter what it is, becomes one if it's taken to the zero power. Now, you tell me it isn't going to change the value in an addition or subtraction problem."

Okay. Holly had asked for that. She knew better than to get Tessa going about anything to do with math. It wasn't that Holly didn't understand the subject; it was simply too early in the day for an in-depth analysis of algebra. Or, she shuddered to imagine, trig.

"I'm going to get dressed. You can have the bathroom first." Before Tessa could spout off any more mathematical words of wisdom, Holly scooted into her bedroom.

Her cell phone rang just as she was fastening her skirt. She was afraid for a moment before she remembered Jack Wallace was in jail. Regardless, she checked caller ID.

"Good morning, Luke."

"Good morning, Holly. So, you're finally getting in the habit of checking your caller ID?"

"Nope." The dog edged as close to Holly as he could get, being nosy. "Clarence said he had a feeling you were going to call."

A chuckle emanated from the phone. "Well, did Clarence tell you Mrs. Pickler's goats somehow made it all the way to my yard last night?"

"How did they do that?" Mrs. Pickler's property abutted the south edge of his farm. The goats would have either had to come through a big soybean field and pasture or around on the road. It didn't make sense either way. "Do you think they had some help?"

"If they did, I think it was a prank, plain and simple." She could hear the smile in his voice. "I checked everything, and besides the daffodils Mom planted, nothing was bothered. I guess the goats thought they were dessert."

"It's a good thing it's too early for your rose bushes to bloom. The goats would have ended up with their mouths full of thorns, and you'd be calling Dr. Waters. You're too soft-hearted to let them suffer."

Yeah, well, I called because I can't get there to pick Clarence up before you leave. Can you tie him somewhere outside for me?"

"No." She didn't mean to be so abrupt. "I'm sorry, Luke. It's just I can't imagine tying Clarence. I'll leave him in the house."

"How will I get him?" His voice was laced with amusement. "You have to lock your house, and while my dog has many talents, I don't think opening doors is one of them."

Holly thought for a minute. "I'll leave a key outside the back door. It'll be under the mat. You may as well keep it. That way, we won't be on such a tight schedule every morning."

"I don't like the idea of you leaving your key outside, Holly."

"You won't be that long. And Jack Wallace is in jail. I'll put it beneath the northeast corner of the mat, and if it's moved, you'll know it. Okay?"

"I still don't like it." For a moment, Holly thought he was going to argue, but then she heard him sigh. "I'll get there as soon as I can. Leave it where you said you would, and if it's not in that exact location, I'll do a walk-through of your house before I leave."

"That sounds like a good plan." It was a beautiful day, and Holly refused to let her buoyant mood change.

"Okay. I'll get off here so I can take care of the goats."

"Bye, Luke."

"Good-bye."

She turned and looked at Clarence. "You will be all alone in my house. If I find out you were on my bed, I'm going to hold you down and tie ribbons all over you. You'll look like a girl dog. Got it?"

Holly impulsively hugged the dog when he appeared to nod. Sometimes she had to wonder exactly how much he understood.

"Are you talking to that dog again?" Tessa stuck her head in the door. "I believe Luke's right. You're part owner of a dog."

"Luke just called." Tessa stepped the rest of the way into the room as Holly went on to explain the goat dilemma.

"Does he think somebody brought them to his house?" Tessa frowned. "I mean, Mrs. Pickler's goat pen is a long way from his house. The goats would have had to pass lots of tempting shrubbery along the way, whether they came through the field or on the road."

"Can't you see it?" Holly had a sudden vision of the scenario. "All those goats walking down the road, intent on visiting Luke."

"Holly, what about somebody bringing them?" Tessa's frown grew.

"I asked that, too." She sat on her bed and slid her heels on. "Luke checked everything, and nothing has been bothered. Except the goats ate some flowers Anita planted."

Tessa still seemed skeptical. "I guess it would be pretty pointless to drop off a herd of goats."

"That's what he thinks." Holly slid her watch on and picked up a hairbrush. "He's going to be late picking Clarence up, so I'm leaving a key under the mat for him."

Tessa's frown was back in full force. "Holly, we don't know for sure Jack Wallace is the man stalking you. Leaving your house key outside is inviting trouble, if you ask me."

"Luke and I have a plan." She grimaced as the brush caught on a tangled mass of hair. "I told him exactly where I'm leaving the key. If it's not there when he gets here, he's going to check the house. I imagine he'll check the house even if the key is where I left it. Just to be safe."

Tessa still didn't look too happy about it. "It's your house." She produced a small smile. "You can have the bathroom now."

Holly returned her friend's smile as she headed for the other room. Today was going to be a spectacular day. She just knew it.

Chapter 26

This had to have been one of the craziest weeks Luke ever experienced. On Monday, he spent two hours loading goats into the trailer and hauling them back to their pen at Mrs. Pickler's. And unless the eighty-seven-year-old woman decided to free her goats, he couldn't figure how they got out.

Then yesterday, he went to take his tractor to the north field only to find it parked facing forward inside the locked machine shed. He was positive he backed it in. He always did. But his bedroom window was open the night before so he would have heard if anybody started it. And there was no way at all a person could have pushed it. It just didn't make sense.

Now, to top it off, he was looking at his ATV—parked smack dab in the middle of the pond. It had been locked in the machine shed, and the key for it was hanging on a hook in the mud room. At least, the pond was shallow enough it hadn't damaged the motor. Somebody had to have driven it out there, but there were two problems with that theory. Keys to the machine shed and vehicle had been inaccessible, and the driver had left no footprints. No human being was going to walk out of a pond without leaving footprints.

As silly as all this seemed, he called Mitch anyway. Maybe he'd see something Luke was missing. To his credit, Mitch didn't act like Luke was overreacting. He said one of those things might be a strange fluke, but all three together suggested tomfoolery. Luke should head for the house to wait on Mitch, but he couldn't seem to stop staring at his Gator, trying to determine how it got there.

He must have lost track of time because Mitch's shouted greeting broke his concentration. He turned to see his friend nearly there, having walked from the house.

"Now there's something you don't see every day," were the first words Mitch spoke upon arrival.

"Tell me about it." Luke started to walk around the pond again, keeping his eyes focused on the muddy edge of it. "Am I missing something here? Wouldn't a driver leave footprints?"

Mitch, studying the pond's edge as they walked, nodded. "Unless they had longer legs than either one of us."

Luke turned and looked at him. "We're both pretty tall." Luke was six-two, and Mitch a couple of inches taller. "What would this guy have to be? Seven feet?"

"The ground is too hard up here, but I don't see how even a tall person could have a long enough stride to step over the mud." Mitch seemed as perplexed as Luke was.

"It's almost like somebody drove it out there and floated away."

Mitch appeared to ponder the concept. "You know, Luke, I've seen kids figure out how to do a lot of strange things. Remember last year, when Mr. Graham's car ended up on the roof of the school? I know students did it, but I never figured out how."

"But why would teenagers want to play tricks on me?" He felt like he was missing something important, but it was just out of reach. "The youth group went fine. Ronnie was even telling those other boys who helped hold onto Jack Wallace, they should come to our bowling tournament next week. I think he called it cool."

"Those were six freshmen." Mitch knelt and seemed to study something on the ground. "Looks like a log impression," he muttered before raising his voice. "There's a whole high school full of teenagers. Just ask your girlfriend."

"Please don't call Holly my girlfriend." As good as it sounded to Luke, he was afraid of what Holly's response would be. "She knows how I feel now, but she wants to get past all the stalker drama and know it's over for good before she figures out how she feels. I have to be a patient man if I want that woman to marry me."

"I'm not that Dr. Phil guy Missy watches." Mitch straightened and grinned. "But if Holly's not in love with you, I'd like to see how she acts when she does fall in love."

Luke's heart soared. "I pray you're right, Mitch."

Mitch's grin faded. "How are you planning on getting your ATV out of that pond?"

Reality came crashing back as his gaze returned to the green vehicle. "I'm going to wear my waders out there and drive it out. Can you stick around a few more minutes? I might need to hook a chain to my truck and pull the thing out. I'm afraid I'll bury it to its axles if I try to drive it without help."

"Sure." Mitch keyed his radio to make sure it was on. "Do you want me to go get the truck?"

"I will. I have to get my waders anyway."

Thirty minutes and with what seemed like a ton of mud and water spewed all over the place, they finally had the ATV back on dry ground.

"Okay." Mitch put his hands on his hips. "Now I'm convinced they used a different way to put it in there. Look at the mess we made getting it out. It wouldn't have been much easier driving it in."

"Is there anything I can do?" Luke was at his wit's end. "Whoever this is, they're not damaging anything. They're just making extra work for me. And I'd like to know how they're getting my keys. I double-check the locks on all my buildings since the spray-painting incident."

"I'll have the guys keep their ears open. If kids are doing this, I guarantee they'll be bragging about it. We should have Tess and Holly listening, too."

"I'm not sure if I want Holly to know." Luke had considered it carefully, but still not made a decision. "She's so happy right now. She really believes Jack Wallace is her stalker, and this is the first taste of freedom she's had in a while. If I tell her this, I'm afraid she'll start worrying all over again—over something harmless."

Mitch frowned. "It's up to you, of course, but I think you should tell her. She knows kids better than either one of us. She'll understand what's going on, and probably be able to make suggestions we would never think of."

"I hadn't thought about it like that at all. Besides, I'm not going to win her heart by keeping secrets."

"That's for sure." Mitch looked at his watch. "I'd better get back to work. I need to get my day finished early if I want to make it to Bible study with Tessa this evening."

"You're starting Bible study?" It surprised Luke. He knew Mitch was a Christian, but with Mitch's hectic work schedule, he wasn't able to attend church functions regularly.

"You're not the only one trying to win a woman's heart." He winked at Luke before he hopped in the truck. He was driving it home so Luke could drive the ATV. At least, neither Luke nor the vehicle could get any muddier. He'd have to use the shower in the mud room and throw the clothes he was wearing right into the washing machine. He'd still probably smell like mud at Bible study this evening.

Oh, well. Such was the life of a farmer.

Chapter 27

"So, will everybody please keep your ears open? Somebody is playing some pretty elaborate tricks on Luke Walker's farm, and Sheriff Landon thinks it may be some of our students." Holly sat back down beside Tessa. She had just addressed the entire faculty during their weekly meeting. Hopefully, they would get some results. Things weren't slowing down at Luke's place.

Thursday, he found every electrical cord in the machine shed braided with others. It took him most of the morning to untangle his drills and saws. He even had to unsnarl the portable generator's cord, which somebody had to have plugged in since he only ran the outgoing cord if he needed it.

Then, this morning he walked out of his house to discover every piece of lawn furniture and decor he owned turned upside down. The only thing damaged was the huge flowerpot his mom planted petunias in every summer. It had fallen over and busted. Luke didn't think the destruction was intentional. Someone was simply having fun at his expense. Luke was the most patient man Holly knew, but she had to wonder how many more stunts even he could handle without it getting on his nerves.

"I didn't get to finish telling you about my talk with Jen after Bible study Wednesday night," Tessa said so only Holly could hear her. Not that anybody was paying any attention to them. The meeting was over, and this was the time everybody caught up with each other.

"I'm sorry." Holly felt guilty. "I saw her headed for you and Mitch, so I steered Luke in the other direction. I just wasn't up for her enthusiasm when I dread the reunion."

"I still don't understand what happened. You were just starting to get excited about it, and then suddenly you don't want to go. What changed?"

"I wish I knew." Holly kept her eyes on the meeting agenda as she folded it precisely. "Maybe it's because I'm afraid it will be just like when we were in high school. They'll all see a homely, chubby farm girl with a total of two good friends."

Tessa reached over and stilled Holly's movements. The paper was folded into a small triangle. "I'm telling you, the very people who used to act like you didn't exist are going to be blown away when they see you. You are beautiful, inside and out. They're going to regret that they didn't realize it sooner."

Holly knew her friend was trying to help, but she was only succeeding in making her feel even more self-conscious. "I'm going, anyway, Tess. I promised Luke, and after all he's done for me, I'm not about to let him down."

Tessa scooted forward in her chair. "Well, let me tell you what Jen said. Brent Dasher owns a chain of restaurants across the state of Alabama. Do you know what he calls them?"

"I can't imagine."

"Fast Food for Giants." Tessa giggled. "You know, unless he's grown a foot taller and bulked up, he was about as far from a giant as a man gets. Remember when he climbed…"

Tessa's words faded into the background as Jack Wallace's hate-filled voice echoed, "Guess your giant hero man can't be everywhere you are, can he?" She'd forgotten that. Was he talking about Luke? But he wouldn't refer to a man he towered over as a giant. Even Mitch, the largest man in Holly's circle of friends, was probably an inch or two shorter and not quite as muscular. Maybe she was exaggerating Jack Wallace's size; after all, she'd been terrified.

"Hey, Holly." Tessa's voice startled her. "You okay?"

Holly looked into the concerned eyes of her friend and started to tell her about the giant. But, then she thought of all Tessa had gone through with her. Why bother her with what was probably a reference to the sheriff? "I was daydreaming, I guess. Sorry."

Thankfully, Tessa was too excited about the upcoming reunion not to accept Holly's answer at face value.

"So, Jen said Tom Dwer called just to ask if Kevin Tripp was coming. You don't suppose those two will be up to their old tricks, do you?"

Holly pictured the two boys, so alike in appearance, yet complete contrasts in personality. "You know, I always kind of felt sorry for Kevin. He seemed so shy, and Tom was obnoxious. Maybe Kevin felt like he had to pull those pranks just to keep the only friend he had."

"Weren't you his project partner in adult living our senior year?"

"I'd forgotten, but I was." Holly remembered now. "Mrs. Wilcox paired us, and she made sure we were with people we wouldn't choose."

Tessa leaned back and rubbed her neck. "We didn't have enough boys in the class, remember? I was paired with Jeannie Singer, She Who Knew Everything. Her speedy checkbook balancing method almost made me flunk that semester."

Although she hadn't thought about it in a long time, Holly easily recalled the war zone in Tessa and Jeannie's corner. And wasn't there something... "I remember Tom went right up to the front of the classroom and got on his knee to propose to Mrs. Wilcox. He sang some silly song about her being her his widow woman bride."

"He thought he was so funny." Tessa frowned. "How did you get through that class? I can't imagine Kevin saying enough to help with any assignments."

Holly searched her memory. "I don't think he ever said too much, but I'm pretty sure he did his share. He must not have done too poorly since I earned straight A's that year."

"Well, I just hope he and Tom don't go stringing somebody's underwear up the flagpole." Tessa reminded Holly of a bulled-up child, sitting with her arms crossed tightly in front of her. "Then, Jen got on a kick about Wes Stevens being married so many times already, and how it was too bad that you and I are still single." Tessa uncrossed her arms, and a contrite expression appeared on her face. "You know what? I shouldn't have stood there and listened to so much gossip."

Holly couldn't help but grin. "Talking to Jen is an exercise in avoiding gossip. Don't punch your nose too hard."

"Excuse me."

Holly looked beside her to see Mr. Roper, the maintenance man, standing there.

"Hi, Mr. Roper." Holly liked the nice man. She didn't know what his salary was, but with his duties, it couldn't be enough.

"I just wondered if I could talk to you for a minute." He looked awkwardly at Tessa. "In private."

Holly gave her friend an apologetic look and stood up. Every so often, her job extended to counseling faculty members. Mr. Roper had never asked for help before. "I'll see you in a while, Tess."

"Sure." Tessa turned around and joined a group at the next table.

"Why don't we go to my office?" Holly suggested.

"That'll be fine." He walked beside her until they reached her office. Then he waited while she unlocked the door.

"Have a seat," she invited him once she was behind her desk.

Mr. Roper looked at the floor and shuffled his feet before meeting her eyes. "I'll just stand."

"Okay." There was something truly troubling the man in front of her. "How can I help you?"

"If I talk to you, it stays between us, doesn't it?"

"Unless it's endangering you or others, or it's illegal, whatever you tell me will not go beyond these four walls."

"That's what I thought." The older man sank into the chair, his bushy gray brows lowered in a frown. "You see, I have a problem. I may have misplaced a few things, and now I can't find them."

"What have you misplaced, Mr. Roper?" He was much too sharp to be suffering dementia. Maybe he had been working too hard.

"I always store the unused shop class equipment. Right now, Mr. Glendon is teaching the students about electrical appliances. He needed all the auto mechanic equipment out of the shop. There's a big room under the gym where I store it."

Holly was confused. "And you seem to have misplaced some of the equipment? I'm sorry, but I don't understand."

"I have a photographic memory, Miss Morris." Sudden sadness overtook his features. "Or at least I used to."

"And..." she prompted him.

"I took art supplies into the room yesterday. Storing them for Mrs. Boynton. And when I walked in, the equipment wasn't right."

"What was wrong with it?"

His eyes sharpened. "There are empty spaces where equipment should be."

"Perhaps Mr. Glendon needed some things and didn't want to bother you," Holly suggested.

The maintenance man shook his head. "The shop was the first place I checked. There isn't any automotive equipment in there."

"Could somebody have just walked in and moved stuff around?"

Mr. Roper pulled a heavy-laden key ring from his pocket. "The room stays locked, and there's only one key besides this one. The principal's secretary keeps it in her desk."

Holly would offer to help search the building, but a lug wrench and jack were the only automotive tools she could identify. She would be no help. "What do you think could have happened to it?"

"I don't know," he sadly admitted.

Something wasn't making sense, but one thing Holly was sure of. "Mr. Roper, I don't believe for one minute you've misplaced that equipment. I think somehow, somebody is playing a trick on you." Luke would commiserate with him. "My friend is going through something similar."

"I suppose I'll be put on leave when the superintendent finds out it's gone, though." His sad expression nearly broke Holly's heart. "With Maude needing her treatments, I can't afford to miss my salary."

Holly thought for a minute. Unless somebody in the staff or administration had decided to get their jollies by tormenting the janitor, the culprits had to be students. "Let's not say anything just yet. Let's do the same thing we're doing to try to help my friend. We'll listen to the students. If some of them have done this, they won't be able to resist bragging."

Mr. Roper's gratitude was immediate. "Thank you, Miss Morris. I figured you'd know what to do."

"You're welcome."

After assuring her he wouldn't tell anybody else and would pay extra close attention to the students while he cleaned during late afternoons, he left to get busy at his job.

What on earth was going on in Shadow High School? If Mitch was correct, a group of students was vandalizing Luke's farm, and now there was an excellent chance students had removed or relocated shop tools. Holly started to pick up the phone. Maybe Luke would have a suggestion for what she could do. But then she thought of all he was dealing with. Besides caring for her safety and doing his farm work, he was dealing with his own pranksters. No. She would enlist Tessa on this one and not put it on Luke's shoulders.

Please, Father, help me with this problem. It seems like my life is never going to get back to normal. I ask you to help me remember you're always with me. Please help Mr. Roper accept your comfort, too. Thank You. Amen.

Chapter 28

"This is really yummy." Holly used a sing-song voice. "Are you sure you don't want to try it?"

Luke looked at the spoonful of tapioca pudding Holly was offering him and shuddered.

"I thought we agreed to disagree about that stuff." He shifted his gaze, intent on eating the good old peach cobbler in front of him.

Holly laughed and stuck the spoon in her mouth. As soon as she swallowed it, she scooped up another bite and waved it under his nose. "You don't know what you're missing."

What he did know was the little lumps in the stuff looked too much like tiny fish eyes. And the one time—clear back when they were in grade school—she persuaded him to try it, he actually gagged.

Luke tried to look stern as he returned her gaze. It was a lost cause, though, when he saw the mischief lurking within her smile.

"Okay, okay." She ate another bite of pudding. "I'll eat this scrumptious dessert while you sit there and eat boring cobbler."

"I didn't know food had to be exciting to be good." He was not an adventurous eater. If he liked something, he stuck with it. He decided to change the subject. "So, are you glad we went ahead and came out to eat tonight?"

"Yes," she answered with no hesitation. "If I stayed home, Tess and I would have just ended up parked in front of the TV. And she probably would have talked me into trying a new hairstyle or something."

"I understand why you wear your hair up when you're at work, but I really like it this way." Maybe he needed to compliment her more often. Besides, the long, flowing strands looked like spun, coffee-colored silk. He knew firsthand it was as soft to touch as it looked.

Holly gave him a self-conscious smile. "It's just too easy to pull back into a ponytail. I don't know why I don't brush it out and leave it like this more often."

"You should."

"Walker? Luke Walker?" A man standing at Luke's side was addressing him.

"Yes." He looked vaguely familiar.

"Man, you haven't changed a bit." The lean man had hair too blond and skin too tanned to be natural, in Luke's opinion, but he tried not to judge people by their appearance.

"I'm sorry." He just couldn't figure out who the other man was. "I can't seem to place you."

The man grinned. "I'm Clay Richmond. We graduated together. Remember?"

Clay Richmond. The guy every girl seemed to go for. "Of course. How are you?"

"Great." He glanced behind him. "I'm here with Jen Ewing and her husband. She found out I arrived this morning and insisted I join them for dinner." A slight grimace marred his handsome face. "She sure hasn't changed, has she?"

Luke couldn't think of a prudent thing to say, so he indicated Holly. "You remember—"

"Hey." Clay had just taken his first good look at Holly. "You've gone and found yourself quite a beauty. Please tell me she's not wearing a ring." Before either of them could respond, he spoke to Holly. "Let me tell you, your fellow here has developed much better taste since high school. Lots of girls went after him, but he just hung out with some homely girl nobody would date."

Luke's first instinct was to slug the guy for insulting Holly. She had a weird look on her face. He had to fix this.

"I spent time with that girl because I liked her. And this is her, Clay—Holly Morris." He hoped he didn't sound as aggravated as he felt.

"Holly..." Clay grinned again. "You're not that pudgy little girl. No way."

Luke abruptly stood. "Look, Clay, I don't know where you're living now, but in Shadow, gentlemen still have manners. If you're going to talk to Holly that way, I see Jen and Dennis sitting over there. Maybe you should just join them."

The other man had the grace to look ashamed. He turned to Holly, and Luke watched as right before his eyes, the rude, cruel-mouthed man became the Romeo who enticed girls in high school.

"I'm sorry." His smile would melt butter. "I'm just nervous around beautiful women, and baby, you are beautiful."

Okay. This wasn't what Luke intended to happen, either. He most certainly did not want Clayton Billings Richmond III to flirt with the woman he loved. "Clay—"

"Sir, your party is ready to order. They've asked you to join them." A waiter had arrived in the nick of time.

Clay's smile was for Holly. "I'll look forward to seeing you at the reunion tomorrow." He gave Luke a cursory glance. "See you, Walker."

Luke sat back down, uncertain of what just happened, but aware of the fact he didn't like any part of it.

"I'm sorry, Holly." What was the look on her face?

She smiled dreamily. "Clay Richmond just called me beautiful."

Yes, he did. After he called her a homely, pudgy, little girl nobody would date. This wasn't right. "Of course you're beautiful. You've always been beautiful. You are the most beautiful woman in the world, as far as I'm concerned."

Instead of responding to his compliments, Holly was surreptitiously looking over her shoulder at the table Clay had gone to. Luke's world tilted on its axis. Where was his level-headed, practical Holly? Where had this...*schoolgirl* come from?

"Luke?" Mitch's voice coming from his other side startled him. He probably looked deranged when he turned to his friend.

"What?"

"Tess told me I'd find you here. I need to speak to you." Mitch looked at Holly, who had turned back to face them. "I'm just going to borrow him for a few minutes. Okay?"

No way would Holly let them talk without her. She'd want to be involved if it had anything to do with the pranks being played on him.

"I'll wait here." She was already looking over her shoulder again.

It was a bewildered man who followed Mitch into the quiet hall joining O'Leary's dining room with its private banquet rooms.

"I don't understand." And he didn't.

"What?" Mitch seemed as confused as Luke felt.

"Holly." Maybe his friend would be able to shed some light on the situation. "Clay Richmond shows up and insults her like crazy. Then after one compliment, she can't take her eyes off him. I don't understand."

"We've got more important stuff to worry about than Holly making eyes at Clay Richmond." Mitch's brisk demeanor finally got through to Luke.

"What's going on now?"

"It's Wallace." Mitch shifted on his feet. "He's confessed to a lot of stuff; he was close to Holly even more times than he first admitted. But, he's adamant he doesn't know where you live, and he only made the one phone call."

"He's probably lying." It was the only thing that made sense to Luke.

Mitch shook his head. "I don't think he is. He stole that old junk truck of Harvey Mead's and has been holed up in a deer shack on George Gibbons' place. There's no electricity, running water, or telephone." The sheriff shifted on his feet. "Luke, he says some guy is after him."

Luke didn't like the expression on his friend's face. "You can't think it was me. If you even believe the maniac."

"I know you're not who he's talking about."

"But you believe him."

Mitch's solemn expression concerned Luke. "Remember what scared Holly so badly she didn't look in her backseat? The man she heard running toward her?"

Luke mechanically nodded, his mind trying to absorb this situation.

"Wallace will testify in a court of law that even though he didn't see the man's face, the guy chasing Holly that night came after him. Jack showed me a nasty cut on his shoulder, where he says the guy he's calling Holly's 'hero giant' almost got him. He's only alive because of a good hiding place and he was pretty sure that man wouldn't do anything in broad daylight."

The impact of what Mitch was saying hit Luke like a ton of bricks.

"The stalker is still out there."

Mitch looked grim. "I'm afraid so, Luke. I think he's been so focused on the man who tried to hurt 'his Holly," he hasn't taken the time to call."

A hot coal began burning in Luke's chest. "And now with Jack Wallace behind bars, he's free to come after Holly again."

"Yes." The sheriff looked at the door they'd come through. "The description I have is a man my size, maybe a little bigger, and stronger than Wallace. There's no way to identify the man."

"So, we're right back where we started."

"And I don't know what the best way to handle it is."

Just go get Holly and lock her away someplace where nobody could get to her. Keep her safe. That's what Luke wanted to do.

He rubbed the bridge of his nose and thought. "Mitch, tomorrow she and Tessa are getting their hair and all that other stuff done. Then, she'll be with me. We'll all be together at the reunion, so she should be safe, shouldn't she?"

Mitch seemed to consider it for a minute before he nodded. "As safe as she's going to be until we catch this guy."

"Then, let's not tell her until Sunday. Let's let her have some normalcy. She deserves to enjoy herself tomorrow, not spend all day jumping at every sound." Holly would be angry when she found out what they'd done, but she'd just have to get over it.

"I like that idea." Then Mitch seemed to think of something else. "But how are we going to make sure she stays with one of us, without her realizing something is wrong? We can't have her going off by herself."

Mitch had a point. What could they do? Then the answer came to him. "We'll tell Tessa. Then, between the three of us, we can make sure she's not left alone, or in a dangerous situation."

Mitch sighed. "Short of placing her in protective custody, it's the only plan we have. Clarence is still there every night, isn't he?"

"I've been taking him home on Saturday morning and not bringing him back until Sunday evening." The image of Clarence pouting and moping around the house brought a smile to his lips, despite the situation. "I can fix that easy enough, though. I've been talking about leaving him all weekend, so I'll just start doing it."

"Okay. After church on Sunday, we'll sit down and establish some rules for all of us to follow to keep her safe. And if she refuses, I may just have to take her into custody for her own sake."

Luke was surprised. "You'd really do that?"

"No," the other man shamefacedly admitted, "but she doesn't have to know that, does she?"

"She's going to be shooting sparks." Holly had never been one to lose her temper quickly, but when she did, she did so with gusto.

"We're going to keep her safe. That's what matters."

It *was* what mattered. How much longer was this man going to get away with this?

Luke just wished they had an answer.

Chapter 29

Holly checked her makeup one more time and decided she looked as good as she was going to. Luke should be there to pick her up in about fifteen minutes. If he picked her up. She wouldn't blame him if he didn't. She behaved deplorably at O'Leary's the evening before. What had gotten into her? She knew better than to swoon at the first compliment a man paid her, even if the man was Clay Richmond.

And before the compliment, what had he been talking about? She was so thrown off by his presence, she hadn't really heard a word he said before he told her she was beautiful. She noticed Luke looked angry a couple of times, but she didn't know why. Maybe it had something to do with Clay talking about Jennifer. Maybe Clay was as bad of a gossip as she was.

"You look stunning." Tessa stood in the bedroom doorway.

"Thank you." Tessa had acted strangely all day. She insisted on taking care of Clarence's regular outing this morning, even though she and the dog still weren't the best of friends. Then, at the beauty salon, Tessa actually switched her appointments around so the two of them were together throughout the entire treatment. Tessa even let Joni do her nails, so she would have them done while Peter was doing Holly's. And the last time Joni did Tessa's nails, her friend spent the next two hours complaining about streaks and removing every fleck of polish she could find.

That wasn't all, either. Tessa visited the salon's bathroom with Holly. They hadn't done that since they were teenagers. It was like Tessa was her shadow or something.

"When is Mitch picking you up?" Maybe she'd get a breather if Mitch picked Tessa up before Luke got there.

"Oh, didn't I tell you?"

Why did Holly think she didn't want to hear this?

"We decided to double. The guys thought it would be fun, and since we're all going to the same place, it doesn't make any sense to take two separate vehicles, does it? Besides, we always have fun when we're all together. We even had fun before Mitch and I became a couple. Don't you think?" Tessa took a deep breath.

"I think you're prattling on like you do when you're nervous." Holly stepped directly in front of her. "What's going on?"

Tessa quickly broke eye contact, but not before guilt appeared.

"What are you not telling me, Tess?"

Tessa's smile looked forced. "Nothing. I just don't think it's fair to Luke if you flirt with Clay Richmond. Mitch said something about you flirting with him at O'Leary's last night."

"I didn't flirt with him," Holly denied. "I was so nervous, I don't think I said two words." She felt her face warm. "I think he may have flirted with me a little, though, and I acted like an awestruck schoolgirl."

"Holly." Tessa's disapproval was apparent. "You're supposed to be figuring out how you really feel about Luke. The man who loves you. Not some guy you haven't seen for ten years, and who wasn't even nice to you then."

Guilt lapped at Holly's conscience, for she knew Tessa was right. She promised herself to show Luke he was the only man in her life, and then went loopy at the first sight of a man she barely knew. Tonight would be different. "I'll be with Luke this evening. Everybody will know we're together, so it won't do any good for there to be flirting of any kind."

Chapter 30

Luke was running late. He was in his suit, hair combed, dress shoes on, and ready to go…but he couldn't find his dog.

"Clarence!" He stepped past the machine shed and yelled as loudly as he could. "Here, boy!"

The dog's favorite tromping grounds were the north and west fence rows, but he never went without Luke. Never.

He tried to push away the horrible thought that had been edging into his mind, but it was too powerful. Clarence had already been the stalker's target once; what if his dog was out there in danger again?

His phone was half out of his pocket when a loud rustling in the tree line was followed by a horrendous howl.

"Clarence!" Luke took off at a dead run, easily spotting the area of brush the movements and wails were coming from.

Picking his way past briars and brambles, he finally had Clarence in sight. "Clarence, you're all right. Come here."

The howls became whimpers. Luke felt the pocket of his suit jacket catch and didn't even pause when it tore. "Clarence, boy, I'm coming. Hold on." Why wasn't his dog coming to him?

He knew the answer to that question when he finally pushed his way into a small clearing with Clarence. The huge dog was tangled up with a tree—no, he was *tied* to the tree.

"Who did that to you?" Luke froze, trying to hear movement, but it was no use with Clarence's pathetic whimpers echoing around him.

"Okay, Clarence." Luke ran his hands across the dog's head and down his back. Although he checked thoroughly, he found no signs of an injury—just a rope hooked through Clarence's collar and tied around the tree. And whoever tied it knew what he was doing; the knot

185

was some sort of intricate looping and turning Luke wasn't sure he could untie.

At least, Clarence had stopped whimpering and was content nuzzling Luke's side while he worked.

He soon reached a conclusion. Two, actually. He was going to have to leave Clarence and go back to the house for a knife, and he needed to call Holly because he was going to be late.

Clarence was friendly, but not to someone who meant harm. So, who would be able to get close enough to the dog to tie him up without being chomped into puppy chow? Who was doing this?

Chapter 31

They were at the reunion a total of fifteen minutes before Holly felt like standing on a chair and announcing she was Luke's date. His *date*. A *real* date—as in girlfriend. Because Patty Waterson, Sabrina Bower, Natalie Beason, and Lisa Hawke had been flirting with Luke as if she weren't even there since she and Luke walked in thirty minutes late. It assuaged her anxious heart that Luke was being polite, and nothing else. Nevertheless, for the second time in her life, she was plain jealous. It was not a feeling she intended to get used to.

"Okay! Can I have everybody's attention?" Up on stage, Jen Ewing shouted into the microphone.

It took a few minutes for the din to lessen. Holly stood closely beside Luke. She was a bit surprised by a sudden, childish urge to look around for those annoying women and point out Luke had his hand on *her* back.

"You all know you filled out those questionnaires?" A less than enthusiastic rumble went through the crowd. It appeared most of them shared Holly's level of appreciation for the document.

"My husband, Dennis, has fixed up a special show for us to watch. If somebody will please get the lights, we'll sit back and enjoy."

It took a few minutes for everybody to get situated, but soon they were all seated so they could see the drop-down screen.

The first picture on the screen was a group picture, their freshman year, Holly thought. A montage of candid snapshots began. Holly expected to see pictures primarily of classmates like Sally Young, Lucy Phillips, and Clay, so she was surprised when everyone seemed to be represented. Holly, with either Luke or Tessa beside her, appeared several times. Luke must have sensed Holly's melancholy since his hand found hers under the table and held it reassuringly.

Finally, the screen froze on the graduation group photograph. Dennis's voice came over the sound system. "We used the 'Dreaming of the Future' papers you wrote before you graduated for this part of the presentation."

The image of Sally Young's face grew until it filled the screen. "Sally Young wanted to be a model when she grew up. Her favorite memory of high school is when she was crowned homecoming queen."

Across the floor, a well-endowed, platinum blond woman smiled condescendingly at her table mates, making Holly glad she wasn't one of them.

When Kevin Tripp's face filled the screen, Holly was shocked by how large he was. Even back in high school, he was more broad-shouldered than most adult men. She glanced around the gym, but in the dim light, couldn't see him.

"Kevin wanted to design houses." Murmurs at a table across the floor told Holly that was probably where he was sitting.

She had to fight off a major fit of giggles a few minutes later when the image of Lucy Phillips Armstrong filled the screen. A heavy-set woman wearing her red hair in an up-do befitting a much older person was obviously her. Holly made the supreme mistake of making eye contact with Missy, who nodded knowingly and mouthed the word, "girdle."

Holly probably just about cut off circulation in Luke's fingers as she squeezed his hand to keep from laughing.

The presentation went through the same routine with a different student being the subject each time. Holly was surprised by hers. She'd forgotten she wanted to be an animal psychologist. Tessa leaned over and stage whispered. "With some of our students, you probably feel like you are." The others at the table heard her and began laughing. With Holly's held-back giggles finally breaking free, the group's volume grew quickly. It only increased when Jennifer gave them the evil eye.

"Shhh." Luke's smiling admonition calmed them.

Holly's interest was piqued when the screen was filled with Luke's picture. Of course, he had wanted to be a farmer from the time he knew what one was.

"Luke's favorite high school memory is the senior homecoming when he finally persuaded Holly Morris to dance with him."

Chuckles and murmurs ensued, and Holly didn't know whether to be embarrassed or flattered. How long had he felt more than friendship for her? Their eyes met, and Luke's glowed with an intensity she'd never seen before. Monkeys took up ballet in her stomach until she finally forced herself to break eye contact with him.

Holly managed to put it out of her mind and enjoy the rest of the presentation, particularly Tessa's goal. She planned to be a mathematical entrepreneur, regardless of the fact no such career existed. Mitch hugged Tessa's shoulders as the gym erupted with laughter.

Finally, the last student, who happened to be Tom Dwer, was highlighted. Again, Holly was surprised by his size, and also a remarkable resemblance to Kevin Tripp. How could he and his cohort look so much alike? Maybe they were cousins or something. She nearly missed hearing his dream of settling down and having a family. Perhaps he achieved it.

She blinked as her eyes adjusted to the lights coming back on. Jennifer was once more onstage behind the microphone.

"Okay. We're finished with our walk down memory lane, so we're going to give some prizes out. Everybody, get up and gather in front of the stage." Holly's hand felt empty when Luke released it to stand. She found herself wishing he'd take it back as they gathered with their classmates in front of the stage. Maybe he intended to comfort her, but for some reason, their fingers laced together stirred up other feelings in Holly. Feelings that reminded her of the kiss he gave her…feelings like maybe she wouldn't mind if he turned and gave her another one right now.

"Are you okay?" Luke's quiet words in her ear made Holly realize how close she was to him. He probably felt like she was about to shinny up his side.

"Yes." His hand slid farther around her waist and held her in place when she would have stepped away. She pushed away the sudden urge to turn and move into his arms. What was wrong with her? Taking a deep breath, Holly forced herself to focus on the stage.

Jennifer, still at the microphone, looked questioningly at Rob Sanders, who was sitting at a small table with several papers in front of him. He nodded.

"All right. We'll start with the person who traveled the farthest to get here." Rob handed her the paper. "From China of all places, Kevin Tripp!"

It seemed like everybody started talking again while a tall, broad-shouldered man with coal-black hair walked up to the stage. When Holly got her first real look at him, she knew she was looking at a wealthy person. His haircut hadn't been done in any barber shop, and if the suit he was wearing didn't cost more than Holly's entire wardrobe, she was Peppermint Patty.

"Thank you." It appeared Kevin didn't like to speak any more now than he had in high school.

"So, tell us, Kevin. What have you been doing in China?" Jennifer all but bounced with excitement.

Kevin looked embarrassed as he answered. "A company over there bought some software I designed. They hired me to move there and work for them."

"So, you'll be heading back soon?"

"No. I'm back in the states."

"Which state?" Jennifer asked.

Now, he was definitely blushing. "I have a few houses—one on the West Coast and one in the East…central United States…I don't like hotels, and I have to travel, so…"

"Wow!" Jen fanned herself. "We have a wealthy alumnus."

"Here's your prize!" Rob's wife, Annie, made quite a production out of carrying a large envelope onto the stage and handing it to Kevin.

He opened it and produced a small smile before he held it up. It was a world map coloring book.

Still red-faced, he made his way back down to the gym floor.

Jennifer once again quieted everybody. "Now, we have a prize for the person who traveled the shortest distance." She smiled broadly. "I don't even have to ask Rob for this one because Mitch Landon's house is three blocks away. Mitch, come on up here!"

They went through the same routine as Kevin's, with Mitch telling everybody about his job since so many had moved away. His prize was an over-sized plastic compass.

Then, it seemed like the prizes were never going to end. An extremely embarrassed Wes Stevens, who was there with his fourth wife, won a floral wedding planner for being married the most times. Personally, Holly thought it was an inappropriate award. Divorces weren't something to celebrate.

Jen went through youngest looking, oldest looking, moved the most times, most children, best-dressed female, and best-dressed male—which resulted in Kevin Tripp once more visiting the stage.

"Our class sweethearts during our senior year were Tyler Brady and Sally Young. This was a difficult decision, but we finally agreed. Mitch Landon and Tessa Lincoln need to come up here." As Holly's blushing friends made their way to the stage, Jen went on. "We've all known these two were made for each other for years. Looks like they finally realized it."

Holly heard Luke's hearty laughter and followed his line of vision to see what was so funny. She had to laugh with him when she saw Tessa bury her face against Mitch's chest, too embarrassed even to look at her classmates. Mitch had one arm around her and was laughing right along with everybody else. Holly laughed even harder when Tessa peeked at everyone and promptly reburied her face. She couldn't remember ever seeing her friend this bashful, as long as they'd known each other. This was a first.

"And here's your prize." Annie handed Mitch a gift bag, and he was finally able to maneuver Tessa around so they could remove its contents. More laughter erupted when everybody saw two stuffed monkeys sharing a banana.

"We could shut the lights back off," Luke observed. "Tessa would light the gym for us."

"I know." Holly had to speak into his ear to be heard over the crowd. "I've never seen her like this."

A few minutes later, Tessa and Mitch had just found their places next to Luke and Holly when Jen announced the next prize.

"Who has changed the least?" Her eyebrows went up. "While we've all gotten older, from what I understand our prize winner hasn't changed his ways at all. He's still a trouble maker—Tom Dwer!"

His black hair was longer than he'd worn in high school, and there was the hint of a thicker waistline, but Tom hadn't changed very much at all.

"You'd better explain what you mean," he instructed Jennifer. "It's been many years since I plotted a nefarious deed."

Jen smiled brightly at him. "Okay." She faced her classmates. "I don't know how many of you have heard of Prankster Toys Limited." There was a consensus most of them had. "Well, you're looking at the owner and CEO of it. This man runs the company that manufactures those cute little robot dogs you see on TV, and just about any kind of gag gift you can imagine."

"And probably some we can't!" somebody shouted.

"And you're located where?" Jen waited for Tom to answer.

"The great state of Rhode Island!" he proclaimed.

"Well, here's your prize." Annie handed him a book entitled *Good Manners Won't Kill You—They'll Just Make You Sick.*

Tom laughed good-naturedly as he walked back down the steps to the gym floor.

"And, now our most difficult prize. Who has changed the most?" Jennifer looked at the group of people. "Kim, you've changed quite a bit, and so have you, Jason. However, our winner has changed in more than her looks. She used to be so shy, she barely spoke. Now, she speaks out and helps our kids. She has blossomed into a beautiful person, inside and out, and I'm proud to call her my friend. Holly Morris, come on up here!"

Holly was stunned.

"Go on," Luke urged.

Holly looked at the smiling and applauding people. She thought recognition of her improvements would make her happy, but instead she was embarrassed and ashamed. All but a few of these people wouldn't have spared a smile for high school Holly—hadn't, actually.

"I don't want to," she murmured to Luke.

His brows rose. "Why not?"

"Because, they—"

The lights went off, surrounding them with darkness before the screen lit up.

Chapter 32

Why were Jen and Rob embarrassing Holly like this? Slide after slide, each with a different photo of her, covered the screen.

"She's not that pretty." Sally Young's "whisper" carried across the floor. Holly had heard her, too, if the way she backed up against Luke was any indication. Her self-esteem was fragile with these people.

"Hey, Jen! Holly's easy on the eyes, but she ain't a movie star. Let's get on with it." Rock Grayer, the class clown, was probably the only person in the room who could say that in a kind manner.

"I'm sorry," Jennifer spoke into the microphone. "We didn't do this. Dennis is trying to figure out what's going on."

Didn't do this?

Holly's eyes were brown circles when she turned and looked at Luke. "Luke?"

Luke's attention was drawn over her shoulder, where Tom Dwer and Clay Richmond had joined Dennis on stage. All three were huddled over the laptop, talking and pointing.

"It's him." Mitch's deep voice came from Luke's left. "Look around and see if anybody is on a smartphone."

"Luke Walker did *not* protect Holly Morris. *I* did." The room went dead silent as the eerie, computer-generated voice echoed over the sound system. "Luke Walker did *not* avenge Holly Morris. *I* did."

A collective gasp filled the room when the photo on the screen switched to a video.

"That's Wallace." Luke would recognize the monster anywhere.

"He's in the jail cell." Mitch stepped closer to the screen. "Is this live feed?" He raised his voice. "Dennis, could this be a live feed?"

"I don't know," the frazzled man said as he looked up from the trio's latest efforts. "I have never seen anything like this. The system has been hacked, and I have no control whatsoever."

"Oh!" Screeches and shouts sounded throughout the room.

Luke looked at the screen, only to see Wallace writhing on the floor of the cell, a half-eaten sandwich in his grip.

"Take. That. Down. Now!" Mitch was no longer asking.

"I can't," Dennis repeated.

"Well, I can." Kevin Tripp hopped onto the stage and walked behind the computer. Luke wondered what he would do, but then Kevin showed them all how complicated they were making a simple problem. He unplugged the electric cord.

The screen went dark, and miraculously, somebody hit the light switch.

"We have to get Tess and Holly out of here," Mitch ordered Luke. "I'll drop you off at Holly's, and then I have to get to the station."

Luke grabbed a silent, and he knew furious, Holly's hand and Tessa's with his other and headed for the door.

He heard Mitch talking on his phone as he followed them out.

"I don't care if it's not your job, Crystal. If you want to *keep* your job, get back there and check on our prisoner. Now."

They were almost to Mitch's car when the unmistakable sound of a horrified female scream came from Mitch's phone.

Holly froze.

"Come on, Holly." Luke opened the door. "Please get in the car."

Holly spun to face him. "Jack Wallace isn't my stalker."

This wasn't going to be pretty. "No."

"You knew."

"Yes."

Her eyes went to Tessa, who was gnawing her lower lip. "You knew."

Tessa's voice quivered. "Yes, but—"

"And I don't even have to ask about you," she told Mitch.

Her eyes were full of anger as her gaze shifted between Luke and Tessa.

"I can understand why Mitch wouldn't tell me; he's the sheriff. But you...you are my best friend and the man who supposedly loves me. And, both of you lied to me all day...you lied to me."

"We didn't exactly lie," Tessa said in a soft voice.

Holly glared at her. "Are we really going to play with semantics, Tessa? Because, that's not your forte."

"Get in the car, all of you. I have a dead prisoner." Mitch wasn't in the least bit interested in their drama.

Holly silently turned and slid into the back seat.

As badly as he wanted to explain, Luke knew that expression. Fear was fueling her rage, and he and Tessa were the easy targets. She would have to work it out in her mind.

Please, God, I just wanted to let her be happy for one day longer. If it's your will, help her find forgiveness and understanding in her heart. Please don't let my act of kindness turn her against me. Amen.

Chapter 33

"Don't gimme less; gimme Shemar." Holly recited the silly limerick as she stared at her old poster of Shemar Moore. Before she graduated, she researched and thought she'd join the FBI as a profiler. Of course, she came to her senses when she realized neither Derek Gordon nor Spencer Reid were actually in the Behavioral Analysis Unit.

When had this bed gotten so small? She turned to her other side, trying to get comfortable. Maybe her conscience wouldn't let her rest because she skipped church this morning to stay at her parents' and pout.

A stab of guilt hit her chest as she remembered Tessa's tears when she left for her parents' home. Holly was too angry to be with her, though, and afraid of what she might say.

"You still awake?"

"Yeah, Mom." Holly pulled her extra pillow over and made a cushion to lean on. "I can't sleep."

Susan turned on the pink-shaded bedside lamp and then sat on the edge of the bed.

"I don't think it's in you to go to sleep angry, Holly."

"I did last night."

"You were exhausted." Susan placed her hand on Holly's shoulder. "Will you tell me what Luke and Tessa did? Honey, your dad and I can only think of one thing, and I just can't believe the two of them would go behind your back and—"

"They didn't do that!" Holly would laugh if she wasn't so close to crying. She closed her eyes and willed the tears away before opening them. "Mom, Jack Wallace isn't my stalker."

"I know." Confusion was visible on Susan's face.

"Yes, but you only knew after Mitch called to tell you to be on the lookout." Those wretched tears burned the backs of her eyes again. "They knew Friday, Mom. Tessa and Luke knew Friday, and they kept it from me. Now, I don't think I can ever trust either of them again."

"Why didn't they tell you?"

No matter how much Holly ignored her, Tessa kept up a running monologue during the entire drive. "Supposedly, they wanted me to have one last happy day before I had to deal with my stalker again."

"Honey, that seems like a kind thing to do."

"But, Mom, if I had known, those slides and watching Jack Wallace…" He tried to hurt, maybe even kill Holly, but no human being should suffer the way he did. "I might have been a little prepared."

Uh oh. Holly knew the stern look on her mother's face all too well.

"Holly Elizabeth Morris. Do you mean to tell me, if you knew your stalker was still out there, knowing he photographs you in just about every area of your life and that he tried to murder somebody wouldn't bother you?"

"Of course it would have still bothered me." Holly hated to feel this defensive. "But I wouldn't have been so shocked."

"Seeing a man nearly die would shock you no matter how prepared you were, and you know it," Susan said. "Look at it this way. The reason Luke and Tessa kept it from you was because they love you; not out of spite. That should be reason enough to forgive them."

Her mom was right about Jack Wallace. His purplish, mottled face was forever ingrained in Holly's mind, and would be for many years—maybe the rest of her life. Thankfully, a seasoned deputy, Wayne Daniels, showed up and was able to perform CPR. A federal agent had shipped the criminal off to a prison hospital, where he was recovering. Mitch instructed the few who knew the man was alive to be quiet about it; it might provide another chance to trick the stalker into showing himself.

Her mom was also correct that Luke and Tessa weren't trying to hurt her; they were trying to do something nice.

"You're right."

Susan smiled broadly. "Wait a minute while I go get my phone. I want a recording."

Holly felt her own lips wobble into a small smile. "Thanks, Mom. I love you."

"I love you, too." Susan kissed her cheek. "And, I'm sorry for trying to keep you my little girl. You've amazed me with your courage, you know. If I had been in your place when this started, I would have come running back to the farm and locked myself in the bedroom. Forget college or a career. I'm proud of you, Holly."

The tears laughed at her puny efforts to stop them, and they erupted. "Thank you," she said again. Her mom finally told her what she had wanted to hear for nearly ten years.

A smile was her mom's response. "Get some sleep, and I'll drive you to Luke's in the morning before you go to work. We'll catch him before morning chores. And, you can fix things with Tessa during lunch. Okay?"

"Okay."

Susan's method worked because Holly soon found herself drifting to sleep.

"Aruuga! Aruuga!" The car horn ringtone had to go. She sleepily answered before she realized it might be her stalker.

"Holly." It was Luke.

"Yes."

"Don't say anything; just listen. I've been fixated on you since we were kids. I'm sorry, but after tonight...the way you acted, things just aren't the same. It's time to find out what it's like to date other women. Puppy love ends, Holly."

The line went dead.

Holly sat straight and stared at her phone, still lit from the call. Luke wanted to date other women; he outgrew his puppy love for her; he didn't love her. Luke didn't love Holly.

But she loved him.

She didn't even try to stop the tears this time.

Chapter 34

"Come on, Holly. I know you're mad, but you don't mean that." Luke was talking to a dead line.

He flopped back on his bed, still gripping the phone. Had Holly actually said those things?

You've been so close, I've never had the chance to be with another man. You're smothering me, Luke. I want to see what's out there. I'll see you around.

"I've been *smothering* her?" Clarence's head appeared beside the bed before the giant dog leaped to the empty side. "Clarence!" He wasn't allowed on Luke's bed.

Clarence's brow rose as if saying, "What are you gonna do about it?"

Well, Luke needed to talk to *somebody*. "How have I ever smothered Holly? It's not like I flew to Massachusetts and visited her in college...or showed up at her house every single time I thought of her." He would have lived there if he did. "And if our weekly routine was too intense, all she had to do was say something. Why didn't she say something about being together too often if I was smothering her? Don't you think she should have, Clarence?"

The dog appeared skeptical.

"The ring. It was too much." He looked at his pet. "Do you think that's what pushed her away? The ring?"

But she acted happy about it, and told him "yes" was a possible answer. If he were smothering her, that gave her the perfect opportunity to say so. It's not like he would have thrown himself on the floor and sobbed for hours—at least not while she was still there.

Something about this wasn't adding up. "She's at her mom and dad's, so I know she wasn't forced to say those things. But, I can't believe she did, Clarence. I thought after the way she acted at our reunion—holding my hand and snuggling against me—I thought she was going to tell me she loved me. And here she up and tells me it's over because I'm smothering her."

He pulled the pillow out from under Clarence's head and covered his face with it. Maybe he could smother himself. And he would die with a mouthful of dog hair since it appeared Clarence was shedding.

"Smothering," he muttered just as he felt Clarence's head plop on top of the pillow. He hoped he wasn't in the way of his dog getting comfortable. Not that it mattered; he wasn't going to sleep tonight anyway.

Chapter 35

Holly easily spotted him when she let Clarence out for his bedtime routine. Hank Stone was clearly visible sitting in his parked car, probably because he was directly under a pole light.

It had come back to this. Home and under guard. Mitch wasn't taking any chances, though—not after Holly's stalker managed to poison a sandwich somewhere between the time it left the restaurant and when it was placed in his prisoner's hands. And, because the state police were due to pick Wallace up the next morning, Mitch was extra concerned about the possibility of the mystery man somehow infiltrating his office computers.

At least, Holly had been able to move home this afternoon, even without Tessa. Her friend was coming back tomorrow morning, though. They talked during lunch and again after school, and finally made their peace.

Tessa was particularly hurt by the situation because it turned out she protested the men's idea of waiting. She only went along with it after they promised to tell Holly it wasn't Tessa's idea. And, neither of them spoke up when Holly found out and flew off the handle. Holly should have paid attention because Tessa told her all that on the drive to the Morris farm.

If only she could fix things with Luke that effortlessly…No. He ended their relationship, and she had to get over it. It appeared even a distant friendship was out of the question since his dad brought Clarence this evening. Of course, Luke could be on a date. The thought felt like a knife through her heart.

Clarence ran back through the open door and hopped on his favorite spot—the end of the sofa nearest the television. Maybe he was far-sighted and couldn't see the screen from anywhere else. Oh, well.

"Clarence, why do you suppose it hurts so much? Luke being with another woman, I mean."

"I dunno," Clarence said. What others may consider dog throat noises was close enough to speech for Holly.

Their photograph drew her attention, so she walked past the sofa and to it.

Memories were a movie in her mind.

Luke, laughing and holding her hand as he taught her to roller skate. Tumbling head over heels off the back of the sled and sliding down the smooth path on his back, right past her as she sat buried in a snowdrift. His eyes sparkling when he saw her in her homecoming dress their senior year—and his voice telling her not to listen to anybody else; she was prettier than all those other girls combined. Joy on his face when he saw her walk out of the concourse at the airport.

Every important, and not-so-important event in Holly's life involved Luke Walker. Because he had always been in her life. Because he was her life.

"I can't think like that—not after he ended everything. We were good friends. Right, Clarence?"

"Yeah," Clarence said in his dog language.

Her heart thudded to the ground. She was too late. Even the dog agreed with her.

"That's just dandy, isn't it," she asked the dog. "It's like we're living in one of those sappy soap operas my grandma used to watch. Hunter Lumps or some other silly named guy will rush in and save the day." Only, she wanted Luke to rush in and save the day. All he'd have to do was tell her he was wrong; he did still love her.

"Ha Ha Harooo!" A dog howl came from across the room.

Clarence immediately sprang into action, evidently in search of his fellow canine.

"Ha Ha Harooo!" was joined by a much louder "Howww Harooo!"

"It's my phone, Clarence." Maybe a dog howl ringtone wasn't the best idea. With both the phone and dog howling, she couldn't hear herself think.

As she finally answered, Tessa's voice was nearly drowned out by yet another "Harooo! Ha Ha Howwwooo!"

"Oh, my gosh, what did you do to Clarence?" Tessa sounded horrified. "I'm not fond of him, but I would never hurt him."

"Shhh," Holly said to Clarence. "It was my phone, you silly dog."

With a look that could only be described as disgust, Clarence turned his back toward her and lay down.

"I have a dog howl set for my ringtone, and I guess Clarence sympathized with it."

Laughter so loud Holly had to hold the phone away from her ear was Tessa's response.

Finally, Tessa spoke again. "That's hilarious, Holly. I wonder if he'd chase you around the house if your phone meowed."

"I'm not finding out." Holly couldn't stop her own smile. "Did you need something?" Like to tell her Luke called and asked her to straighten things out for him?

"You know how forgetful I am." That was putting it mildly; the car alarm letting her know the door was open had saved her many times.

"Yes."

"My teaching certificate expired last week. The state board gave me an extension after I called and whined and begged, but they need the forms in the office by tomorrow morning."

"Okay."

"They're somewhere in my bedroom, Holly." Tessa sounded guilty. "I remember putting them in a pink envelope from my stationery collection so they would be easier to find, but that's all I remember."

Holly didn't want to ask. "What do you need me to do?"

"Will you find it and have Hank run you to the school? I can fax it and this proof of continuing education to them tonight."

Did she want to wade through the disaster Tessa called filing and find a pink envelope? No. "Yeah. I'll be there as soon as I find it."

"Thank you."

"You're welcome."

She set the phone down and turned to the dog. "Come on, Clarence. You stay in there when you think she won't notice. Help me find a pink envelope with state forms in it."

Over an hour and three pink envelopes containing checks, two with out-of-date rebate forms, and one full of expired coupons later, Holly finally found the right one.

"Okay. I'll be right back."

As she headed for the door, Clarence suddenly jumped in front of her and blocked her path.

"Clarence, I don't have time to play. Now, move."

He stayed put.

"Clarence, I mean it. I'm going outside and walking across the road. A policeman with a gun will be watching me. I'm safe. Now, move."

His expression clearly said, "Make me."

She felt guilty, but what else could she do? "Want a Peppy Pup treat?"

Clarence hopped to his feet, and before he could move, Holly was around him and out the door. Her storm door groaned in protest as the large dog jumped on it.

Holly turned and looked at the forlorn expression on Clarence's face.

"See? You can watch while I walk over to Hank's car. And then, he'll be with me when I come and lock up. Okay?"

A growl began deep in Clarence's chest and erupted in the most ferocious bark Holly had ever heard.

"What's the mat—"

A hand covered her mouth as a strong arm surrounded her chest and pulled her back against a hard body.

"You're mine, Holly."

She began to struggle in earnest, but this guy was strong and she was terrified. She vaguely noticed Clarence had disappeared. Was he afraid of this guy, or did he know him?

"Let me go!" sounded nothing like that with her mouth covered. "Hank!" she tried to scream.

"If you're hoping that Barney Fife across the road will come, well, my Holly, his coffee put him to sleep. Now, come on. I'm taking you to our dream house. You'll love it."

"No!" She managed to pull her face back far enough and bit his hand.

His cry of pain was almost drowned out by the loud sound of breaking glass and crumpling aluminum. Then, Clarence was there.

Deep growls were his only noise as he forcefully shoved his head between the stalker and Holly.

A second cry of pain and hard shove from the culprit told Holly Clarence had hurt him.

She hit the ground hard, the wind knocked out of her. Somehow, her need to know the man's identity gave her the strength to roll over. Unfortunately, by the time she raised her head, all she saw was the silhouette of a man—appeared large—running past the squad car and down the alley. Clarence nuzzled her hand.

"Thank you," she told him before climbing to her knees to give him a hug.

Then she remembered.

"Hank!" What if he used the same poison on the deputy he used on Jack Wallace? She scrambled to her feet and took off at a run with Clarence beside her.

The young officer's head slumped over the wheel, but the door wasn't locked. Holly quickly checked for a pulse.

"Thank you, God." It was steady. And his breathing seemed okay.

Now, what should she do? Not leave him and go home for her phone. She ran around and slid into the front passenger seat and grabbed the radio microphone.

"Hello? Can you hear me?"

"Who is this?" Crystal Stanley's perpetual bad mood was firmly in place. "It's against the law to play with a police radio. I'm sending somebody to arrest you right now."

"Send somebody!" Holly yelled. "This is Holly Morris, Crystal, and I don't care if you send out the National Guard! Hank has been poisoned, and we need help. So, stop griping and get off your high horse long enough to send somebody out here!"

She didn't know how, but Holly could hear a siren before she was back out of the car.

"Help is coming, Hank. Hold on."

Please, Dear Lord, don't let this man die because he was protecting me. One man has already nearly died because of me. I'm asking from my heart, heal Hank. Amen.

Hank was in God's hands.

Chapter 36

"More coffee, Luke?" Sandra Kinsey held the pot over his cup, prepared to pour.

He had probably already drunk an entire pot, but he just wasn't ready to go home yet. "Just one."

He came to town after supplies. His south fence was down again, only this time it wasn't an accident. Unless one of Mrs. Pickler's goats had learned how to use the discarded wire cutters he found next to the fence row.

If things weren't so lousy with Holly, he'd have waited and picked Clarence up when he made this trip. He hadn't, though. Instead, this was his second trip to Shadow this morning.

At least, Wilkins Diner wasn't busy. The breakfast rush was over, and it was too early for the lunch crowd. Only a couple of the other tables were occupied.

"Sure you don't want a piece of pie?" Sandra asked. "Maisie baked them fresh this morning. The apple just came out of the oven."

"No thank you." He didn't even have an appetite for apple pie.

"Let me know if you change your mind." Sandra turned and walked away. She was a permanent fixture in the diner, having worked there as long as even Luke's dad could remember. With her gray hair and sparkling blue eyes, she was one of those people whose age was impossible to gauge. She reminded him of Aunt Bee on the Andy Griffith show. He never could tell how old she was, either.

"Excuse me." The softly spoken words brought Luke's head up to look at the man standing across from him.

"Hi, Mr. Roper." Luke had always liked the school maintenance man. "Have a seat."

The older man sat down. He didn't say anything more to Luke until he allowed Sandra to fill his coffee cup and told her he didn't need anything else. Then he turned clouded eyes to Luke.

"Do you have any ideas about the missing equipment?"

Missing equipment? "I'm sorry, Mr. Roper. I don't know what you're talking about."

Mr. Roper was noticeably surprised. "Miss Morris told me she wouldn't tell anybody else, but I assumed you were an exception."

"I guess I'm not." At least, not anymore. "But if you want to tell me something, I promise it will stay between us."

"I don't know." The janitor's voice was hesitant, but then he seemed to reach a decision. "Maybe you'll have some ideas." He nodded. "I told Miss Morris about some equipment that's gone missing from the big storage room in the school basement. At first, I thought maybe I moved them and didn't remember. You know, with my Maude being so sick and all. Now I'm sure I didn't. No, sir." He shook his head. "Somebody's taken those things."

Luke knew the kind man well enough to know if the janitor were responsible for the loss of equipment, he would willingly admit it. He believed Mr. Roper.

"What's missing?" Maybe it would help to know. It was a logical place to start, at least.

Mr. Roper spoke with assurance. "Some chains—at least six of them, eight floor jacks, six pulleys—the large ones, and the swivel base."

It was an odd combination. "What is a swivel base? I'm not familiar with that piece of equipment."

"It's new on the market. Mr. Glendon had to go to the board four times before he persuaded them to buy him one." Luke could tell the loss of this particular item bothered the older man more than the rest combined.

"What does it do?"

"It looks like a giant floor jack, with a saddle about six feet in diameter. You can roll it under vehicles and use it to lift them. After it's up, a man can actually swivel the car until it's facing a different direction. Mr. Glendon wanted it so he could fit more cars in the shop for the students to work on."

Luke was trying to picture such a tool. "It'll lift cars?"

Mr. Roper nodded. "It's hydraulic. Mr. Glendon said if a bus weren't so long, it would even lift that, too."

Luke shook his head in amazement. He kept up on new equipment for his farm, but it always amazed him when something like what Mr. Roper described came along. Yet, what would anybody have to gain with those things? What could they be used for?

"Do you have any ideas?" he decided to ask the maintenance man.

"Not one," Mr. Roper admitted.

Luke thought again. Floor jacks, pulleys, chains, and this swivel base. "Maybe we should consider what somebody could do with them."

Mr. Roper frowned. "I guess they're all tools to help lift something. But, you'd need a hoist to use the pulleys. And I can't imagine a bunch of kids wanting to move a car in a circle. They'd only succeed in turning it sideways or backward to what it was."

A thought was at the edge of Luke's mind, but he couldn't quite grasp it. "With all those tools, they could stabilize something heavier or shaped differently long enough to use the swivel base."

The other man slowly nodded. "Like a bus."

Then Luke knew. "Or a tractor."

Puzzlement wrinkled Mr. Roper's brows. "I don't follow you."

"I can't explain right now, Mr. Roper, but I'm pretty sure I know what the equipment is being used for." He quickly pulled enough money out of his wallet to pay for his and the other man's coffee. If Luke were right, the janitor had just helped clear up a situation that was driving him crazy. "Thank you," he told Mr. Roper. "I appreciate this more than you know."

He stood and left a puzzled man sitting at the table. Instead of climbing into his pickup, he walked the three blocks to the station. It wasn't until he saw Mitch's squad car in its customary spot that the thought his friend might not have been there occurred to him.

"I need to speak with the sheriff," he told Haley Johnson, who was at her regular post.

"Just a min—" was all he heard as he walked on past and into Mitch's office.

Mitch looked up from a photocopy he was studying. "You heard about last night?"

Last night? "No. I'm here about the nonsense at my farm. I'm pretty sure I know what's going on, even if I don't know exactly who's doing it."

Mitch slid the paper to the side of his desk and gave his full attention to Luke. "Let's hear it."

Luke explained what Mr. Roper told him, and what the swivel base was for.

"My tractor. If some kids were using the tool, they'd have been able to turn my tractor around without starting it."

Mitch slowly nodded. "They could have used the chains and pulleys to stabilize it since its weight wouldn't be evenly distributed." Then he frowned. "But what about the ATV?"

Luke's brows furrowed. "The only things I can think of are those chains and pulleys. Somehow, they used them to pull the ATV into the pond. I haven't figured out exactly how, though."

Mitch seemed to consider Luke's theory. "It makes sense. But who has the equipment?"

"That's the twenty-five-thousand-dollar question, isn't it?" And the one he had absolutely no answer to.

"Before you go, Holly didn't tell you about last night?"

Luke's heart broke a little each time he said it. "Holly has ended things with me. We don't talk."

Mitch frowned. "Not even when you drop Clarence off or pick him up?"

"Dad dropped him off, and she just sends him out the door when I pick him up."

"Well, you better sit back because you're liable to launch when I tell you what happened."

Luke wasn't sure if he wanted to know. "Just tell me."

"Last night, Holly's stalker slipped something into Hank's coffee—they had to pump his stomach, but he'll be fine."

Hank. "Hank was watching Holly." Fear hit him in the solar plexus.

Mitch nodded. "The guy had Holly, Luke, until your dog busted through the door. She's certain he's nursing a dog bite or two this morning."

Luke started to rise. "She's okay? Tell me she's okay."

"She's furious," Mitch replied. "Her dad came to town and got Cliff to open the hardware store so he could replace Holly's door last night."

"She wasn't hurt."

"Not at all. But, she bit him, too." Mitch grinned. "Too bad we can't just drive around looking for dog bites on arms or legs and a human bite on a finger."

Luke sank back to the chair. "Did she…did she ask for me?"

"Not that I know of."

"Figures."

"You sure she ended things?" Mitch's doubt was evident.

"I wish I wasn't, but she made things pretty clear. Said I smothered her."

Mitch frowned. "That doesn't sound like Holly, Luke."

"I didn't think so, either," Luke said. "But I heard her; it was Holly."

Mitch still looked doubtful. "If you say so."

"I do." But, oh, how he wished he didn't.

Chapter 37

Given that the moon was full, Holly should have been prepared for anything. Yet, when she arrived on Monday morning to discover star senior quarterback, Sammy Lewis, anxiously pacing the floor outside her office, it surprised her.

"Miss Lincoln hates me." He voiced his complaint before she had her door open. "She hates football players—all of us."

Finally inside her office, Holly turned to the belligerent teenager. "Why do you say that?"

Like a race car waiting for the green light, Sammy shifted into hyperdrive. "She waits until a couple months before school ends and gives us too much homework. And she grades them wrong—changes my answers and gives me D's and F's."

The poor boy evidently didn't know who Miss Lincoln's housemate was. "How is she changing answers on homework you're not turning in, Sammy?"

The proverbial hand in the cookie jar look flitted across his face before he tried again. "She throws my homework away." He nodded, enthused about his newest concocted complaint. "Yeah. I work real hard on that stuff, and I saw her throw it in the trash like it was nothin'."

Well, she was the one who insisted on coming to work today. Dr. Potter would have gladly written her an excuse for the week, due to the stress she'd been under, if nothing else.

She walked around her desk and sat down. "Sammy, if you can't lie any better than that, give it up."

His chest expanded, but before he could speak, Holly was ready. "Acting isn't your thing, either. We both know you haven't been doing your homework, so knock it off, Sammy. Before I write a detention slip for the rest of the year."

The teenager slumped into a chair, but he still wasn't ready to give in. "Miss Morris, I'm going to be a pro football player; everyone knows that." His tone was that of a genius talking to a simpleton. "I don't need math, so I shouldn't have to do those assignments."

Unaffected by his attitude, Holly nodded. "Uh huh. So, when the reporters ask you how far you ran to get that touchdown, you'll just grin and say, 'Oh, I'm Sammy Lewis—I don't need to know how far. I just run when they throw me the ball.' You do realize how that sounds, don't you?"

She watched as her point sank in, only she didn't get the hoped-for response.

"I don't care what you say. It's stupid, and I shouldn't have to do those assignments."

Okay. It appeared to be time for cold, hard facts.

"Sammy, I'm going to lay it on the line for you." He appeared surprised by her sternness. "Pro football scouts aren't exactly flocking in droves to Shadow, Illinois. If you want to be noticed, you need to play college ball. You have to graduate high school to attend college. And you, Sammy Lewis, are not going to graduate unless you pass math. To pass math, you have to turn in the papers you're late on. You should be grateful you have a teacher willing to let you make them up. She doesn't have to. And on top of that, I know for a fact Miss Lincoln is eating her lunch in her room so any of you who need help catching up, can go in there and get it. So, pull up your big boy pants, and do your assignments."

"It's not fair," Sammy muttered as he stood and walked out the door. But Holly saw his expression before he left; he'd heard her. Only time and Tessa would tell whether Holly had helped the situation.

Breathing a sigh of relief, she slid her purse into its usual desk drawer. When she straightened, her heart jumped into her head as she discovered Tasha Hart standing there.

"I'm sorry." The girl placed her hand over the growing baby she carried. "If it's a bad time, I can come back later."

The eleventh grader who refused to name her baby's father wanted to talk? Holly would gladly listen.

"It's okay." She mustered a smile. "Have a seat, Tasha."

The teenager sank into the chair closest to Holly's desk. She seemed to be searching for words before finally speaking.

"Mom and Dad want me to tell them who got me pregnant."

Holly was well aware of this entire situation. "Honey, they can't afford to raise your child, and his father should help. I'm sorry, but I think he should help, too."

"He wants to."

This was the first time Tasha even admitted the boy knew about the baby. "Why doesn't he, then?"

Tasha raised a shaking hand to push a stray, auburn curl from her face. "He can't tell…his mom and dad will be disappointed because they're really wonderful parents. They raised him going to church, and he knew it was wrong—we both knew it was wrong, and we cried after it happened. It's not like we're a couple of partying kids sneaking around. It happened one time…one time, Miss Morris."

"Tasha." Holly didn't have to tell her one time was all it took. "If his parents are Christian, they may be angry, and yes—disappointed—but they love their son and will forgive him. They'll love their grandson, too. How much longer before he gets here?"

"Seven weeks." The girl's eyes welled with tears.

"Listen." Holly stood and walked around to sit beside her student. "Just think about what I've said; talk to your baby's father again…for your child's sake. He'll need a dad." Tasha told her parents in no uncertain terms if they tried to make her give this baby up, she would run away. The situation was sad. "This is school, but can I pray with you right now?"

The teenager wordlessly nodded.

"Father, you know what is best for this baby, and for his parents. Please give everyone involved strength to love past pain and disappointment and forgive as you forgive us. I ask especially for you to calm this precious young lady's heart and give her a peace only you can provide. I pray all this in Jesus' name. Amen."

Holly looked up into tear-filled blue eyes. "Thank you, Miss Morris." Then, without another word, Tasha stood and walked out of the room.

"I should have stayed home." Even as Holly uttered the words, she knew they weren't true. The young adults at this school depended on her to help them, and when she accepted the job, she accepted that responsibility.

A knock on the door brought her out of her musing. At this rate, she wouldn't be surprised to discover Harriet Iverson was suddenly compelled to confess the meat in her meatloaf came from a can. A total of ten students ate a school lunch the last time it was served.

"Come in." She stood and headed back to her chair.

"You gotta help me, Miss Morris." Adam Mayes planted his hands on her desk and leaned forward. "Please, you can't let this happen."

Adam was one of Luke's youth group boys and, while not an angel, wasn't troublesome either.

"Have a seat and calm down," she instructed firmly. "Then tell me—slowly—what's wrong."

"Mom got an e-mail saying I have to take summer school. That'll make me ineligible for summer league baseball. Can you talk to Mr. Graham, Miss Morris? I'll stay after school every day for the last two weeks, and I'll come in on Saturdays if he'll let me. I don't want summer school. Please."

"Why are you being placed in summer school?" Reasons varied; in Holly's opinion, guidelines were too flexible and sometimes students were enrolled more for a behavior problem than academic.

"I don't know. The e-mail didn't say. It told Mom to come in this afternoon for a conference. She's really upset, and with Ted—I just thought if I can fix it before she gets here, it'll help."

While summer league was undoubtedly the leading impetus, the teenager seemed sincere about not wanting to disappoint his mom. The thought niggled at her memory, but she pushed it away. "I'll look into it, but a lot depends on why you've been registered. So, I'm making no promises."

Following a busy morning of woes ranging from a boy's locker plastered with photos and posters of some famous male pop star she understood to be quite unpopular at the moment to a diatribe on how the school should offer and mandate hourly administration of breath mints because everybody—and this particular student meant everybody—had bad breath, she decided to make Adam her first afternoon project. She typed in her password and pulled up Adam's transcript and records on her computer. It was strange. He had been getting A's and B's during the first three quarters of the school year, and during this last quarter, his grades plummeted to D's and F's across the board. It effectively ruled out a teacher-student personality conflict, which happened more often than Holly liked.

"What happened, Adam?" she asked quietly. She needed to get him back in her office and talk to him again. The sooner, the better. She was a little aggravated none of his teachers notified her of the situation. His grades had undergone too drastic of a change in an unusually short length of time. It should have set off alarms for every one of them, even if each was unaware of his other class grades.

She was just picking up the phone to have his science teacher send him back down when a soft rap sounded on her door. Holly sighed as she replaced the receiver. Adam would have to wait.

"Come in."

Billy Andrews walked in, quickly closing the door behind him.

"Good afternoon, Billy." She hoped he was doing okay at his grandmother's.

"Miss Morris, if I tell you something important, do you have to tell people I'm the one who told you?" It looked like the teenager was getting directly to the point.

Holly carefully considered her answer. "I guess it depends on what you tell me. Can you explain it a little more?"

Billy looked like he was about to turn around and head out the door, but slowly, resolve settled on his face.

"If I tell you some kids are going to do something wrong, and you tell Sheriff Landon, do you have to tell him I'm the one who told you?"

Billy thought this was going to require Mitch's involvement? Again, she was careful to answer honestly. She was pretty sure what Billy was really worried about, anyway.

"I can't promise not to tell Sheriff Landon, but I can promise nobody will tell the 'kids' you're talking about it was you."

Holly waited patiently while he stared at the floor and decided what he was going to do.

"I have to tell," he blurted out, "or Mr. Roper will get in trouble for something he didn't do."

This had something to do with the maintenance man? "We wouldn't want that to happen," she gently agreed.

"I forgot my English book, so I had to go back to the locker room to get it." Holly could see Billy was frightened by what he was telling her, but he continued. "There were some boys down there. They didn't see me. I didn't mean to listen. I was just waiting for them to get dressed and leave so I could go in and get my book. Seniors get mad at freshmen if we bother them in the locker room. They don't like it 'cause some of us have PE with them."

"I understand. You weren't eavesdropping."

"They were talking about a room in the school's basement. One of them said they needed to put the stuff back before somebody found out it was gone. But, another one said it didn't matter. Everybody would just think Mr. Roper took it. Only he didn't call him Mr. Roper." He looked solemnly at her. "I can't repeat the word he said, or you'll have to give me detention."

Holly was trying not to prod him, but this had to be something to do with the equipment missing from the supply room. Her heart sped up. "You don't have to tell me exactly what he said."

"Okay." Billy took a deep breath. "They got into an argument. Some of them want to get more stuff out of the room. Just one says they should put some of it back. They told him to shut up because they decided to sneak in tonight and get some more things." He looked down. "I'm sorry I don't know what room they're talking about, or what they're getting."

Remain calm. "Billy, did they say how they were getting into the room?"

He frowned for a moment. "One of them said they had to put the key back in the desk tomorrow before his aunt found out it was gone."

Billy didn't know how much he already helped, but she still needed to know one more thing.

"Do you know the names of the boys you heard?" She decided to rephrase it. They were in the same PE class, after all. "Will you tell me their names, please?"

He looked into her eyes. "Can I write them down? Then nobody can say I told."

Now was not the time to discuss semantics with this boy. Holly pulled a piece of paper off her printer and slid it and an ink pen across the desk.

"Just write them down." She smiled encouragingly at him. "The sheriff might want to talk to you, but he won't tell the boys it was you."

Billy's hand was shaking as he wrote on the paper and didn't stop when he held it out for her to take.

A quick glance at the names was all she allowed herself for the moment. Right now, the young man in front of her was more important.

"Thank you, Billy." Holly waited until he made eye contact again. "What you are doing is a brave thing, and I'm very proud of you." This boy, with his far from happy home life, rescued her from Jack Wallace, and now he was helping keep Mr. Roper out of trouble.

"Let me sign your pass." He reached into his jean's pocket and handed her a crumpled piece of paper. "Let's get you back to class. Don't say a word about this to anybody else. Especially Adam, and not even Ronnie. It's too easy for people to forget they're not supposed to say anything." She did not want him hurt.

Holly waited until Billy left before she picked up the phone and called Mitch. It was time to put an end to the thievery of the five boys Billy named, two of whom surprised her. One of the struggles she'd gone through that morning had most likely been pointless.

Chapter 38

Luke stretched his leg as far as he could without making himself visible. He and Mitch had been sitting in the dark storage room of the high school for over an hour, and it was growing difficult to remain immobile.

He was grateful when Mitch arranged for him to be there. He still couldn't believe how everything fell into place once the sheriff received a call from Holly. It all made sense. And then Mitch had come up with a plan.

They knew the boys were supposed to come tonight, but not what time. So, one of Mitch's deputies and two state police officers were stationed at various points around the exterior of the building, hidden from sight. And the two of them were in the room.

When one of the state police officers expressed concern about letting a civilian participate, Mitch explained his reasoning. Luke was their target. If they saw him with the police, Mitch hoped it would startle them to realize they had been caught red-handed. Not just for breaking in and stealing things, but also for what had been done to Luke. The officer conceded, seeing there was no reason to suspect danger to Luke, and complimented the sheriff for his idea.

Of course, if Mitch hadn't been able to leave Hank watching Holly, Luke wouldn't have come. No matter how she felt, he still loved her. He couldn't sit back and do nothing when she was in danger. He could have parked out of sight and kept an eye on her place himself.

Clarence wasn't enough protection anymore, but Mitch said nobody wanted to point it out to Holly. Mitch just quietly extended Hank's hours of protective duty. Luke figured Hank would have a party when the stalker was caught. The poor guy was working crazy shifts.

"I'm getting too old for this." Mitch broke the cardinal rule of a stakeout and spoke. "My legs are cramping worse than they ever did when I played football."

Luke kept his voice as soft as Mitch had. "I know what you mean. Where are these boys' parents, anyway? They shouldn't be out this time of night."

"Two of them have good families. I'm sure they don't know what their sons have been up to. It's going to break their mothers' hearts."

Mitch had a list of who the boys were, but Luke hadn't seen it. All he knew was they were all seniors. At least it wasn't any of his youth group boys. He didn't know how he'd handle that.

He just kept asking himself why. Why would five high school seniors steal equipment, and then single him out to vandalize? He never had run-ins with any kids, let alone high school boys. Sure, he'd been toilet-papered a time or two, and sicced Clarence on the pranksters. Even so, there had been nothing with results that would make boys want to get even with him.

Luke sighed. Hopefully, they'd have some answers as soon as they caught the young men. Which couldn't be soon enough. His back was going to be stiff in the morning. He started to say something to Mitch, but hushed voices outside the door stopped him.

He watched as one, two...All five boys walked stealthily into the room. He held his breath as one of their flashlight beams missed landing on his foot by less than an inch. That's all they'd need—him and Mitch with their stiff legs, trying to run down five teenagers.

The boys were well into the room when the dark shadow Luke knew to be Mitch stood and silently walked to the door. He reached out and touched the wall.

As the lights came on, the boys froze for a split second before they turned to run. Mitch's large frame planted firmly in front of the door made them rethink their plans.

One of them assumed a cocky stance. "We ain't done nothing. You can't arrest us."

Luke stood but didn't say anything. He was waiting for Mitch's signal to make his presence known.

Mitch spoke loudly. "Rod Hirsh, Trevor Bayne, Dustin Gray, Sammy Lewis, and Ted Mayes...You're all under arrest for breaking and entering, and stealing school property."

The boys exchanged startled glances. They hadn't been expecting the sheriff to know who they were. The one who appeared to be the ringleader spoke again.

"We ain't stealing anything. And we have a key. We didn't break in."

"You have the key you stole from your aunt's desk, Trevor. And I know you're in possession of chains, pulleys, floor jacks, and a very expensive piece of shop equipment. I believe the value of the stolen items might bring this up to a felony."

"Wait a minute." One of the other boys spoke up. "You can't do anything to us. We're minors."

"You might only be seventeen, Dustin, but Rod, Trevor, and Sammy are eighteen. Besides, you're all old enough to arrest."

"You can't prove we have any stolen property." Trevor was starting to sound desperate.

Mitch nodded toward Luke, who stepped out of the shadows.

"I imagine if I look hard enough, I'm going to find all those tools somewhere on my farm. And they'll be covered with your fingerprints." For the first time, fear appeared in some of the boys' eyes. One of them looked particularly familiar, but he couldn't figure out why. He didn't have time to dwell on it as the boys exchanged frantic glances with each other.

"I told you we shouldn't do this." The boy who looked familiar spoke to Trevor. "You just wouldn't listen."

Trevor snarled at him. "You needed the money just as much as the rest of us did, Mayes. We ain't the ones with a pregnant girlfriend."

Mayes. "You're Adam's older brother." Luke spoke softly, but the boy's reaction was immediate.

"My brother doesn't have anything to do with this."

"So, why don't you tell us where money is coming into this," Mitch suggested. "You stole equipment and used it to vandalize Mr. Walker's home. What does that have to do with money?"

"I'm not talking." It was Trevor speaking again. "None of us is saying anything."

"Fine." Mitch spoke in a matter-of-fact manner. "We'll just go on down to the station, and I'll talk to you there—after you've been arrested and processed."

"We didn't steal any money." The boy with long, blond hair spoke for the first time.

"It was the man." The Mayes boy ignored Trevor's glare as he spoke. "He paid us to do it. We didn't hurt anybody or anything. I even tied your dog to a tree when he wouldn't stop following us. We just wanted to have fun."

Of course. Clarence wasn't around them often, but he loved children. He would have thought they were there to play with him. That explained how he got tied up the day of the reunion.

Mitch picked up his radio mike and called his deputy. "Wayne, we're going to run these kids in. You and the other officers can come get them."

"I don't want to go to jail!"

"You should have thought of that before you stole something, Dusty." Mitch showed no sympathy for any of them.

"Listen, it was a man." Trevor was finally admitting to it. "None of us saw him. He called and told me if I got some guys together we could make some money."

"What did you have to do?" Mitch asked.

"Just keep that guy working." Trevor gestured toward Luke. "The man told us to have fun and keep him busy. He told us about the stuff in this room and how we should get the key out of my aunt's desk."

"How did he pay you if you never saw him?" Mitch looked skeptical.

It was Adam's brother who spoke again. "There's a storage locker at the bus depot. Number three-twenty-three. He left the combination in Trevor's mailbox. We go to the locker every Saturday and there's money in it."

"How much?"

None of them answered Mitch.

"Sammy, do you want to tell me how much before, or after, I call your parents?" Mitch was addressing the long-haired boy. "This is going to mess up your football plans, buddy."

"If I tell you, can we forget it?" Sammy looked desperate now. "So I can go pro like I planned."

Mitch wasn't making deals. "All actions have consequences. It just so happens stealing and vandalism have pretty big ones. Now, is somebody going to answer my question?"

"He left a thousand dollars. We each got two hundred a week." The Mayes boy spoke.

Mitch exchanged a glance with Luke that told him they were thinking the same thing. It was a lot of money to pay kids to pull pranks. There was something more to this story. Something maybe the boys themselves were unaware of.

They were interrupted by Wayne and the two state police officers entering the room.

"Take them all to the station and, before you process them, see that their parents are called." Mitch ignored pleas from the boys.

As soon as they were all cuffed and out the door, Luke asked Mitch the question bugging him. "Why would a man pay them that kind of money just to 'keep me busy'?"

Mitch shook his head. "We don't even know this man exists. Those boys would make up anything if they thought it might get them out of the mess they're in. Instead of admitting it was their idea, they may be inventing a scapegoat. We won't know more until I sit down and question them individually."

"Thank you for letting me be here."

"I'm just sorry you had to be the target of this, no matter the reason." Mitch walked through the door. "I'll let you know what we find out," he said over his shoulder.

"I appreciate it."

Luke drove by Holly's house on his way home, relieved to see Hank sitting in his own car across the road. With Clarence to announce any visitors, and Hank to provide protection, she was as safe as she could be.

He couldn't get the night's events out of his head during his drive home. And the one question that rose above all the others. Why?

Chapter 39

"Girls' night," sang Tessa as she sashayed across the living room floor. "Ha ha, Clarence. You're stuck here while we go out and have fun."

Clarence yawned to show how impressed he was.

"I'm still not sure this is a good idea." Holly had finally given in to her friend's pleas after enduring a solid Saturday morning of whining.

"We're partying."

Holly sat on the sofa. "I don't feel like partying." She reached down to Clarence, who had laid his head across her lap, and scratched behind his ears. His thumping tail told her thank you. "Not when five of our seniors were expelled this close to graduation."

"They'll be lucky if they don't end up in juvenile detention or jail, Holly." Tessa lost her carefree attitude. "Those boys broke the law. Just think what might have happened had they gotten away with it. It was easy to steal and not get caught this time, so why not try it again? I tell you, that's how a life of crime gets started."

"I still can't believe Ted is the father of Tasha Hart's baby. And Adam, of all people, has been his confidant. No wonder the boy has had trouble focusing on his grades." Holly blinked away her tears. "Do you think Sammy or Ted will even have a shot at college now?" It still broke her heart to see them lose their dreams.

Tessa sat down beside Holly and spoke seriously. "Holly, you have to accept it. They took over ten thousand dollars' worth of equipment and vandalized Luke's farm. Each one of them will have that on their record for the rest of their lives. And it's because of the choice each one of them made. Any one of them could have said no; he wouldn't go along with it. But, not one of them did."

"I understand." Holly sighed. "My mind knows it, but my heart is having a hard time accepting it." She leaned down and hugged Clarence. "Did Mitch find the tools where the boys told him they were?"

Tessa frowned. "Not even forty feet into Luke's woods. Mitch said the equipment was covered with a net the boys had laced with grass and leaves. Homemade camouflage, I guess."

Clarence nuzzled Holly's leg, reminding her he was still there. "Why are you here so early tonight, Clarence?" She had heard a couple of doors close while she was in the shower, and was greeted by the dog as soon as she entered the living room.

"Luke just said he had something going on this evening and needed to leave him here now." Tessa smiled a little too brightly.

"Is he okay?" Holly asked quietly.

"Other than being as daffy as you are?" Tessa crossed her arms and tilted her head back. "I should get Mitch to lock you two in the same cell and not release you until you work this out."

Holly's eyes burned. "Work what out? He doesn't want to be with me anymore."

"I am not having this conversation with you again." Tessa suddenly grinned. "Nice try, sister, but we are going out. Now get a move on. You'll see. We are going to have f-u-n!"

Two and a half hours later, Holly had to admit Tessa was correct. They had gone to a movie that had them both laughing so hard there were tears involved. And then Tessa insisted they stop at Tibbles for pizza. The subs they had for supper weren't enough.

Holly was laughing at her friend trying to get a string of cheese into her mouth when she looked up, and her heart stopped.

Luke was walking in, and he wasn't alone. A pretty woman with long, extremely dark brown hair was with him. He had his arm around her, and as Holly watched, he gave the woman a hug before pulling out her chair and getting himself situated beside her.

"What's the matter?" Tessa let her cheese hang. "You're not going to pass out, are you?"

Holly shook her head, tears blinding her. "No."

"Then, what—" Tessa looked over her shoulder and then very slowly turned back around. "I don't believe it. I just don't believe it."

A single tear ran down Holly's cheek as, for the first time, she accepted the truth—no more pushing it away. She had been fooling herself for years. Friends, indeed. A woman didn't want to share every moment of her life with a man because he was her friend. She didn't want to be wrapped tightly in a *friend's* arms and kissed silly. All this time, she considered him an important part of her life, but she was wrong. Luke Walker *was* her life. Holly was deeply in love with the man. But, now it was too late. "I waited too long."

"No." Tessa looked back at the couple. "There has to be an explanation for this."

Holly sniffed and lifted her chin. "There is. He offered me something very precious, and I took him for granted. I've always taken him for granted." She knew the words were true as she spoke them. "Luke deserves to be happy, and if he needs to be with...her...or any woman to do so, he should be."

"Oh, nonsense!" Tessa put her napkin on the table. "I'm going over there and finding out exactly what is going on."

"Please don't." Holly put her hand on Tessa's arm. "If he's found somebody who appreciates him and makes him happy, I don't want to ruin it. Please just leave them alone. Let me keep some of my self-respect, and give him at least that much. Please, Tess."

Tessa slowly sat back in her chair. "Okay." She put her napkin back in her lap and picked up her pizza. "But just for the record, I think you're wrong with a capital *w*."

Holly wished she were, but she could still hear his voice: "Puppy love ends, Holly."

"Good evening, ladies." Tom Dwer stood beside Tessa.

"This is a surprise." Tessa set her pizza back on the plate. "What are you still doing in town, Tom?"

He smiled. "I'm working on a project that will be easier to develop here. It should be finished in a couple of weeks."

"What's the project?" Holly could distract herself by focusing on Tom.

He lifted his index finger and wagged it back and forth. "It's a secret, Holly. Don't you know good businessmen never give their plans away?"

"Sit down and have a slice of pizza." Tessa gestured toward the chair he was standing behind.

"If you're sure?" Tom gave Holly a questioning look.

"Please join us." She looked pointedly at Tessa. "If we don't eat all this pizza, Tessa will take it home and try to sneak it to the dog. Even though he's not supposed to get table scraps."

"What kind of dog do you have?" Tom sat down and helped himself to a slice of pizza.

Holly deliberately avoided looking at Luke. "He's not really mine."

"Don't listen to her." Tess took a bite of pizza. "She and Luke have joint custody of Clarence. The mutt is so spoiled, it isn't funny."

Tom's gaze sharpened. "You and Luke share a dog? I knew you two were close, but I didn't realize—"

"We're not." Holly spoke quickly. "He's...loaning me Clarence for a while. That's all."

"I think people would have to be pretty close to share a dog." His gaze was full of skepticism.

Always good at changing topics, Tessa spoke. "I'm glad you're still around." She reached across and touched his hand. Her voice dropped to a near whisper. "What you did—letting Mitch tell the others you set up that film as a joke—was one of the nicest things I've ever seen."

He shrugged. "I pulled a lot of stunts in school. Who better to blame?"

To maintain the illusion the film was a hoax, Mitch had asked Tom for help. The former jokester immediately agreed. It gave Holly a headache trying to keep the sheriff's logic straight—the stalker would know the film was live feed and think Wallace was dead. Mitch hoped he would give himself away.

"So, Tom, before the …movie, did you enjoy the class reunion?" Holly thought Tessa's question was silly; she didn't see how anybody could have had a good time.

His gaze slowly shifted from Holly to Tessa. "It was nice to see everybody."

"It was, wasn't it?" Tessa asked.

"We had a good turnout," Holly offered.

Tom frowned. "I think Jen made a little too much over the fact Kevin is such a success."

Holly wondered if the two remained friends. It looked like they hadn't. "So, where's home?"

"I live in Rhode Island." He looked happy to share the information. "You'd like my house. Everything computerized; it practically maintains itself. And the design is unbelievable—two-story with a walk-around porch completely encompassing it. The view from the upstairs balcony is unbelievable. A dream house"

"It sounds very nice." For some reason, Holly couldn't picture Tom living in the house he described. She would have thought he lived in a more modern house, or even a condo or apartment. "Do you have any family?" She didn't remember any mention of a wife, and he wasn't wearing a ring, but that didn't necessarily mean anything.

His smile faded. "No. There's someone special—very special. However, we have a lot of stuff to work out before I can convince her she and I can make a go of it."

Holly exchanged an uncomfortable glance with Tessa. She hadn't expected such a personal answer and was more than a little embarrassed by it.

"So, Holly and I both work at the high school." It looked like Tessa was saving the day again. "It's kind of strange to work in the same place we attended."

"You must be a very good guidance counselor." He set his pizza down and gave all of his attention to Holly. "Jen told some of us she had a special presentation planned for you because you've gone through a rough patch. It didn't have anything to do with that movie, did it?"

She wasn't sure what Mitch told Tom about the incident, but he obviously didn't know everything. "No."

"Then, can I ask what happened?"

"Nothing important." There was no way she was going to explain the situation to Tom. "I hate to be a spoilsport, but I'm getting sleepy, and we do have to get up for church in the morning."

She looked at Tessa and hoped her friend would go along with it.

"Yes. We'd better go." Tessa picked up her purse and dug out a couple of dollars. "Please finish off the pizza, Tom. I really shouldn't feed it to the dog."

"The dog Holly shares with Luke." There was an expression on Tom's face Holly couldn't quite read. It looked like either displeasure or disapproval, which made no sense. Why would he care if she and Luke shared a dog? She looked over Tessa's shoulder to see Luke deep in conversation with his companion, and was suddenly too tired to try to figure it out.

The image of Luke and the mystery woman was still stuck in Holly's mind as she pulled back her blankets a while later. Maybe it was why she didn't check caller ID when she answered the phone.

"Hello?"

"You're mine. I love you, and you're mine." The caller's voice was tender as he crooned. "We'll be together very soon, my Holly, and everything will be perfect. You'll see."

"Tess?" Holly sank to her bed, her phone dropping to the floor. "Tess!"

Tessa, pajamas on, appeared in her bedroom door. "What—Holly, what's wrong?"

"He just called. He said he loves me, and we're going to be together soon." Pure panic hit her. "He's coming back for me! He's going to take me!"

Tessa knelt in front of her and framed Holly's face with her hands. "Listen to me, Holly."

Holly looked at her friend, still more frightened by this call than any of the others.

"To get to you, this guy has to get past Hank, Clarence, and me. We can go to your parents' house if you want. Would you feel safer with your dad?"

She had to get a grip on it. "No." She took a deep breath. "I'm sorry. There was something different about his voice this time. Like he was trying to be romantic. Or maybe because I still feel his touch. This was worse than when he sounded threatening, Tess."

"Lie down." Tess waited until she was comfortable on the bed before she pulled the covers over her. Then Tess turned to Clarence. "Get up on the bed and keep her safe, you walking Chia pet! You know you want up there, anyway."

Clarence looked at Tess for a moment, and just like that, jumped up on the foot of the bed. Holly felt him snuggle against her legs and lay his head across them. She immediately felt better.

"I'll be right back." Tessa left the room.

Holly didn't know how long her friend was gone before she showed back up with a cup in her hand.

"I made you some herbal tea. It will calm you." She waited for Holly to sit up far enough to drink some of it, and then helped her get cozy again. "I'm going to go call Mitch. He needs to know about this call. It might be something significant. He might even want to give Hank a heads up."

"Okay." Holly watched her friend turn to leave. "Tess?"

Tessa turned back around.

"Please leave the light on."

Chapter 40

"Luke, are you in here?" Mitch's voice came through the open barn door moments before he did.

"Hi, Mitch." Luke turned back to the tractor. "I'll be with you in a minute. I've just about got the fan belt back on."

"Busted fan belt?" Mitch came over and looked at what Luke was doing.

"Yep." Luke finished tightening it and looked up to see Mitch's concerned gaze. "No vandalism this time—unless the culprits left mouse droppings."

Relief immediately flooded Mitch's face. "Good."

Luke picked up a towel and wiped his hands. "So, what are you doing out here today? Any new information on the man the boys claim hired them?" It was Thursday, over a week since they'd caught the boys.

"Yes." Mitch nodded. "The warrant finally came through. We opened the locker the boys said they used, a couple of hours ago."

Luke's interest was piqued. "What did you find?"

"Ten one-hundred-dollar bills, just like the boys claimed."

"So, they weren't lying." Maybe it would make the judge go a little easier on them. The boys needed to answer for their crimes, but Luke hated to see their lives completely ruined. And, they had given Mitch the best information yet.

"Who is the locker registered to?"

"That's just it." Mitch looked confounded. "First of all, there's no record of the locker having been rented. The bus company doesn't have any idea how the boys, or this man, could have gotten the combination."

"Maybe something on a computer somewhere?" Luke speculated.

"Maybe," Mitch agreed. "But the bus depot has a couple of security cameras aimed at the lockers. Difficult to see if you aren't looking at them."

"Cameras?" If they had a film of someone putting money in that locker, this should all be over.

"The depot owner gave me the security DVDs without a warrant. He knew about Holly's stalker. Turns out she helped his niece with a problem at school, and he was glad for a way to pay her back."

Luke couldn't stop the surge of pride at one more person appreciating Holly's skills.

"Do you want to come to the station and watch some movies?" Mitch presented him with a small grin. "There are at least a dozen, and I can only spare one deputy to help. Haley already has a disc in the dispatch computer, and she's not impressed by what people do when they think nobody is watching."

"I'll be glad to help."

An hour later, Luke rethought those words. So far, he had observed a harried mother sneak over by the lockers to change her son's diaper—dirty diaper, a man change from street clothes into a waiter's uniform, and he fast forwarded through the newlyweds making use of a little privacy.

"If we knew how much ahead of time he left the money in the locker, we might have better luck finding him." Mitch looked like a hypnotized man, staring at the monitor. Luke would still rather have the desktop than this tablet. He had to zoom in for details too often, and saw some things too up close and personal.

"Hey, Mitch!" Haley yelled from the dispatch desk.

Even in these circumstances, Luke couldn't stop his smile. The intercom system on Mitch's desk was used so seldom, a thick layer of dust lay undisturbed on it. He had observed Haley and Mitch's method of hollering back and forth too often.

"Yeah?" There went Luke's right eardrum.

"I found something!"

Both men bumped and bungled their way past Mitch's desk and the table Luke was using, to make it out of the office and over to Haley's desk.

"Look." She pointed to the monitor.

Mitch squinted at the computer. "Haley, that picture's so dark, you can't see anything but shadows."

"I know." The lovely blond sounded exasperated. "The security lights all just went off. But, watch."

Luke hunkered down on the opposite side of Haley and focused on the nearly black screen. And, then he saw it—a flash of light.

Mitch stood and pointed. "That could be one of those alien babies floating around."

Haley turned to her boss. If looks could drill holes, Mitch would have an extra nostril. "Mitch, I told you to watch. I'll slow it down and lighten the contrast."

This time, the light seemed to barely move as the video played.

"Now, look." Haley froze it and pointed at the screen.

"Haley, I'm sorry, darlin', but all I see is a neon green blob." At least Mitch managed to sound regretful.

"I'll darlin' you," she muttered. "Here, you blind old bat."

That brought a chuckle out of Luke, even though nothing about this was funny. Mitch was his age, a ripe, old twenty-eight.

As the image grew, it became clearer. And then, Luke saw what she meant.

"Is that a logo on the back of a jacket, Haley?"

Haley sent a dirty look Mitch's way before turning with a smile to Luke. "Yes, it is. And, I used a variation of our facial recognition program to find what the logo is for. Here."

She handed Luke the printout of a neon green whoopee cushion, and what looked like a diving board—or very long skateboard. Underneath it were goofy looking letters reading, *Pull a Prank or Walk the Plank. Prankster Products, Limited.*

"Prankster Products...why does that sound familiar?" Luke knew he'd never bought anything from them before. He couldn't think of how he would know the company name.

"You're right." Mitch stood straighter. "It rings a bell. I've heard it somewhere, but where?"

Luke decided to look at it logically. "Okay. We both heard it, so it has to be someplace we both were."

Mitch suddenly grinned. "Did the Prayer Committee decide to start playing pranks instead of giving thanks? We're both at church a lot."

Luke couldn't help but chuckle. It didn't seem like he'd done that very often lately. "I think the members want to help people, not give someone a whoopee-cushion-induced heart attack."

"Okay. So where else have we both been?"

"The hospital." Luke searched his memory. "But Tony and Susan Morris were the only ones there with us, and I know they didn't talk about Prankster Products."

"Luke, I feel like we're missing something here. Something right in front of us." Mitch looked at the screen again. "They sell gags, right? Like somebody would put it out as a joke."

"Joke." Luke suddenly saw an image of Jen Ewing with a man beside her. "Our class reunion. Isn't Prankster Products Tom Dwer's company?"

"That's it." Mitch's look of satisfaction faded into confusion. "But what could Tom's business have to do with this mess?"

"A Thomas Ian Dwer is the sole owner and CEO of Prankster." Haley was using a small tablet. "But, it looks like he's on the verge of declaring bankruptcy. A quote from him reads, 'It's not over until the fat lady screams…and I haven't scared my grandma lately."

She looked up at Mitch with a huge frown on her pretty face. "Who is this guy? He's about as funny as the backside of a donkey race."

"Did he go to that locker?" Mitch pointed at the monitor again.

"I can't tell, but it's sure strange how the lights go off; the jacket is there; and it's gone a few minutes later when the lights come back on." Haley must have made sure of what she saw before bothering her boss.

Once more, Luke felt like he was at the edge of something important…if he could just remember it.

"Tom…I talked to him. What did he say?" Luke tried to think; something Tom told him had made him uncomfortable. What was it? "Wait a minute." Suddenly, things clicked into place, and Luke's heart went into double time.

"Mitch, Tom told me there's a woman. She doesn't live near him. There was something about another man, but Tom thinks he can persuade her to be with him." A sense of growing dread filled him. "Where does Tom live?"

"Rhode Island." Haley and Mitch answered together.

"I remember because Clay Richmond made an idiotic joke about island living," said Mitch.

"Rhode Island and Massachusetts are right next to each other. He could have been talking about Holly. It all makes sense."

Mitch picked up on Luke's train of thought. "His company makes all kinds of computerized junk; he could have rigged everything. And he paid the boys to keep you busy—away from Holly."

Luke grabbed Mitch's arm. "Tom Dwer might be Holly's stalker."

Mitch took a step back and held up his hand. "Slow down, Luke. I'm on board with you, but I can't go arrest the guy because he lives in New England and has girlfriend problems. Anybody could be wearing a jacket with his company logo. We need proof."

Luke thought for a minute. "Maybe Holly knows something that will help—something she's not aware of. Like a chance meeting with him while she was in college. It may have slipped her mind, but it would prove he was there."

"There are still holes in our theory," Mitch warned him. "We have the six year gap with no contact."

"Maybe he didn't know where Holly went after she graduated. That she'd come home to Shadow." Luke didn't really think it was a plausible explanation, but too many other facts were lining up. "We have to talk to Holly."

"Come on." Mitch started out the door. "You can ride with me."

A sense of urgency suddenly came over Luke. Forget her feelings for him; he needed to get to Holly. Fast.

Chapter 41

Holly set her iced tea on the end table and stretched out on the sofa, the latest Mary Connealy novel in her hands. She sighed as she made herself comfortable and opened her book. She was home alone.

It was a fluke, and Mitch would be furious if he found out, but it would only be for an hour or so, in broad daylight. And it wasn't really anybody's fault. Hank let her know he'd been called home to help his mother and would be back soon. She wasn't to step one foot out the door while he was gone.

Then, when Tessa announced she needed to go back to school and enter some grades on the computer, Holly hadn't seen the need to inform her Hank had already left. After all, the world did not revolve around Holly Morris.

So, for the first time in weeks, she was completely by herself. The only problem was, the house was too quiet without Clarence plodding around. She had gotten more attached to the dog than she ever imagined she would. Luke wouldn't be bringing him for a few hours yet. If Luke brought him.

Luke. She had been offered a very precious gift—Luke's love. And she let it slip through her fingers, not realizing its true value until it was gone.

I know I'm too late, but, please...Luke deserves to be happy. Please give him a woman who will never take him for granted and treasures the man he is. I'm sorry I didn't realize what a gift you were giving me. Please...

Tears began to fall. It was a good thing God knew what was in her heart because at the moment, it hurt too much to put into words.

The ringing phone broke through her misery. *I should have checked caller ID* she thought as she pushed accept. It was too late.

"Are you ready for our wedding?"

Holly's first instinct was to hang up. But if he was talking to her on the phone, he wasn't there with her. And he knew her, so maybe she knew him. If she could be brave enough to talk to him, perhaps he'd slip and give himself away.

"I'd like to order wedding invitations, but you've never told me what name to put on them." She hoped he couldn't hear the quiver in her voice.

His low laughter came across the line. "We're going to be happy, my Holly. I have our dream house all ready. It's a perfect place for us to live and raise our children."

She fought back the revulsion she felt at listening to this man talk about having children together. "Where is our house?"

"Now, if I tell you that, you might go see it, and then it won't be a surprise. I've worked too hard to make it perfect. I want to see your face when I bring you there the first time."

"When—when do you plan to do that?"

"Aren't you impatient? Our wedding night, of course. I knew if I waited long enough you'd get past all that nonsense."

Keep him talking. "What nonsense did I get past? I want to know so I don't do it again."

"Luke Walker. You aren't meant for him, and you never were." The voice was angry now.

"Okay."

"You know how he tempts you, yet you came right back to him. I trusted you. You should have been faithful." He was in a rage. "I was getting things ready for you, and you were here, cheating. After we're married, you'll never cheat again. You are mine, Holly. Mine!"

The line went dead.

Holly was shaking so badly she could barely put the phone on the table without dropping it. She forced herself to calm down and think about the conversation. Had there been something—anything familiar about the man? His voice was obviously disguised. It couldn't have been a recording this time, though, since he responded to what she said.

I have our dream house all ready. It's a perfect place for us to live and raise our children. Aside from the outright horror that statement instilled, there was something about it she thought she should know. Something familiar...

She jumped a mile when a loud knocking sounded on her front door.

She glanced at the clock on her way to the door. Hank was probably letting her know he was back. She'd have to tell him about the call. She braced herself as she opened the door.

Tom Dwer stood outside.

For a moment, Holly was stunned into silence. Then her manners kicked in. "I'm sorry, Tom. Please come in."

Tom walked through the open door and on into the living room. There, he turned to face Holly.

"I have to tell you something, Holly. Something serious." His words were slurred. Holly took a good look at him. His eyes didn't look right, and now that she was closer to him, she could smell alcohol.

"Tom, why don't I call a cab, and you can come back later? We'll talk then." She didn't want him to say something he'd be embarrassed about after he sobered up.

Holly involuntarily took a few steps backward as he walked closer.

"I have to tell you now. I've waited too long."

She spoke more firmly, for the first time realizing how vulnerable she was. "Tom, I must insist you leave. You can come back when you're sober."

He reached out to touch her. "No. Your life...the house...marriage and…"

The house. His house. His perfect, two-story dream house with a wraparound porch and second-floor balcony. The perfect place to take a wife and raise a family. Holly was suddenly terrified.

"Leave, Tom. Now. There's a police officer watching the house, and he'll be in here any moment to make sure I'm okay. Leave." *Please, God, I need Hank to get back and realize something's wrong. Clarence isn't here to rescue me. I'm more afraid than I've ever been in my life.*

Undeterred, Tom stepped even closer and put his hand out as if to touch her shoulder. "I have to tell you, I can't live with this anymore. I need you—."

When his shirt tail moved to show a cell phone in his pocket, sheer terror took over. All sense of logic and every last vestige of courage disappeared. She screamed louder than she ever had in her life.

"Don't." Tom's hand was on her arm now. "Don't scream."

She squeezed her eyes tightly shut and produced an even louder one. The pressure of his hand abruptly disappeared, and when Holly drew a deep breath she heard a commotion. She wasn't taking time to inspect it, though. The sudden, ridiculous memory of her phone's ring after Ronnie programmed it spurred her on, and she let loose again. She'd put that phone to shame.

"Holly!" Arms reached around her.

"No! Don't touch me! Let me go!" She shoved Tom away.

"It's me, Holly. It's Luke. I've got you. You're okay." Luke. Luke was here. She was okay. This time when his arms went around her, she collapsed into them.

"Hank, you're going to have to help me get him out to the squad car. He passed out." Was that Mitch talking?

"Mitch?" Her voice trembled.

"He's got Tom. He's taking him to jail. You're safe." Luke looked over his shoulder and spoke. "I'll stay with her and make sure she's okay. Can she wait to give you her statement?"

Mitch said something, but she had no idea what it was. Her legs suddenly gave out, and she collapsed. She didn't fall, though. Strong arms went under her and scooped her up.

"I've got you." Luke's voice was tender as he carried her to the sofa. Holly curled up on his lap and buried her face against his neck. "I'm not going anywhere until you feel safe. I promise."

His voice soothed Holly and made her feel protected. Her heart finally slowed down, and her breathing became less labored. She slowly came back to her senses. The embrace he meant to be comforting was beginning to feel good for other reasons.

"Luke?" She reluctantly raised her head.

He drew back from her far enough to see her face. "Are you okay now?"

"I think so." She slowly swung her legs around and cautiously stood up.

Luke stood with her. "Can I get you something? Is there anything more I can do to help you?"

"No. I think I just need to process this. Tom Dwer is my stalker?" Holly still couldn't believe it.

His expression was grave. "Mitch and I think so. There is evidence linking him to the boys, and some other facts tying it all together."

She tried to stand straighter. As much as she wanted him there, it wasn't right to keep him. "I'll be okay now. Tess will be home any minute. You don't have to stay." She looked into his troubled eyes. "Thank you, Luke."

He smiled sadly. "I told you I'd do anything for you. I'm sorry I smothered you, though. I didn't mean to." He turned and started for the door.

Smother her? "I'm sorry you stuck with your puppy love so long."

He turned back and looked at her, a frown on his face. "Puppy love? Holly, what are you talking about?"

They spoke at the same time.

"Why didn't you tell me I was smothering you?"

"Why did you say your puppy love was real?"

They practically harmonized on, "What?"

"Holly, what are you talking about—puppy love? Do you think I love Clarence more than you?"

She shook her head. "No. You told me you were over me; that you wanted to see what other women were like because your puppy love died."

"Now, hold on." All of a sudden, Luke looked angry. "You told me I was smothering you and I needed to back off."

"I did not." Holly was aggravated now. "Why are you making something that ridiculous up, Luke? I didn't argue with you when you broke up with me. You don't have to lie to make me leave you alone."

"I'm not lying. But this puppy love...have you made that up to make yourself feel better?"

"I didn't make that up! Luke, you broke my heart. I realized I love you, and then before I can tell you, you turn around and tell me it's over. You want to be with someone else." She blinked back her tears. "I saw her, Luke. She's beautiful."

"You love me?" There was a light in his eyes. "Not just as a friend?"

"I've been in love with you for years. I just didn't realize that's what it was." She managed to produce a shaky smile. "I hope she appreciates you."

Suddenly, she was swooped off her feet and swung around in a circle before being placed gently in front of Luke.

"You love me!" Luke's smile would have lit the sky as he steadied her.

"You have a—"

"You must have seen me with my cousin Ellie. She was in town overnight, so I took her out for pizza. There's no other woman for me except you. I am crazy in love with you." He held her tightly for a moment before he released her to look in her eyes. "I'm so thankful you decided I'm not smothering you."

It was Holly's turn to be confused. "Luke, I promise, I did not tell you that. Why do you think I did?"

"You called me." A baffled look was on his face.

"You called me and told me about the puppy love ending."

He shook his head. He put his hands on her shoulders and looked into her eyes. "Holly, the kind of love I have for you is the kind that doesn't go away. Because God put it in my heart a long time ago. You're the woman I'm meant to be with for the rest of my life."

"I don't understand." Holly knew he called her, and he wasn't a liar so he sincerely believed she called him.

Suddenly, he smacked his head with the palm of his hand. "That voice changer, Holly. Tom used it to make us think we called each other."

"But why…" Then, she knew. "To separate us. He grabbed me after that happened."

"Mitch told me. I'm so sorry I wasn't here."

"Clarence was." She managed a smile.

"I love you, Holly." His grin was enormous. "I can't believe I can just say that now. I love you."

"I've been a fool." Holly's eyes filled with tears of happiness. "I took you for granted. I promise I will never take you, or your love, for granted again. Because I love you the same way you love me. The kind of love that lasts a lifetime. God put it in my heart, too." She suddenly laughed. "God just answered a request I made right before all of this happened. I prayed that you would end up with a woman who loved and appreciated you. And, you can believe me, Luke. You have."

"I'm taking you out to O'Leary's tomorrow night. We're celebrating." His smile faded and the look that appeared in his eyes weakened Holly's knees. "I love you very much, Holly."

She steadily returned his gaze. "I love you, too."

Luke lowered his face to hers and stopped with their lips barely touching. "My love." He laced his fingers through her hair and kissed her. Really kissed her. Holly could feel the love Luke had been waiting to show her for a long time, and she returned it with joy. The kiss deepened, and his arms slid down and held her tightly for just a brief moment. His lips slowly left hers as he loosened his hold.

The look on her face had to be mirroring the one on his. It was full of wonder and happiness. Holly had never even imagined any feeling could be this intense.

"You'd better go." She reluctantly took a small step backward. Now wasn't the time to start something they had no intention of following through with. Holly didn't want anything to mar their relationship.

His hands trailed down her arms as he released her. "I'll call Dad to come pick me up. Will you be okay?"

"Tess will be home anytime." Her knees still felt weak as she managed to turn and walk away. They shook the entire time she dug her keys out of her purse. "Take my rental car. We can get it all squared away tomorrow."

His thumb captured her fingers as she handed him the keys. "Okay."

It was all she could do not to step up to him and take up where they'd left off, but she dug deep for strength and lowered her hand beside her.

His eyes told her he shared her inner struggle. "Goodbye, Holly."

"Goodbye, Luke."

She walked to the door and waited as he pulled out of the driveway and drove away. Her heart was soaring. God answered her prayers in a much better way than she ever expected.

The door was barely closed when a knock sounded on it. Luke was probably back; they'd forgotten to make arrangements for Clarence. She still wanted him nights, even though she no longer needed his protection.

She walked to the door and was smiling brightly as she opened it. She couldn't stop the strong arms that grabbed her, or the hand that held the sweet-smelling cloth over her nose and mouth. Her world faded.

Chapter 42

Make a joyful noise unto the Lord. It was a good thing the scripture didn't specify it had to be on-key because Luke was slaying his favorite hymn as he walked through the back door of his house. There was an excellent reason Luke had never joined the choir, and the look on Clarence's face said he would attest to that. The poor dog was liable to start howling in agony any moment.

He couldn't remember ever feeling this happy before. Holly was finally safe, and she was in love with him. His prayers were being answered.

"Before too long, you'll get to be with Holly as much as you want," he told Clarence. "We'll be a family."

A family. Holly would marry him, and when they were ready, they would have children. Holly would have his children. That was a blessing he'd never dared to contemplate before. His heart soared.

Then he thought of Tom Dwer. Luke needed to let go of the anger he felt toward the man and try to forgive him. Tom was obviously disturbed. Something nobody knew about might have happened to him, to cause him to do the things he'd done. No matter what, he would get the help he needed now.

Did Tom have any family still around here? Luke seemed to remember his parents and sister moving away shortly after graduation. He hadn't known where Tom went, or what he was going to do. And he hadn't bothered to find out.

His ringing phone pulled him out of his musings.

"Hello?"

"Luke, are you still with Holly?" Mitch was unusually abrupt.

"No. I'm at home. Why?"

"She's in danger. Tom is not her stalker."

Luke couldn't believe what he was hearing. "But he was there, at her house. And the locker...He was at Holly's house."

Mitch spoke firmly. "He was at Holly's, trying to tell her who her stalker is."

Luke's heart jumped into his throat. This couldn't be happening. "Who is he?"

Chapter 43

Holly felt like her mouth was full of cotton as she slowly managed to open her eyes. What happened? Had she passed out? No. She had to think. Remember. Luke left. He had come back...It hadn't been Luke. Somebody grabbed her.

She quickly sat up, only to be stopped by thick strips pressing painfully against her skin. Terror started to overcome her as she realized she was tied to some sort of chair.

No. She had to calm down. Panicking would not help. She looked around the room. The Victorian armchair she was sitting on matched the sofa and love seat a few yards away. As her eyes scanned the room, she wondered if maybe this wasn't some sort of dream after all.

The room looked like a picture taken from a storybook. There were throw pillows and knickknacks...even magazines spread out made it look like somebody lived there. There were pictures on the wall, including what appeared to be enlarged snapshots and family photographs. One of them caught her eye.

"What?" she whispered. It was a photograph of Luke and Holly taken after her college graduation. Only it wasn't Luke's smile she saw. Another face had been edited in. It was...

"Ah, my Holly. How are you?" Kevin Tripp walked into the room and sat on the sofa as if nothing were out of the ordinary. "It's been a long day, hasn't it?"

This wasn't happening. Holly couldn't process it. Kevin Tripp was sitting with one arm across the back of the sofa and his legs casually crossed, making conversation with her—while she was tied to a chair. Though she tried to stop them, hysterical giggles bubbled up and burst forth.

They turned into full blown laughter when he sat, unmoving, staring at her with a silly smile on his face. He reminded her of a mannequin. If she weren't tied up, she'd walk over there and poke him in the stomach to see if he was alive. That thought added to the hilarity, and her hysterics increased. She may never stop laughing. He would be sorry he kidnapped a lunatic. Kidnapped. She'd been kidnapped.

Slowly, Holly came back to her senses. She wasn't going to accomplish anything this way. She needed to be rational and use her brain if she were going to get out of this. She took a deep, calming breath.

"Kevin, you don't have to do this. I'll be your friend."

He acted as if he hadn't heard her. "What would you like for dinner this evening? I thought I'd cook something special for our celebration."

She had a horrible idea of what they were celebrating. But maybe, if she played along, she could get out of this mess.

"I'm not hungry, thank you." Holly tried to smile. "But I'll help you in the kitchen. If you just untie me, so I can get up."

"You know; I knew on the very first day we worked together, how you felt about me."

Keep him talking. Maybe help would come. "How did you know?"

Kevin smiled happily. "You looked at me. I saw the way you looked at me. It was in your eyes, as plain as day."

Was he serious? "Do you mean when we were partners on the project in Adult Living? In high school?"

He chuckled. "Of course, it was our secret, wasn't it? All those smiles, secret touches, longing looks…It was nearly impossible to contain our feelings, the love was so strong. We were teenagers, though. Now, we're adults, My Holly, so we can show each other how we really feel."

"We were working on assignments. I may have smiled, or even touched your hand when I gave you a paper. But what you're describing is in your imagination."

"You loved me then, and you love me now." Kevin seemed certain of his claim. "You told me marriage lasts forever, and then you signed it. Now, all we have to do is honor those promises we made to each other."

What was he talking about? Since the purpose of the assignment was to show them what it would be like to live as adults, the teacher had instructed them to complete assignments like real couples would. And had the subject of marriage come up in a discussion, Holly could easily see herself stating it would last forever. But the promises?

"You're imagining things. None of that happened—at least, not like you remember. Now, untie me and let me go."

"I have a special gown upstairs for you, My Holly. Such a lady, so innocent and pure, saving yourself for me on our wedding night." Was that really a tear on his face?

It seemed her tactics were a failure. She only seemed to be feeding into his fantasy.

"Kevin, listen to me." It was time to try another approach. "You need help. Let me go, and I'll find somebody to help you. I promise I'll get you the help you need."

Her heart stopped when he stood. As hard as she willed him to turn around and leave, he slowly walked straight over to her. "You really are beautiful." He reached out and softly touched her hair.

Holly's fingernails dug into her palms as she fought the urge to flinch. "Let me get help for you, Kevin."

"My Holly." Kevin leaned down, and for one horrific moment, Holly was afraid he was going to try to kiss her. Instead, he ran his fingers down the side of her face. "We're going to be so happy together.

We'll start our family right away." A look that made her skin crawl appeared in his eyes. "I have our room ready. You'll like our bed."

No! Everything inside of Holly screamed. Somehow, she managed to keep her voice calm and firm. "We will never share a bed, and I'm not having children with you, Kevin. We are not together. You kidnapped me. What you are doing is wrong. Now, let me go."

Kevin laughed softly before he turned and walked to the large picture window on the opposite wall. "You'll like our other home. I know you don't want me to spoil you, but you deserve our homes. We can stay here when you want to visit your parents."

"I'm not going to share even one home with you." She had a sudden realization. Tom! "Tom Dwer was at my house." *Please, God, don't let me be wrong.* "He knows about you, and he's with the sheriff. He'll tell them where we are."

He turned and smiled apologetically. "I should have talked to you first, but I invested in a business venture with Tom." He held up his hand. "I know you'll say I shouldn't have, since he used to order me around so much, but now I'll be the boss. He'll have to listen to me." Kevin took a few steps toward her. "Please say you forgive me. Since you're my wife, Tom works for both of us now, anyway."

Tom worked for him? Her hopes plummeted to the ground. She couldn't give up, though. "I'm not your wife."

His smile made her nauseous. "Don't be silly, my Holly." He reached into his jean's pocket and pulled out a ragged looking piece of paper. "You are. See?" He held it down where she could read it.

It took her a moment to realize what it was. "Kevin, that is the corner of an assignment we did. I only wrote my first name, but you wrote both of yours. Your last name ended up under my first name. Tripp isn't now or ever was my last name."

"Oh, my Holly, this is our wedding day. We've waited for this day for a long time."

The man was delusional. He had an entire relationship developed in his mind, and something else was wrong—he wasn't even keeping his fantasy straight. First she was already his wife, and then this was their wedding day. Not that her semi-professional observations made a whit of difference; nothing she said was getting through to him.

"Please, Kevin. Just let me go."

"You know, when you didn't come home from college right away, I knew why."

"Why?" Maybe if she kept him talking, he'd somehow come to his senses, or run out of air and pass out. Either would be fine with her.

"You wanted to test our love. But, then when you came home that summer, I got your message and followed you back to college."

Now, his garden was growing hogweeds "I never gave you any message. I don't even remember seeing you."

"At the pool, my Holly. You told me you didn't know what you would do without me. I knew you needed me all the time then." He reverently folded the torn off corner of a ten-year-old school assignment and slid it back into his pocket.

"What happened before I said that?"

"I dove in and got your phone."

She remembered now. She was showered and dressed, ready to leave, when a boy from another school grabbed her phone and tossed it over the fence. The splash made her feel sick; her parents couldn't afford to replace it, and she liked the security of having her own phone.

Then, she saw Kevin dive in, and the next thing she knew he handed her the phone. "Just put some dry rice in with the battery; it'll be okay."

Thank you. I don't know what I'd have done without you.

She was going to scream. "Kevin, that was just an expression of gratitude for getting my phone."

"And, then, when I saw you with that boy who looked like Luke Walker, I had to let you know I was there to keep you safe. Luke Walker tempts you, my Holly, and so did that boy."

"Kevin, please listen and try to understand. This isn't real. What you think you and I have is *not real*."

He didn't even seem aware she had said anything.

"When you graduated, I got the job in China. I told you I would work for a few years and save enough money to keep us in style without having to leave each other to work. But, when I got home, you were gone. And, where do I find you? Back with Luke Walker."

He was getting worked up.

"Kevin—"

When I saw how Luke Walker stood by and let that man hurt you, I decided he isn't even worthy of your friendship. And I protected you! I avenged you!"

Now probably wasn't the time to announce he hadn't succeeded; Jack Wallace was still alive. "You murdered a man!" she yelled. "He was in jail and would have paid for his crimes, but you— you're worse. You're a murderer, Kevin Tripp! Now, let me go!"

It was no use; his quartet was shy of four singers. He stepped closer to her. "A love like ours doesn't come along very often. I'm so happy you love me. We'll go upstairs soon so you can show me."

Holly couldn't listen to him anymore. She channeled her fear into cold, dark anger. "The only thing I will show you is how hard I'll fight you off. I have never loved you, and I don't love you now! I love Luke!"

Finally, he appeared to process her words. His response was immediate.

"Luke! Luke Walker is in the way! He's always in the way, tempting you to stray! He'll learn you belong to me and realize the truth. And if he doesn't, I'll take care of him!"

Panic struck her. "Don't hurt Luke. I love him."

His returning smile was belied by the anger in his eyes. "We'll leave for our home in the mountains first thing in the morning, after we enjoy our wedding night. It's a beautiful house, where nobody will be able to bother us. Once we're there, you'll have time to get used to your new life. You'll be so happy you won't even want to visit this town again."

"Kevin, please." It was all she could do not to cry. "We aren't married, and I'm not going anywhere with you. My home is here in Shadow. With Luke."

"You're talking nonsense again, my Holly." He walked over to the door. "I'll come back when you're ready to admit the truth."

"If you mean the truth as you see it, you may as well not come back." Her words were born of desperation.

He didn't respond at all as he opened the door.

Holly had mixed emotions as she watched him leave the room. On one hand, she felt safer with him gone, but on the other, she was alone and defenseless in a strange house, and who knew what he was preparing for her.

I know I'm asking for a miracle, God, but you perform miracles all the time. Please help me get through to Kevin, or send somebody to save me. Please. I'm so frightened. I know I'm not alone, though. You're with me. You're with me.

Holly couldn't stop the lone tear from trickling down the side of her face. She was totally at the mercy of Kevin, but God was right there with her. She had hope.

Chapter 44

"I don't care how busy you are," Mitch spoke sternly into the phone. "Pull everything you have on Kevin Tripp. I want to know where he was the last time he sneezed."

Luke tried to ignore the desperation he could hear in his friend's voice because it only added to his own. Instead, he focused on the computer screen. Mitch set him up in his office so Luke could do his own research on Kevin. Of course, other police officers were doing the same thing. But at least Luke wasn't sitting idly by, waiting.

They had arrived at Holly's house to find her front door locked, but when Luke let them in with his key, they discovered a too-quiet, completely empty house.

"Where are you, Holly?" He couldn't let himself think of what Kevin Tripp might be doing to her.

Hank stuck his head in the door. "Sheriff?"

Mitch and Luke both looked at the young deputy. "Did somebody find something on Tripp?" Mitch asked.

"Not that I know of," Hank replied. "But, I've finally poured enough coffee down Tom Dwer that he's making sense."

"I'll be right in to question him." Mitch stood up. "Hank?" The deputy came back to the door. "Good work."

Hank nodded. "I'd hate to see something bad happen to Holly. She's a special lady." He smiled grimly at Luke. He turned and walked away.

Everybody who knew Holly cared about her; she was that kind of person.

"I know it's breaking protocol, but please, Mitch. Let me go in there with you." Luke couldn't bear the thought of waiting and not knowing what was being said.

Mitch gave him a measuring look. "Technically, he's not under arrest. I'll bend the rules on this one. Come on."

Luke breathed a sigh of relief as he followed Mitch out of the office.

As they walked into the room, Tom lifted his head from the table and looked at the men through bloodshot eyes.

"Dwer." Mitch was brisk. "I need to know everything you can tell me about Kevin Tripp. Now."

Tom looked straight into Mitch's eyes. "I went to Holly's to tell her everything."

"So tell us," Mitch ordered.

Tom raised his hands as far as the cuffs allowed. His eyes glazed over when he stared at them as though trying to figure out what they were.

"Dwer!" Mitch's shout would have jolted Tom off his chair if he hadn't been secured. At least, he appeared to come back to his senses.

"Kevin has been obsessed with her ever since they did some project together in high school. I always thought it was all talk until this morning."

Luke clamped his mouth closed so Mitch could do his job.

"What happened this morning?" Mitch's frustration was knocking on the door. Tom better hurry up and get to the point.

"He took me to a house. I thought we were going there to finalize a deal for him to invest in my company, but he just wanted to show me the place." Tom looked from Mitch to Luke. "Called it their dream house. It's all fixed up for her. It looks like somebody is already living there. He's sick, Mitch. Really sick."

Mitch and Luke exchanged glances before Mitch asked the next question.

"Where is this house? What is the address?"

Tom's head drooped to the table, muffling his voice. "I don't know." Then he sat back up. "But I'm pretty sure I can take you there. I think I remember the way."

Mitch was already around the table with a key out to unlock Tom's handcuffs. "Let's go."

"Luke." Tom spoke softly as he stood. He waited until Luke looked at him. "I'm sorry if this is my fault. When I tricked her into signing that fake marriage certificate, I didn't know Kevin thought it was real. Not until I saw it framed and hanging in …a bedroom. He saved it all these years…you have to know I never intended for anybody to get hurt, especially somebody like Holly."

Luke didn't have time to worry about blame and fault. "It doesn't matter right now. What matters is that we find Holly."

"Come on," Mitch ordered as he steered Tom through the doorway. "We don't have time to waste."

Please don't let us be too late, Lord. It was the only prayer Luke could come up with, so he prayed it with all his heart.

Chapter 45

A heavy door opened somewhere behind Holly. Kevin must have gone out another door and was coming back into the house from outside. He would be in this room with her in seconds.

I'm sorry, Father. I've lost my courage, and I can't be strong anymore. I'm frightened. She began to cry. This was going to end badly because there was no way she was going to be a "wife" to Kevin. She cried harder as she realized she would never get to be Luke's wife now. She would never have his children.

She heard Kevin's footsteps. She would keep telling Kevin no, so it was inevitable he would snap sooner or later and hurt her. *I'm in your hands.* She closed her eyes and waited.

"Holly." The whisper came from behind her. "Sit still while I get you untied."

"Luke?" Holly thought she must be imagining things.

"Shhh." She could feel the cords tighten and loosen as he worked on them. "Mitch is trying to find a back way in. We're getting you out of here."

"Thank God," she whispered softly.

It seemed like hours before Luke's movements stopped, and Holly felt the cord finally fall free from her body. Luke helped her out of the chair, but then her legs shook so badly she couldn't stand. After waiting a minute for her trembling to lessen, she was able to walk with Luke's arm tightly around her waist. They had just taken a few steps when she heard a door slam open behind them.

"You are always in the way!" Kevin's voice was so full of rage, it was nearly unrecognizable. "Holly is my wife! You're not going to tempt her anymore. I warned you."

Luke stopped walking and slowly turned them around to face Kevin.

"Just let her go," Luke slowly started to push her behind him. "Let Holly leave."

It was then Holly saw the pistol Kevin was holding—aimed directly at Luke.

Kevin snarled. "You won't ever get in the way again!"

Holly used every last bit of strength she had and broke free from Luke. She stepped in front of him.

"No! I'll go with you, Kevin. We're m-married. I'll stay with you. You don't have to hurt Luke." She felt Luke try to move her from in front of him, but she stepped out of his reach, toward Kevin.

"Right." Kevin didn't lower his gun. "You're lying. You'll lie until he's not tempting you anymore. Move, and I'll get rid of him."

"You don't have to do that." Holly took another step toward him.

"Holly." Luke's voice was full of agony. "Don't."

"I...I want..." Bile rose in Holly's throat. "I want to be with you, Kevin. You were right. Let's leave him here and go. We'll go to our other house. Let's leave right now. I can't wait anymore."

For the first time, Kevin looked uncertain. The gun wavered for a moment before he jerked it back up.

"I don't believe you." He sneered at her. "Why don't you come over here and prove you're my wife?"

Please help me do this. It's the only way I can save Luke. Please help me do this. Please.

Holly took another step toward Kevin. A few more, and she'd be within his reach. As she looked desperately at him, a movement caught her eye. Mitch! He was creeping up behind Kevin. But, if Kevin turned his head the least little bit, he would see Mitch. Then Kevin might shoot him.

She had to keep Kevin distracted. She had to keep his attention on her.

"How many bedrooms does our mountain house have?" She'd get him talking. "I hope it has a bunch since I want a big family. Does it?"

Kevin's gun wavered again. "Six. It has six bedrooms." He straightened his arm. "But you don't want to have my kids."

"What makes you say that?" She had to do this, or one of the other men could get shot. "Remember when I looked at you in that special way?" Mitch was only a few feet away. "I'll look at you that way every day from now on. Let's leave right now so we can get started on our—"

"Hit the floor!" Holly heard Mitch, but she froze. Her brain couldn't comprehend what her eyes were seeing. The two men locked in a struggle with a pistol being jerked between them.

Just as a loud crack sounded, Luke seemed to come from nowhere and push her to the ground. She felt him cover her body with his, and realized he was protecting her.

It wasn't very long before the scuffling sounds stopped.

"Okay." Mitch's voice sounded strained. Holly turned her head to see him holding a prone Kevin on the floor, his hands cuffed behind his back. He picked up his radio. "Officer needs assistance." Then he gave an address totally unfamiliar to Holly other than Shadow.

She turned her head the other way. "I'm okay, Luke. You can let me up now." Only Luke didn't lift himself off of her.

"Luke?" She nudged his chest with her shoulder. "It's over. We're okay."

Something was wrong. He wasn't moving. She managed to free her hand and was horrified when she felt a warm, sticky substance.

"Mitch! Help! Luke is bleeding!" Pure panic set in again.

Mitch appeared at her side. When he gently turned Luke over, blood was pouring out of his abdomen. "Here. Hold this tight against him." He'd pulled an afghan off the sofa. "Just hold it tight and try to stop the bleeding."

Holly knelt over Luke, and while she held the blanket and prayed, she was vaguely aware of Mitch radioing for an ambulance.

Please, Father. Don't take him away from me now. Not when we can finally be together. You've shown me how much I love him. Please give me a chance to show him. Please.

Chapter 46

Luke woke up with a terrible ache in his side. What happened? Had Tony's cantankerous bull finally chased him down? The old guy had been trying to for years.

He opened his eyes and looked around. He had seen this place before. He was in the hospital. Only instead of being on one of those uncomfortable chairs, he was lying on an equally uncomfortable bed. And from the feel of things, he wasn't adequately dressed.

A soft noise drew his attention. Holly was curled up on the chair next to his bed, sound asleep. The circles around her eyes and pallor of her skin told Luke she needed the rest. However, she needed to be in her own bed, not a hospital chair.

As if his attention woke her, he watched her beautiful brown eyes open. A smile lit her face when she saw he was awake. She quickly uncurled and stood so she could walk over and stand next to his bed.

"How do you feel?" Worry was evident in her eyes.

Luke tried to chuckle and found it was too painful. "Like Horatio gored me. What happened?"

Holly's smile disappeared. "You were shot. The bullet went clear through your abdomen, but the doctor said it was a miracle. It didn't hit any internal organs. God was watching out for you."

He looked into the eyes of the woman he loved. "Are you okay?"

She steadily held his gaze. "I am, thanks to you. You protected me, Luke. If you hadn't pushed me down, the bullet would have hit me."

"So, my patient is awake." Luke hadn't heard Dr. Potter come in, but there he was, smiling brightly as he approached Luke's bed. "Just in time for my rounds. How considerate of you, Luke."

"You know me." Luke couldn't take his eyes off Holly. "I always aim to please."

"Well, let's have a look at that wound." Holly stood on his left side as the doctor lifted the gown. After he had fussed with a bandage on the front of Luke's abdomen, he had Luke roll onto his side so he could examine the exit wound on his back.

"How is he, Dr. Potter?" Holly's eyes were still focused on Luke.

"Both wounds look good. I don't see any sign of infection in either of them, and there has been no further bleeding."

That sounded fine to Luke. "So I can go home?"

The doctor burst into laughter. Then he must have seen the puzzled looks on Luke's and Holly's faces because he stopped and looked at them incredulously.

"You were joking, right?" Luke barely shook his head. "Well, young man, you have been shot. You will be in this hospital for at least three weeks. And then it will take up to six months for you to completely heal. This isn't a bicycle scrape."

"That long?" Luke couldn't begin to imagine being out of commission for anywhere close to that length of time.

Dr. Potter nodded. "And when you first go home, you'll require around the clock care. It's a good thing your parents live so near."

Luke looked at Holly, who suddenly looked...happy? She couldn't be happy his recovery would take this long.

"I'll stop back by in the morning. Don't hesitate to let the nurses know when you need medication for the pain. It is bound to hurt."

"Thank you, Dr. Potter." Holly *was* happy! Well, as much as Luke loved her, he was not going to get himself shot every so often just to please her. Maybe he was missing something.

Mitch and Colonel Sanders' identical twin walked in just as the doctor left the room.

"So, how's my gunshot victim?" The sheriff looked worriedly at Luke.

"Frustrated."

"It's not that bad," Holly admonished Luke before she told Mitch what the doctor said.

"Well, if you're up to it, Luke, I thought we'd fill you two in on the case." Mitch's gaze traveled between Luke and Holly.

"I can handle it, but it's not up to me." Luke turned to look at the woman sitting closely beside his bed. "Holly?"

"Please tell us everything." Holly's steady voice and calm demeanor surprised him.

"This is Rex Towers. He's a behavioral analysis specialist, on loan from the Federal Safety Administration. He's examined everything we have on Tripp and spent several hours with him. I'll let him tell you what he's learned."

"First, I'd like to say I'm sorry either of you had to go through this. Stalking is a very traumatic ordeal, and, in this case, you were dealing with a very disturbed individual." Rex appeared to be a plainspoken man, and Luke liked him right away. "It didn't take long to determine that Kevin Tripp is extremely delusional, and I'm positive he will be diagnosed with one or more psychological disorders."

Apparently, Mitch had already made his own diagnosis. "No disrespect, Agent Towers, but from what I saw, the man is a certified kook."

Holly's giggles were music to Luke's ears. "Kook?"

Mitch nodded solemnly. "He's nuttier than my Grandma Baker's fruitcake."

A smile appeared on the somber agent's face, as he waited until Holly stopped laughing before he continued. "Tripp and Holly have been married since a class assignment, when you signed a fake marriage certificate."

"Tom Dwer tricked you, Holly." Mitch spoke before she could ask. "He's been helping us as much as possible, and has apologized too many times to count. If it means anything, I really don't think he ever meant harm."

"Tom was a teenager." Holly still didn't seem the least bit rattled. "And, as soon as he found out what Kevin was doing, he tried to help. Maybe not in the best way, but he tried." She nodded. "I'm not sure it's in any way his fault, but you tell Tom there are no hard feelings…right, Luke?"

With the peace glowing within her eyes, Luke only had one answer. "No hard feelings at all."

"I'll tell him." Mitch smiled stiffly. "I think you'll want to hear the rest of what Rex has to tell you."

Luke dragged his gaze from Holly to the agent. "Go ahead."

Rex nodded. "So, Holly, when you went to college, he was here, selling his computer programs via the Internet and fixing up your special house."

"That was his maternal grandparents' place. The federal computer guys are still tracking the trail he hid his ownership behind." Mitch frowned. "So smart, and he wastes it on stuff like that." He gave a small nod to the agent. "I'm sorry. I didn't mean to get started. Please, go ahead and tell them the rest."

If Rex was aggravated, it didn't show. "So, Holly, I understand you had an incident in which you told him you didn't know what you'd do without him?"

Holly sighed. "At the public pool, he got my phone out of the water and told me how to fix it. I said it, but only as an expression of gratitude."

The agent smiled kindly. "I was certain it was something like that. People in Kevin's condition attach significance to the smallest touch, glance, or words."

"He talked about me touching him and giving him special smiles. That's why he felt that way, then?" If anything, Holly seemed even more relaxed.

"Exactly." Rex was clearly satisfied, if not pleased, by Holly's comprehension and acceptance. "The first time he really became upset was when he saw you with a man he claims looked like Luke."

"Patrick." Holly's voice was soft as she looked into Luke's eyes. "A student named Patrick was in one of my study groups, and he always reminded me of you. I barely knew him, though."

Luke grasped her hand and squeezed reassuringly. "It was Kevin Tripp's imagination."

"He began calling to remind you to be faithful." The FBI agent's eyes were sympathetic.

"If that's why he called, why didn't he want me to know who he was?" Holly seemed completely unaware she had moved to sit on the edge of Luke's bed.

"On a very deep level, he knew your relationship was a fantasy," Rex explained. "And he knew if you found out who he was, it would be over."

Rex walked closer to Luke's bed. "When Holly graduated, the offer from China had just come through. In his mind, Holly was coming back to Shadow to prepare their home while he went off to earn their keep. I think the different environment and culture of another country may have temporarily brought Tripp to his senses, and he stayed longer than he intended. He didn't even attempt to contact her during that time. But then his job was finished, and he hadn't been back in the states more than a week when the invitation reached him. Something— the town's name, the school emblem...who knows...something triggered his obsession."

"Only, this time it was worse?" Luke asked.

"He came back and managed to stay under the radar long enough to see the two of you together. You were tempting her to stray, Luke. You know what he did about that."

"Wait until you hear how," Mitch said.

"The man is a genius." Agent Towers slid what appeared to be photographs out of an envelope Luke hadn't even noticed and handed them to him. "The university's security did little to stop him from discovering Holly's phone number, and the tiny microphone he used to disguise his voice was completely his design."

"Are you talking about this spring with a pencil eraser stuck on the end of it?" If Luke had happened to come across such a thing, he wouldn't have given a second thought to throwing it away.

"Its functionality has been verified. That next photograph is another device Tripp designed and built himself, to copy a key. It uses paper." Something resembling admiration appeared in the agent's eyes. "He inserted special paper into a lock, and when he pulled it back out, it gave him the pattern for the key." The contraption looked like a plastic wallet to Luke. "As long as it wasn't locked with a deadbolt, he could get into any building."

Judging by the look on Mitch's face, he would prefer Towers not be so happy about Tripp's accomplishments. Then the sheriff turned an uneasy look Luke's way. "About where he's been staying..."

Luke handed the photographs back to Towers. "Yeah?"

"The old home site between the northwest corner of your field and the woods..."

"My great-grandparents had a small house there. It's been torn down for years." What were the pictures the FSA agent was holding out now?

"You'd never see it unless you know it's there, but Kevin made use of the cellar. He had a generator and water system. He couldn't find a place near Holly, so he stayed close to you."

Luke looked, first with disbelief, and then with anger. He practically threw the offensive pictures at Rex. "I want all of his stuff out of there." Somehow, it sullied his great-grandparents' memory.

"It's a crime scene right now." Mitch seemed genuinely regretful. "As soon as we're finished processing it, I'll haul everything to the evidence locker, myself."

"But the house?" Holly's hand was on Luke's arm, and she seemed unaware of her nails digging into his skin. "Didn't he live in that awful house?"

"That was for you and him together." Rex's voice was sympathetic. "He wouldn't dream of sleeping there without you."

"Luke would never have let that happen." Luke's spirit was buoyed by the strength and confidence in Holly's voice.

"You have to hear about Jack Wallace." Mitch seemed eager to tell them. "Tripp saw Wallace get in the backseat of Holly's car the night of the wreck. I believe he was going to reveal himself to save you, Holly. But when Wallace succeeded in hurting you, Tripp went after him with a passion. He gets quite wound up about avenging his wife. If he's ever sane enough to stand trial, we have a grade A confession."

"We were right then, Mitch? Tripp stopped calling because he was after Wallace?" Luke couldn't help but think how complex this was turning out to be.

"That's how it appears." Mitch glanced at Rex and back to Luke. "Crazy or not, Kevin Tripp is smarter than any person I've ever met."

"And the boys?" Concern for her students filled Holly's face.

"He freely admits to paying them to harass Luke." Mitch still spoke. "Trevor Bayne told the truth; Tripp called him and offered to pay a good amount of money for a group of boys to have fun, as he put it. Besides telling Trevor about the storage room and how he could 'borrow' the key, he sneaked around and left buildings unlocked for them. Then, all he did was encourage them to use their imagination. He brags like he had those boys do something wonderful."

What's going to happen to them?" Holly asked quietly.

"I won't lie, Holly." Mitch was dead serious. "They're all five going to see jail time if I have anything to say about it. I know they're your students, and you care about them, but there have to be consequences for their actions."

"I understand." But Holly's sadness was evident. "What will happen to Kevin?" Her voice was once more firm and steady.

"He will be tested for competency." Rex sounded reassuring. "I believe he most likely will be admitted to a secure psychiatric unit for strict supervision and intensive therapy. Then, if he is ever declared competent, he will stand trial. With all the evidence, as well as his confession, he will be given a lengthy sentence. He won't ever be a danger to you again, Holly."

Holly drew a deep breath. "Is this my fault? Did I do something wrong?"

"No." Rex's answer was immediate. "I'm confident it will be determined Mr. Tripp has been ill for most of his life. Mitch told me how he acted out in high school. That tells me he was already living in some sort of delusional world, where consequences didn't matter."

Luke felt Holly finally relax. He caught her eye and gave her a reassuring smile.

"It's over, Holly."

Her smile wobbled for a moment before it grew bright. "I know."

Then she turned back to Rex. "I don't know what your beliefs are, but I believe in miracles. I'm going to pray that God heals whatever is broken inside of Kevin."

For the first time, a real smile appeared on the staid FSA agent's face. "Holly, miracles have gotten me out of many bad situations. I'll be praying for the man, too."

Mitch asked if either Luke or Holly had any more questions. Luke wasn't surprised when Holly said she didn't. He knew she was at peace with what had happened.

A few minutes later, he and Holly were once more alone in the room.

"I'm surprised by how well you're taking this." Luke raised his hand to the back of her neck. "Are you really all right?"

She leaned over and kissed his cheek before standing. "I'm better than all right. It's over, Luke. I'm not going to give even one more second of my life to that man." The expression on her face lightened his heart. Gone were the signs of constant stress and worry. Holly was truly happy, and all was right with the world.

Well, almost all. Now, he just needed to quit being so negative about his situation. "I guess I'll stay with Mom and Dad while I'm recuperating. I can hire somebody to take care of the farm for me."

Holly's fingers softly traced his cheek. "I was thinking Billy Andrews and a couple of your youth group boys would be good help for you this summer. Your dad may have to show them how to do a few things, but I'm sure they'll work their hardest for you."

Luke thought the idea over for a few minutes before coming to a decision. "If their parents agree, that'll be okay with me."

"So, that takes care of the farm." Mischief sparkled in Holly's eyes. "But I have a better idea for somebody other than your parents to take care of you."

"Who?" Luke couldn't imagine who she would suggest.

Her smile growing brighter, she pulled something out of her jean's pocket and held it out for him to see. "I found this in your pocket."

He looked. She was holding his family ring. His eyes met hers. "I just couldn't stop carrying it. I keep it with me all the time, praying someday you'll accept it."

"So?" She waited expectantly.

Was she saying what he thought she was? He couldn't believe it. His voice shook just a little when he asked, "Holly, will you marry me?"

"Yes." Her response was instantaneous. Then she leaned over and kissed him gently.

After their lips parted, Holly straightened up. Luke took her hand in both of his and slid the ring back on the finger it was made for. It looked perfect.

Luke was ecstatic but now confused, too. "What does your accepting my proposal have to do with—Holly, my fiancée cannot stay at my house to take care of me."

She softly kissed him again. "No, but your wife can."

He had to be asleep and dreaming. Then, common sense picked that moment to close the gate. "I don't want you to rush into marriage just because I need somebody to take care of me."

"Good." Holly seemed unbothered by his declaration. "Since I'll be marrying you because I love you and don't want to waste another minute being apart."

"But what about a fancy wed—"

Her fingers over his lips halted his words. "I've always wanted a small ceremony. Pastor Rollins can marry us right here in the hospital chapel. It's plenty big enough for our families, and Mitch and Tessa."

Luke started to protest, but then he took a really good look at Holly. She seemed happier than he'd ever seen her before. "Okay, but I'm not marrying you until I can wear pants."

She presented him with her heart-stopping Holly smile. "I love you, Luke."

As long as he lived, he would never get tired of hearing those words come from this woman's lips. "I love you, Holly."

Once more, she leaned down, and they sealed their plans with a kiss.

Thank You, God. You've answered my prayers, and I feel more blessed than I ever have before. Holly is safe. And she's going to be my wife very soon. Thank You.

Epilogue

Holly smiled up at her husband as his arm tightened around her shoulders. Even though the ceremony was short and simple, Luke had already been up and around more than he should.

"Let's sit down," she suggested, slipping out from under his arm and taking his hand.

He grimaced. "Sounds like a good idea." She led him to the sofa, where they sat side by side. He slid his arm behind her and curled it around her waist. "I guess I don't have all my strength back yet."

"Luke!" She couldn't believe what he was saying. "You were shot twenty-five days ago, and just released from the hospital right before our wedding this afternoon. Remember, Dr. Potter said it might be six months before you're completely back to normal."

He grinned lazily at her. "Okay, Mrs. Walker." He leaned toward her. "But I'm not too tired to steal a kiss before everybody gets here."

Holly had driven them straight from the hospital to her house. After giving it a lot of thought, they decided her single-story house was a better place for Luke to convalesce. Once he was able, they were putting it on the market and moving to the farm. He hired the three boys to work for him during the summer, but his dad had gone one step further. The son of one of his childhood buddies was moving to town and needed a job. As a wedding present, Richard hired this man, Beau Harding, to supervise the farm. He had already moved an eighteen-foot camper onto the property. It was a beneficial solution for all of them.

"Have I told you how happy I am you're my wife?" Luke asked after he kissed her.

"Not for at least fifteen minutes," she teased. "But you can tell me as often as you like. As long as you don't get tired of hearing me say how happy I am you're my husband."

"Where do you want the cake?" Susan walked into the room, carrying a small two-tier wedding cake.

"Just put it on the dining room table, Mom." Holly should probably get up and help, but she did not want to be more than a few inches from Luke. It was their wedding day, after all.

"Richard and Anita are right behind us with the wedding presents." Tony, balancing three large bottles of sparkling cider, spoke.

He had barely gotten the words out before Holly's new mother and father-in-law entered the room, both laden with beautifully wrapped gifts.

"I really wish you guys had listened to us." Holly leaned against Luke and sighed. "We already have enough things for two houses. You shouldn't have bought us gifts."

Richard met Tony's eyes. "You didn't tell them yet?"

Tony, having set the juice on the table, raised his hands in surrender. "I was afraid they'd shoot the messenger."

"What?" Luke didn't look any more thrilled than Holly felt at the thought of a surprise.

"Oh, nonsense." Susan walked over and stood directly in front of them. "Your friends all decided you needed a reception."

Holly started to protest. Luke wasn't up for more than the small gathering they had planned.

"Now, just a minute, Holly." Her mom wasn't finished. "Jennifer Ewing came up with the idea of a card reception. It's like a card shower, only most of them attached their cards to gifts. They know and understand Luke needs to mend. They still wanted to share in your celebration somehow, so they sent gifts. Just be thankful for your friends."

"Besides, everybody needs seven can openers." Luke's dad spoke imperturbably.

"Oh, hush, Richard." Anita blushed as she explained to Holly and Luke. "We ended up with seven can openers as wedding gifts. Not any other small appliances. Only can openers."

"So, she took that to mean we could eat out of cans for the first seven years we were married."

Anita swatted her husband's shoulder. "You'll be eating out of cans for the next seven years if you don't stop telling tales."

Holly heard the back door open and close, and then Tessa call from the kitchen.

"Are all the presents off the floor?"

"I'll see." Mitch entered the room and looked around. "There's nothing on the floor, Tess."

What was going on? Why did Mitch look like he was about to burst out laughing, and what was the deal with things on the floor? Holly looked questioningly at Luke, who shrugged.

"Okay!" Tessa yelled.

Suddenly, the familiar thud of four feet could be heard running across the kitchen floor. The sound only preceded Clarence by a few seconds as he happily galloped into the living room and right over to the sofa.

"Clarence! How did you get here?" Holly thought Richard was bringing him in the truck later that evening. Then she took a better look at the dog as she petted him. "What happened to you? Have you been wallowing around with Mrs. Pickler's goats?"

Luke's laughter drew her attention away from Clarence. Her husband put a hand on his side as his laughter grew. Holly followed his line of vision.

Tessa had just walked into the room and what a sight she was! Her once perfectly coiffed hair strongly resembled a dust mop, and her dress was crooked. Holly couldn't stop her own laughter as she took in her friend's disheveled appearance.

As Holly looked at her, Tessa grinned through the locks of hair hanging in front of her face. "I won!"

Thank You, God. So did I.

Coming January, 2016

Living in Shadow
Book 2 of the *In Shadow* Trilogy

Haley Johnson is tired of being "fixed up" with men. God would bring her the right one when it was time, and they would take one look at each other and know it was meant to be. Right?

Wrong.

Beau Harding isn't Beau Harding. Nor is he any of the other names he's gone by during the past five years. A Chicago detective, deep undercover in a well-known syndicate, he struggled with the lifestyle he was forced to live. And, just when he was close to busting the whole operation, circumstances beyond his control forced him to blow his cover. Now, to save his life, he has to disappear until the syndicate is brought down.

The problem is, Haley and Beau are drawn to each other almost from the moment they meet. With secrets he can't share and her desire to stay right there in Shadow, they don't stand a chance of making this work.

Or do they?

A crime wave is hitting the friendly town of Shadow, Illinois. Vandalism turns into murder, and it's going to take the right people to stop it.

Including Beau. There's a chance trouble followed him to Shadow, and nothing will make him leave his new friends and the woman he loves to face it alone. He'll stay and fight...even if it costs him his life.

March, 2016

Staying in Shadow
Book 3 of the *In Shadow* Trilogy

Ellie Walker doesn't remember the past five years of her life—not after driving off a bridge. So, she's come to Shadow and made a new home near her cousin and his wife. She even has a steady boyfriend who seems to mean more to her than he should. Sometimes, Ellie is so content, she's not sure she wants to remember.

Brady Donovan was ordered by the doctors to let Ellie remember on her own, but he's not about to let her forget him. He's banking on her falling in love with him all over again—just as she did before they were married. He knows, no matter how it turns out, this won't be easy.

Ellie was part of a special federal investigative team, headed by Brady, set up to take down a nation-wide child-kidnapping ring. Nobody knows what happened to Ellie the day of the accident, after she rushed out of headquarters.

When it appears the very organization they're trying to stop has set up shop in Shadow, Brady and his team figure it's too much of a coincidence. Ellie knows something important, if only she can remember. But, when her memory returns, will she be the same person? Will she be Brady's wife? And the criminal they've been looking for may turn out to be much closer than any of them anticipated.

Lives are in danger and hearts break as Brady and Ellie search for the truth.

About the Author

Georgia Florey-Evans writes stories readers can relate to—an "Oh, this could happen to me," is the best compliment she receives.

In the Christian Romantic Suspense genre, she has found her niche and voice. Her characters struggle with their faith, and sometimes evil rears its head—but, without preaching (she hopes) God's Love always shines through in some way.

Her husband, Jeff, may roll his eyes, but always answers such questions as, "Would a woman hold a gun this big?" or "What's the difference between a bulldozer and backhoe?" (She's still not sure about that one.)

With "characters" such as Clarence, and Fat Albert (*Slaying in Shadow*), she turns her sense of humor loose. Real life isn't all happy or sad, so neither are these stories.

She would enjoy hearing from her readers. You can contact her and read her blog at www.georgiaevansauthor.com

www.ingramcontent.com/pod-product-compliance
Lightning Source LLC
Chambersburg PA
CBHW032203190626
46810CB00017B/330